**Svin lay very still, ears and**
**gone over the blur and hit**
**which direction dan**

Her fingers curled whiteknuckle-tight over the cableplug that fastened into the 70's belt. It was the channel output jack, and without it, the onion-reeking Yarker bitch was shouting into the wind. The sardies would think she was dustsick, or crazed by being too close to a rifter, and if there was one thing about frontline troops, it was their tendency to beat the shit out of a target first and find out why it wasn't responding later.

It was, Svinga decided, not a bad way to start her first real day out of prison.

# PRAISE FOR THE WORKS OF
# LILITH SAINTCROW

## Trailer Park Fae

"*Trailer Park Fae* is what you'd get if you mixed a Bourne film, a political thriller, and a weepy Lifetime movie about abusive, drunken trailer park fathers together, and shook vigorously."
—*B&N Sci-Fi & Fantasy Blog*

"Saintcrow deftly mixes high-minded fantasy magic with rough, real-world rust using prose that veers between the beautiful and the bloodcurdling. Honestly, I wish I'd written it."
—Chuck Wendig

"A true faery story, creepy and heroic by turns. Love and hope and a touch of *Midsummer Night's Dream*. I could not put it down."
—Patricia Briggs

"Painfully honest, beautifully strange, and absolutely worth your time. Lilith Saintcrow is at the top of her game. Don't miss this."
—Seanan McGuire

# CORMORANT RUN

# BY LILITH SAINTCROW

## GALLOW AND RAGGED
*Trailer Park Fae*
*Roadside Magic*
*Wasteland King*

## BANNON AND CLARE
*The Iron Wyrm Affair*
*The Red Plague Affair*
*The Ripper Affair*

## DANTE VALENTINE NOVELS
*Working for the Devil*
*Dead Man Rising*
*The Devil's Right Hand*
*Saint City Sinners*
*To Hell and Back*
*Dante Valentine* (omnibus)

## JILL KISMET NOVELS
*Night Shift*
*Hunter's Prayer*
*Redemption Alley*
*Flesh Circus*
*Heaven's Spite*
*Angel Town*
*Jill Kismet* (omnibus)

## A ROMANCE OF ARQUITAINE NOVELS
*The Hedgewitch Queen*
*The Bandit King*

# CORMORANT RUN

## LILITH SAINTCROW

www.orbitbooks.net

Orbit
Hachette Book Group
1290 Avenue of the Americas
New York, NY 10104
orbitbooks.net

First Edition: June 2017

Orbit is an imprint of Hachette Book Group.
The Orbit name and logo are trademarks of Little, Brown Book Group Limited.

The publisher is not responsible for websites (or their content) that are not owned by the publisher.

The Hachette Speakers Bureau provides a wide range of authors for speaking events. To find out more, go to www.hachettespeakersbureau.com or call (866) 376-6591.

Library of Congress Cataloging-in-Publication Data

Names: Saintcrow, Lilith, author.
Title: Cormorant run / Lilith Saintcrow.
Description: First Edition. | New York : Orbit, 2017.
Identifiers: LCCN 2016053135| ISBN 9780316277969 (paperback) | ISBN 9781478916031 (audio book) | ISBN 9780316277938 (ebook)
Subjects: | BISAC: FICTION / Science Fiction / Adventure. | GSAFD: Science fiction. | Fantasy fiction.
Classification: LCC PS3619.A3984 C67 2017 | DDC 813/.6—dc23 LC record available at https://lccn.loc.gov/2016053135

ISBNs: 978-0-316-27796-9 (paperback), 978-0-316-27793-8 (ebook)

Printed in the United States of America

LSC-C

10 9 8 7 6 5 4 3 2 1

*For the censored.*

# ACKNOWLEDGMENTS

Thanks are due first and foremost to the Strugatsky brothers for their *Roadside Picnic* and to Andrei Tarkovsky for *Stalker*. This book is my homage to them.

Thanks are also due to Devi Pillai, who believed; Miriam Kriss, who kept me sane; Mel Sanders, the best writing partner ever; and Lindsey Hall, who took the book through the final stretch. Not to mention my beloved children, who calmly put up with their mother spending twelve hours or more in other worlds daily.

Last, but not least, once more, I thank you, my faithful Readers. Come in, pour yourself a drink, settle on the couch, and let me tell you what happens when the Rifts open...

# PART ONE

# PREP

# 1
# INTERVIEW

**INTERVIEWER:** *We are here today with Yevgeny Strugovsky, the acclaimed Rift scientist, who has just received a Nobel Prize for his work in unlocking several Rift technologies. His work has proved a foundation for most of what we know about the Rift's treasures. Thank you so much for joining us today, Doctor.*

**STRUGOVSKY:** *Thank you, yes. Yes.*

**INTERVIEWER:** *You must be asked this quite a bit, but it's a good place to start: What do you think caused the Rifts? There are several different theories, including, as it were, aliens. [Laughs]*

**STRUGOVSKY:** *We have no way of knowing, of course. It would be irresponsible to conjecture.*

**INTERVIEWER:** *And yet—*

**STRUGOVSKY:** *All we can say for certain is that one night, eighty-six years ago, there were strange lights in the skies of many countries. Aurora borealis, perhaps. Then, the Event, at a very specific time.*

**INTERVIEWER:** *Yes, the famous Minute of Silence. Four thirty-seven in the afternoon, UTC+2. The Kieslowski Recording—*

**STRUGOVSKY:** *Yes, yes. The point is, we cannot even begin to know what triggered the Event until we have ascertained what, precisely, the Rifts are.* Rift *is somewhat of a misnomer.* Bubble *is also a bad term;* Zone *would be more precise, but still not quite what we're looking for.*

**INTERVIEWER:** Rift *is the accepted term, though.*

**STRUGOVSKY:** *[Coughs] Yes, indeed. The most current theory is that these… places, these Rifts, are actually tears in a fabric we cannot adequately measure. It is not Einstein's spacetime, it is not Hawking's and Velikov's layer cake, it is not the Ptolemaic bubbles of earth and air. When we know what fabric is being so roughly torn, we may begin to reclaim those parts of the Earth's surface.*

**INTERVIEWER:** *Do you believe in reclamation, then? The Yarkers protest that it's against God's will.*

**STRUGOVSKY:** *Their religion does not interest me. The human race is staring directly into the face of the infinite on the surface of our little planet. The frequencies and patterns of the Riftwalls—seemingly random, but we do not have enough data yet—have blinded us to the amazing fact that the energy for them must come from somewhere. The artifacts brought back—*

**INTERVIEWER:**—*illegally.*

**STRUGOVSKY:** *Legally, illegally, they are there. And they share this same quality, of clean, near-infinite energy. I say near-infinite because we have not yet managed to discern the half-life of these objects.*

INTERVIEWER: *Can we say "clean" energy, though? The incidences of mutations near Rift borders, the possibility of some radiation we have no means of measuring yet...*

STRUGOVSKY: *Ah, will there be those dying like Madame Curie, of invisible rays in the service of Science? It is perhaps worth the cost. Imagine a world where this energy is free, and we have reclaimed the cities that lay inside the Rifts. The implications for our lives, for the planet, even for travel to other parts of the solar system, now that we perhaps have the fuel to do so, these are what interest me.*

INTERVIEWER: *I see. Can you talk for a moment about the presence of rifters? Most of the data we have has come from those who can enter and leave these zones, these tears in the fabric?*

STRUGOVSKY: *They are mercenaries. It is a sad comment upon humanity that profit is pursued more vigorously than science.*

INTERVIEWER: *But there are some commonalities among them, as your fellow scientist Targatsky has shown.*

STRUGOVSKY: *He is a* psychologist, *not a scientist.*

INTERVIEWER: *Still—*

STRUGOVSKY: *It is the scientists who will solve the Rifts. They must be protected from the mercenaries and the crowds of... [Burst of static]*

# 2
# NURSERY RHYME

⊰╫⊱

*How many years ago did they show?*
*Threescore and ten.*
*How many they come back aroun'?*
*Never see them again.*
*One, two three, four five six,*
*We all go riftin',*
*Pick up the sticks!*

# 3
# EATEN THE BODIES

⤜╫╡

First came the screaming, drowning out blatting alarms and the ear-shattering repetition of the recorded containment protocol. The long piercing shriek cut right through concrete, glass, stone, buffers, and skulls. Most of the on-duty rifters instinctively hit the ground, one or two ended up with nosebleeds, and one—Legs Martell, absolutely sober for once—going through containment passed out and almost drowned in the showers. A couple of scientists got a headache, but whether it was from the noise or the rest of the afternoon, nobody could say.

The wedge-shaped leav* should have come over the border and inched slowly to a graceful halt right inside the white detox lines, hovering at the regulation three feet above pavement. It should have then been dusted with chemicals, nootslime,† and high UV to make sure any Rift radiation or poisonous goo was

---

* Antigrav replacement for a sled, forklift, or truck. Larger ones can be used as helicopters.

† A neutral semiliquid (reverse engineered from glaslime) that soaks up any stray Rift energies or radiation.

neutralized. Instead, it zagged drunkenly over the blur,* spewing multicolored flame and spinning as two live undercells tried to cope with one gyro melted and the third cell pouring toxic smoke. The dumb fucks on tower duty even unloaded their rifles at it, probably thinking it was the Return,† the aliens who left the Rift-bubbles all over the surface deciding to revisit and pick up their dropped toys, with the tower guards first in line to be grabbed for experimentation or whatever. The terrified fusillade popped the leav's canopy and gave the fire inside a breath of fresh air.

The resultant explosion shattered every window facing the containment bay. Klaxons were added to alarms and recorded exhortations to *wash twice, dust down, wash again.* Someone got the yahoos in the towers to quit shooting, but by then it was too late. Any evidence of what had happened inside the blur-wall was well and truly shot to shit, and burned for good measure.

Wreckage that had once been a good solid piece of antigrav equipment drifted on its two remaining cells, turning in majestic, lazy circles and burning merrily. The emergency response team had been playing Three High‡ instead of suiting up as soon as something rippled in the blur and the watching rifters hit the alert, so it took them a good ten minutes to get their lazy asses out there. They foamed the whole thing, and someone got the bright idea of setting out a triangle of dampers. When they were switched on, their flat surfaces coruscating

---

* The shimmering, sometimes almost-translucent border of a Rift.
† Sooner or later, the aliens will come back.
‡ A card game.

with peculiar static-popping blue stutterlight, the leav thudded down, cracking concrete. It was too heavy, as if it had dragged a squeezer*—what the scientists called a localized gravitational anomaly, isn't that a mouthful—out on its back.

There are squeezers and shimmers,† and the pointy-headed wonders call them the same damn thing, when any idiot could guess you'd need to know which was *too much* and which was *too little*. Didn't matter. They kill you just the same. Except there are stories of a rifter surviving a shimmer. You never know.

Anyway, once the foam dripped away, the entire warped chassis of the leav was there, and three shapes glimmered through the smoke. One of them had to be Bosch from the physics department, because one of *that* corpse's legs was two and a half inches shorter than the other. Another one's pelvis was horribly mangled, but it could have been a woman's.

The obvious conclusion was that it was Ashe and the two scientists, with their accompanying sardies‡—who would have been in the secondary, much smaller leav—dead somewhere in QR-715. The gleaming inside the shattered leav was skeletons, turned into some sort of alloy. It took two weeks of patient work by teams in magsuits to free them from the tangle, and they were carted away to the depths of the Institute. Someone did a hush-hush paper on them—the bones were alloy, where the ligaments were all high-carbon flex with an odd crystalline pattern all over. That was the heaviness—the alloy was impervious to diamond or laserik, and incredibly dense. Whatever

---

* A heavier-than-Earth localized gravitational anomaly.
† A lighter-than-Earth localized gravitational anomaly.
‡ Slang, possibly deriving from "sardine" or "Sardaukar."

had crushed the pelvis of the third skeleton had to have been massive, unless it had been done before the transformation.

By then, though, the rifters had already held a wake at the Tumbledown. Anyone who wasn't a rifter got thrown out after the first round, and the next morning saw not a few still-unconscious freaks on the tables or under them, and even more reeling home. Sabby the Pooka got carted to the butcherblock* for alcohol poisoning. Might as well have medicated him for grief, too, since he and Cabra'd been running with the Rat ever since she rolled into town. There was nothing to bury, science had eaten the bodies, and besides, it's what she would have wanted.

That's how Ashe Rajtnik, Ashe the Rat, who held herself to be the best rifter in the world and was certainly one of the luckiest, died. After that, the higher-ups sent a commission. They discharged all the on-duty rifters, and more orders came down: Nothing went into the Rift, anything that came out was to be shot and contained. Afterward, Kopelund once told Morov he'd almost been canned, too, since he'd played loose with the regs to send in even a small research team, not to mention one with a couple leavs.

And yet, a year later, the motherfucker in charge of the complex perched at the edge of the biggest Rift in the world was looking for someone else to go in after the Cormorant.

---

\* Free hospital. Generally avoided except by the very poor or very desperate.

# PART TWO

✳✳✳

# PRISON

# 4
# PERMISSION TO LAND

᚛ᚋᚈᚂᚉ᚜

*his is Juliet-Oscar niner-three-oh, coming in easterly, requesting permission to land."*

With Svinga's cheek mashed against the bubble the world underneath was a green smear, broken by concrete and smoke-stacks belching, scrubbed but still foul greasy-white. The town had moved up the river once the Event hit, factories thrown up slapdash now sporting the swellings of carbon filters retrofitted on the stacks, haphazard main arteries branching like the foot-paths and small surface roads they were built on, the railroad tracks suddenly curving to cross the river here instead of down-stream at the better bend.

Some cities had died during the Event. Others, like this one, just leaned away on the second-most-favorable bit of terrain. The slums that had housed refugees were now higher-grade residen-tial districts, unless you counted the fringe along the riverbank itself. Buildings crawled upstream, figuring it was safer than Rift-filtered water. Even if some assholes bottled and sold the latter—or marketed rusty fluid from ancient taps as Riftwater, good for you, capable of curing cancer or impotence.

The city stopped as if sliced. The deadzone was wider than the mandated mile minimum, clipped down to waste grass, any bushes or bramble ruthlessly shorn, tree stumps taken down to the dirt, all under a threadbare scrim of snow and freeze. The old railroad, now simply a rusted spur, dove through on its way to the better river crossing, the one stuck behind shimmering curtains of randomized energy. A straight shot, right for the heart of the Rift. Any patrol in the 'zone would have the same orders: Shoot to kill.

Whether or not they were relaxed about it was something you could only tell when you got near them. Svin spotted two three-leav groups moving there, bristling with scanners and long penile bankguns.

The leav banked and came in low over the military complex, a reply burbling through the pilot's helmet. Shackles bit Svin's wrists, one of them rubbing against her left ankle, too, and the cut on the bridge of her nose, crack-glazed with dried blood, throbbed.

The beefy Regulation 70* next to her in flexphase perma-plas armor settled her knee more firmly in Svin's back. *Just a routine transfer*, they'd said.

Only for routine transfers you were chained to a benchseat in a malodorous transport hevvy, with a bunch of assholes yelling all around you and flicking snot at each other.

Even criminals never got over school.

Svin took a deep breath, but slowly, filling her lungs in

---

* Transport or private security. Faux-police.

increments. There, at the very edge of her vision, a shimmering. Light bouncing in weird ways, and the space inside her empty-aching like a pulled tooth.

Were the fuckers really planning on putting her down near a Rift? She didn't shut her grainy, insomnia-hot eyes, didn't even blink, her tongue creeping out to touch the slick, almost-gritty clear plas of the bubble. The cells whined as stabilizers kicked in against a sudden airdrift, and the Reg70* behind her exhaled a breath of onions, fear, and petty dominance. Transport dicks were generally a little more easygoing, but this one had a crucisplice† on her cheek and was probably praying as they glided. Goddamn Yarkers.‡ *Satan works inside the Rift*, they said, and the only thing they hated more than the tech dragged out past the blur was the rifters themselves. Consorting with the devil and all that.

Of course, the greedy fucks used the tech, just like everyone else. Leavs, sleds, poppers,§ Mata equations,¶ halone,** triphase plasma—the list went on and on, and they used it all.

This Reg70 had generous hips and wide soft shoulders with hard muscle underneath. She might have even been attractive, except for the fear-stink. And the fact that her hand-cannon was stuck in Svinga's back; no doubt a gloved finger was

---

* International Regulation 70-A, Section 70, authorizing all necessary force against a prisoner arrested for Rift-involved activities.
† Hair-fine filaments braided together and shaped into a cruciform knot before dermal implantation, to denote a particular Yarker denomination.
‡ Slang for a member of an evangelical sect.
§ Small blue spheres that can be "cracked" for energy. Note: They do not actually crack.
¶ The set of cycling equations that make leav "antigrav" cells work.
** A highly addictive drug made from nootslime.

caressing the trigger. Of course, letting a bolt off in here was likely to plunge all three of them groundward in flames, but there wasn't a 70 anywhere without something to prove.

Who *wouldn't* be keyed up this close to a Rift? Even the assholes who'd been predicting Intelligent Life Somewhere Else had been floored by the Event, and all the kooks suddenly "proven" right about UFOs had a field day until the true extent of the casualties sank in. Not the civilians vanished when the Event happened, but the ones who went into the Rifts right after, thinking they were going to be pioneers or some shit. In the end, all the emergency planning in every municipality, county, province, state, country, and continent had only managed sticking-plasters over bleeding gunshot wounds. Excising whole cities from the map was a messy business.

Permission to land was granted with a burst and a crackle of transmission code and the transport leav began to sink gently, gyros whining and its cells glowing with Mata curve differentials. Svin didn't shut her eyes until the slugwall slid out of sight behind a bulky concrete-and-sealed-glass building. A few moments after that, the bump of landing jolted all the way through Svin's bones, and since she wasn't shot in the back she decided the Reg70 behind her had either *some* trigger discipline or a couple dry nerves left. Or maybe she had to finish praying before she shot one of Satan's minions.

Once the bubble lifted, the 70 holstered her gun but kept her knee in Svin's kidneys.

It would, Svin thought, be easy. Pitch forward, getting her legs up behind her, use the 70 to push off against, hope not to chip a tooth or dislocate her shoulder on concrete, but if she *did* pop her shoulder out, the restraints would be easier to wriggle.

Once her hands were in front of her, they might get her from the towers but at least she could get this particular 70's neck snapped before the rounds went through Svin's body. It would depend on how drunk the tower watch was.

Staring at the slugwall's slow, opalescent sheen for hours at a time did bad things to the inside of your head. It was axiomatic that the only way to keep the guards doing it was an alcohol ration, and with the mounted guns, you didn't need accuracy. Just the willingness to shoot even at shadows.

Svin let the moment pass. Let the 70 haul her from the leav, let her entire body go slack. Landed in a heap on pavement blast-cleaned by leavcells and containment chemicals, getting a good look around as she fell and closing her eyes again to fix it all in memory. A standard horseshoe of an Institute, the walls lead-webbed concrete sandwiches, its open end full of U-shaped levvy slots—just lines of white paint on the concrete, nothing fancy, a total of three sleds resting on blocks for moving heavy shit. The actual levvy bays would probably be on the south side, and—

The 70 hauled her up again by the back of her paper-thin prison jumpsuit. "You little shit. Stand up!" The black helmet was fogged on the inside—someone was doing some heavy breathing. Another shake, Svinga's head bobbling on her neck, as if she were only partly conscious.

Whoever was watching might get the idea this particular 70 had beaten the crap out of her prisoner in transport. And the bobbling gave Svin a chance to observe more of the layout.

One of the cargo doors on the northern face was opening, and a flurry of movement started. Scientists? Other rifters? A flash of light—someone wearing glasses, maybe? Had to be vanity, anyone who could afford it got ocular nowadays. Svin let herself stay nice and limp, making the 70 work for every step.

*There.* The bottom of the U—the eastern wall, facing the k-zone* and the blur—opened up a couple of black gaps as well, and security forces came spilling through. The uniforms were black, but the red piping at the shoulders showed they were sardies, frontline troops instead of jumped-up faux-*polizei*.

*Red-eye stripe, yo' ass is wiped*, the saying ran. Right after the Event sardies were hurried into uniform in case it was the prelude to an attack. During the Crash, they were government mercenaries—distinguished from private mercenary armies only in the matter of paymaster and the quality of their rations, and sometimes not even the latter.

If they had this many sardies just sitting around, it must be a bigger Rift. Which narrowed the list.

*Always look*, Ashe said, years ago. *Look. Think. Then and only then do you move even a finger. Even an eyelash.*

Svinga sensed the 70's intent to drop her a split second before it happened and went down again, rolling violently sideways as if the guard had kicked her. Yeah, it was a standard Institute, built a few years after the Event but before the Crash, when funding was sloshing around and everyone was terrified. Another piece of evidence saying *a bigger Rift*. She'd been hooded for the first few legs of transport, so she had very little idea of where she was. Across the ocean from Guan, that was for sure.

---

* The mandated no-man's-land between an Institute's buildings or open bay and a Rift border.

Which was great. The further away, the better.

Now she had the general layout, she could guess at the rest. *Know your ground*, Ashe always said. So Svinga lay on the cold hard landing pad, curled around herself as if it hurt to move. It did, a little, but that was life. If you didn't expect it and hold yourself in readiness, your expiration date would amble up and bite you before you were even close to ready.

That was when she caught sight of the scorch. A looping, blackened path from the blur in, and just like everything to do with the Rift, it looked…different. *Wrong.* A normal person wouldn't be able to tell just *how*, and would look quickly away, maybe with their stomach clenching a bit and a cold bead of sweat forming right at the base of their spine.

Svinga stared. The mark was too black, too thick, and she gapped her mouth, quick sipping breaths. You had to taste things.

There was no hint of anything but exhaust and cold weather. Just a faintly obscene streak burned into pavement, heat-rings rippling at its edges.

*"Stand down!"* someone was yelling, probably at the 70 behind her. The transport goon began shouting something muffled, and there was a crackle of live stimsticks.* She was probably still trying to explain when the first one smacked against her flexphase armor.

Flexphase didn't have anti-stim padding, which made it lighter. An advantage for a transport dick, until it wasn't.

Svin lay very still, ears and eyes open, as if she had just gone over the blur and hit the ground, waiting to see which direction

---

* A crowd- and prisoner-control baton, lightly electrified.

danger would come from. Her fingers curled whiteknuckle-tight over the cableplug that fastened into the 70's belt. It was the channel output jack, and without it, the onion-reeking Yarker bitch was shouting into the wind. The sardies would think she was dustsick,* or crazed by being too close to a rifter, and if there was one thing about frontline troops, it was their tendency to beat the shit out of a target first and find out why it wasn't responding later.

It was, Svinga decided, not a bad way to start her first real day out of prison.

---

* Addicted to powdered, ultra-refined halone, "dust" in street parlance.

# 5
# OUR AGREEMENT

⋈╫⋈

The one-way mirror was filthy with dust and flyspotting, which distorted the view of a sweating concrete room lit by a buzzing fluorescent tube. Thin, nasty light played over a thin woman slumped in a metal chair bolted to the floor. Shackled, deadfish-pale hands rested on the interrogation table; her maroon prisoner's jumpsuit was just this side of threadbare and the flextag with her number and barcode at her left breast lay flat and almost frayed out of legibility. Her pointed chin dropped slightly while ropes of dirt-matted hair swayed forward, then jerked upward, regaining lost ground. Either she was trying to stay awake or she was bobbing to atonal, rhythmless, wholly internal music. Grime lodged under her bitten-down fingernails and along the cuticles, and every once in a while, when her head jerked back up, the tip of her nose showed just as fish-belly as her wrists.

Prison pallor. You saw the sun for an hour a day in max, rain or shine, but not at all in solitary.

"That's it?" Kope's nose wrinkled as he arranged his uniform cuffs. It was a big, generous nose, and its twitches signaled his feelings—or what he wanted you to think his feelings were—at every possible opportunity. "Shit."

"You asked for a good rifter." Zlofter pulled irritably at the cuffs of his shiny new suit, too, perhaps not realizing he was mirroring the larger man. His slick black pompadour almost glowed in the dimness, and his silver earpiece was the latest little gift from the Rift's depths, a high-range Aurovox. Probably a thank-you present from his corporate masters, a shiny collar making sure they could buzz him at any moment with marching orders. A glorified leash.

Kope's disgusted snort echoed in the concrete corners. "And your little knob-polishing buddies send us a washed-out felon? We could have gone into town and picked up a few dozen of those by ourselves." He had to be careful to sound just irritated enough. DynaKrom had no shortage of people *or* funding to throw at whatever their rifters brought out, and government agencies couldn't hope to compete. Especially when standing orders were NINO—nothing in, nothing out. They wanted to "map" the smaller Rifts first.

That fucking decision had probably come out of a committee. It had *idiot* written all over it.

He should have gone into private security instead of the sardie-hole. He'd been telling himself that for years, but his contract was signed and fucking set, and there was nothing to be done but make the best of a bad pile of fertilizer, as his grandfather would have said.

So it was begging for scraps under the guise of "cooperation," and if there was one part of his job that made Kope want to set the entire fucking building on fire and piss on the flames, it was the sucking up necessary to get even *this* halfass kind of quasi-legal support. Of course, if they suspected exactly what he was after, they would probably take over his whole installation, and even though he could cheerfully gut the place, it was still *his*. And he was still capable of oiling the levers right to get what he wanted. The proof of that was sitting in the room on the other side of the mirror.

When this place was built, there was still hope some civilians had survived inside the Rifts and were waiting for rescue. So, thoughtfully, the design had included a couple of debriefing rooms. There was an ancient commjack in the wall in front of them, at knee height. He could have scavenged some equally ancient camera to tape this, if he'd wanted to. God knew there was probably one old enough in the storerooms.

Zlofter's greasy mouth pursed. "How many of those would have been trained by Rajtnik?"

Anticipation had begun, beating right under Kope's overworked heart. He had to go through the motions, make sure this little asshole thought he was dispensing largesse instead of falling right into a carefully prepared plan. "Do you mean *trained* by or *fucked* by? The Rat wasn't very selective." *I need a connection to the Rat, and I need it disposable*, he'd told Zlofter. There was only one possible fit, and he'd let the man arrive at that conclusion himself.

"You didn't even bother to look at the file."

Kope restrained the urge to throttle the whining bastard. It wouldn't look good. "Tatiana Pajari, goes by Svinga, thirty-three, born in Sobzardio, near the Sbardo Rift. Emigrated at sixteen on a false passport, went offgrid until she showed up working the Birmingham Rift with Rajtnik. Pops

25

up again near other Rifts, makes a name for herself, then gets arrested two years and change ago for running poppers illegally near Shasta. Would have been just a thirty-day sentence in lo-sec clinical, but she killed two of the four arresting officers and crippled a third for life. Course, the officers were used to beating every goddamn smuggler to a pulp to teach 'em not to get caught. Didn't bargain on a rifter, and there's some suspicion that a local warboy* had paid to have her—or one of the Rat's crew—erased. They put her in Guan† and threw away the key." Rifters didn't do well in general population, so they'd stuck her in solitary a lot. The file hadn't said whether she'd needed "interrogation."

"I stand corrected." Zlofter's prissy little mouth didn't relax, though. Nor did his manicured hands, the left one bearing a tastefully expensive chaxalloy‡ ring. "I don't blame you, though. She does look a little..."

"She looks like a dust-sniffing whore," Kope supplied. The only thing missing was raw nostrils and a disintegrating septum. By the time they got that thin, dustsluts—especially the males—started to show the collapse right in the center of their face. *Nosers*, some called them. *Sniffbabies*. Or, one of Kope's favorites, *holeyheads*. Like Yarkers, sniffing after God.

The rifter's head jerked up, as if she'd heard him. It dropped

---

* A petty warlord, usually one who has a security contract with a government to keep a certain slice of territory under "control."
† After the double assassination (Sanders-Clinton), Guantanamo Bay never closed.
‡ Alloy made by folding and refolding Rift-harvested spinstrands, light but extremely strong.

by degrees, again, following whatever weird rhythm-free music was playing in her brain.

"I can always have her sent back, Kopelund."

Now was the time to let Zlofter think he'd won. Not too easily, but not too hard, either. Kope shifted his big shoulders under his ill-fitting gray uniform jacket. Finally, grudgingly, he assented to the inevitable he'd been working for all along. "Fine." Now the other man would add what he thought was a trap's closing jaws to the situation.

Right on time, Zlofter opened his oily mouth. The bastard was nothing if not predictable. "And of course, we would like a look at anything she brings out."

Sure they would. Kope kept his face a blank wall, with just the faintest suggestion of a bad smell reaching his several-times-broken nose, which obediently twitched once. "That's our agreement."

"Very well." The corporate man checked his sleek silver atomic chrono. "I have a meeting in town. Ping me if you need anything else."

Kope just nodded, as if he didn't know Zlofter was just going to visit the Rabak, drink all afternoon, and send the Institute the tab. Maybe the little bastard was celebrating getting one over on him and pocketing the finder's fee Kope had scraped out of the budget to pay for this piece-of-shit, washed-up rifter. He barely heard the door shut, Zlofter making a squeaky little remark to the guard outside, or his own breathing.

Once he was gone, Kope grimaced, his face screwing up afresh before it smoothed and he leaned forward, studying her intently through the dirty glass.

Still skinny. Still wearing prison pallor, and that filthy hair hanging in lank matted ropes. The tip of her long nose peeked out again, and the black-and-white Guan ID headshot in the file showed a remarkably ugly woman. The nose was huge, the mouth too broad, the teeth barely fitting in, and her eyes protruded like watery eggs. Her shoulders jerked a little as her chin rose again, and Kope shook his head.

He was hoping Zlofter couldn't smell his excitement. This was the rifter Kopelund had hoped for, Ashe the Rat's protégé, the one Ashe had wanted to get out of lockup before she went in with Bosch and Gunther and three expendable sardie troublemakers for the Cormorant.

Well, the prodigal was here now.

Kope bared his own very large teeth in a white, predatory grin, smoothing his graying hair back.

Time to meet his new acquisition.

# 6
# DEADNAME

⋊╫╍

*T*ired.

Her head kept dropping, and she would surface when the fluorescent's buzz overhead changed a fraction or when the balding, heavyset guard outside the interrogation room's door shifted his weight, his uniform whispering against itself. It was cold, but she'd learned long ago not to shiver—waste of energy, gave away your position, and was a distraction. All things you couldn't afford past the slugwall.

Or in prison.

The grime under her fingernails was black, her skin cringing from the light. She mapped the blue veins on the back of each hand as if they were a slice of Rift she had to traverse, a trancelike alertness requiring her to look, learn, look again, look *again*. If she went deep enough, she might be able to see the slight changes as her blood pressure shifted, the blue lines creep-crawling like a worm or a scuttlesnake.*

---

* A semi-sentient serpentine collection of hunger, scavenged metal, and bad temper.

That reminded her of Ashe and their fourth trip into Birmingham. Or was it the fifth? Her, the Rat, and Connie the Goof with his golden head shaved. His hair was lucky, but the lice had finally gotten too bad, because he was a filthy motherfucker with running sores on his scalp from scratching too much.

Maybe that was why the first half of that particular trip had gone bad. The sound as the Goof was snatched because he didn't drop fast enough, yanked into the air by a passing shimmer, the scuttlesnake following the grav-flux's looping path jerked free of grassy dirt too and snap-crunching as it *fused* with Connie, each shape struggling for primacy before the shimmer dropped them both in a spray of blood, brains, bone fragments, and fragrant glaslime.* Vicious gleaming shrapnel from the scuttlesnake's spinal column had peppered the entire area, but at least Connie's death had been quick.

Sick fear, the tremble in her hands, and a squirming sensation of *serves you right for not listening, Goof,* and crawling forward on her belly after Ashe, testing each hand- and toehold before committing herself, barely daring to stand even when the shimmer was gone and Ashe said *come on up.*

Behind the dusty, flyspotted mirror on the wall to her left, breathing presences loomed. Probably whoever had yanked her out of prison. Maybe Ashe had worked a deal, though that wasn't like her. *Let it drop and on to the next* was her philosophy, and a good one if you could stomach it. Kept the Rat alive and

---

\* GLA slime, an irradiated goop common in Rifts, sometimes exuding from the slugwall in thick, slow-moving streams.

going into the blur, instead of liver-rotted, rotting in a cell, or exploded in a shimmer.

Svin exhaled softly. The cuffs weren't too tight. If she wanted to, she could yank a hand free. It would only cost a little skin, but she was still ankle-shackled to the chair. Wasn't worth it.

Not yet.

So she waited. Lots of life was just hanging around. Wait for a client, wait until the blur moved, wait until the shimmer or the crawling sense of danger passed, wait until someone who had money was at home to buy. Once you got comfortable with the idea of crapping wherever they left you, it was surprisingly easy. You didn't even have to wipe, if they were just going to keep you in a box. Just pick a corner and tune the smell out. If they didn't feed you, though, you didn't shit. Or so Fuller Ginch, the only convict who'd bothered to talk to her in Guan, always said.

Fuller also claimed he'd survived the Event, and going over the blurline* kept him at the same age he was when it hit. Unlike *that* tall tale, the non-shit of starving prisoners sounded pretty believable.

The presences behind the mirror faded. Svin thought about it. The first problem was getting loose of the shackles. After that, there was the guard at the door, and the corridors. If she was running for the slugwall, they might shoot her in the back. Best would be picking up some supplies on the way and escaping notice until she was inside the Rift itself; running in was a good way to get yourself killed.

You had to watch for your moment, wait for the soap-bubble

---

* The slugwall, the coruscating border of energy at the edge of a rift.

shimmer that was the Rift's face to take on a welcoming expression.

Footsteps. She surfaced again, the fine hairs on her nape rising. Inside the blur she would have frozen to assess the new sound, but out here it was stupid-simple: Whoever had pulled her out of Guan was coming to tell her what they wanted. It could just be information, except anything she had was three years old, give or take. Not worth hauling her ass out of deep-freeze and through several hours of transport.

When the door opened she could *smell* him. Big. Meaty. Male. Greasy food but no tang of cigarette, no sourness of metabolized alcohol. So: nondrinker, nonsmoker. Maybe he was into food, fucking, or pain. Everyone had a vice.

She kept rocking a little, her head swaying as her body kept itself upright by making tiny adjustments. They echoed against the bare walls, though. Either you learned how to sit still in solitary, or you forgot it was even possible. Sometimes you could pretend the tiny noises of your own movement were from other people.

Once or twice, she'd contemplated making friends with one of the rats that shared her cell. In the end, it was always better to not get attached.

A flicker of motion. He slapped a red-banded file folder on the dusty tabletop. They didn't use this room often, there was a hole chewed in the baseboard under the mirror. Rats here, too. The place was probably alive with them. A government installation, running down at the edges.

"Miss Pajari." He settled into the other chair, the one that wasn't bolted down. "What did that transport 70 do to you, huh?"

She could have said *I just don't like a gun in my back all the time.* Or, closer to the truth, *I don't care.* They'd broken one of the 70's arms before they got that she wasn't resisting. Svin had just lain on the ground until one of them picked her up. No need for anything else. Not like when they'd tried to kill her in the guise of a simple arrest. They'd charged her after the fact with running poppers, for shit's sake, as if she were fifteen again.

Still, she'd survived. Svin contented herself with a shrug.

"I'm Kopelund. This is Site QR-715, and I'm the resident god. I say what goes here, and I got you out of that hellhole. I can put you back in, too."

She studied his hands, first. Big, blunt, bitten nails and a few scars white against the darker skin. The edge of a dark-gray uniform sleeve—wool, the dress shirt underneath faintly yellow. The red piping was double. A pen-pusher.

*QR-715.* Her heart jumped inside her thin chest, fell back down with a splash. Not just any Rift. *The* Rift. The fucking Cormorant. The place might look like it was falling apart, but it stood in the middle of some of the most heavily guarded dirt on the planet. Now she knew why the deadzone was thick and daytime patrols had been out without even bothering to conceal themselves.

The file folder was stamped with her deadname, and it was pretty hefty. They might even know a thing or two. That red band on it said *government,* too. What flavor of government didn't matter, it was all the same nowadays. The Event turned the whole planet into a kicked anthill, tiny stupid creatures only cooperating in the face of a larger threat, then falling into petty squabbles right afterward.

She examined his chest next. Broad but getting soft. Soup stain on the red viscose neckcloth. Uniform was untailored.

The badge was shiny, though. Gold, the stamped crest of worldwide authority, lovingly polished. So he was a lifer. Rank stripes on his arm, a high mucky-muck. Probably sneered at rifters, but grabbed whatever he could right out of their hands when they came back from the blur.

A long, ticking silence. The fluorescent overhead buzzed, dimming and brightening randomly.

"Did they tear your tongue out in Guan? Ashe never mentioned you being mute."

Svin's head jerked up a little. She studied his big, florid face. Raw slabs of cheek taking up most of the room. Graying hair, clipped close on the sides, the top pushed back and held with some kind of goop. Muddy, indeterminate eyes. You could tell, just from the color of his skin, that he'd never been through the blur. There wasn't enough snap in his eyes to make her cautious, but not enough dull-cow stupidity to make her condescending, either.

Her throat was dry. She hadn't used her voice in a while, so the words sounded like they were being pulled out through a fluxfilter.* "You think she would have?"

He looked slightly pleased at getting a response. His long nose twitched once, twice. "Maybe. She wanted you here before she went in, but..."

"Before she went in?" It got easier. Her throat was still dry. No water for thirty hours or so.

"You want to get out of those shackles? Clean up? Maybe eat something other than prison slop?" Like he was doing her a favor.

---

* A class of filters, packed with treated nootslime, deactivated glaslime, or crisscrossing fibers.

"Just tell me what you want." Because he *did* want something. If Ashe was mixed up in it, and it was QR-715, there were only a few things that could mean.

*Motherfuckers.* She could just hear Ashe's voice, a slight drunken sneer, the night before things got wild. *Everyone's after it, but I know where it is.* When the Rat got to drinking, sometimes you learned things. If you were lucky, you sometimes didn't even get a bruise from the lesson.

The man—Kopelund—shook his big bovine head. "She said you were smart." Maybe he had a few heavy brains in there to roll around, but Svin doubted he had as many as he liked to think.

"She didn't say shit about you."

"Well, neither of us can ask her now." The man tapped his fingers against her file, each one drumming like the fat fucking meatstick it was. "She's dead."

Svin tilted her head back a little. A high-pitched whistling sound, not quite a laugh, slipped between her protruding teeth. Oh, that was just like the bitch. "Blur your fucknozzle."*

He must have been used to rifters, because he understood. "I'm serious, Miss Pajari."

*It's Svin, you dickwit.* But her chin dropped. She let him think she was considering the whole thing, when she'd really made her decision when she'd seen the blurline in the bay. So tantalizingly close. Once she got in . . .

"Fine," she said, the word rasping all the way up from her wasted chest. "You might want to get the shackles off, though. I need to piss."

---

* Common rifter slang, expressing wonder, disbelief, or a peremptory request for immediate silence, depending on tone.

# 7
## NEVER RIFTING

ᛞᚻᚳ

arko ran a soft pink palm over his shaven head. His stomach threatened to growl. "No shit." He blinked, trying to look excited and surprised. "A full team. How long has it been?" *Sit tight and monitor*, ILACentral* had said, over and over. What had made them change their minds?

Or had they? Kopelund wasn't above plausible deniability. Barko eyed the new kid, who had just arrived, breathless and late, from lunch in the canteen. Looked like he hadn't just ingested food but also gossip, as usual. Barko couldn't remember what it was like to get that interested in *anything*, let alone petty news about people he'd known for years, for God's sake. Most of the time, he preferred to be left in the dark.

Aleks's Adam's apple bobbed, just like it did every time he got excited. "Kope's pulling out all the stops." The kid was a bird,

---

* The central, global agency for coordinating responses to and research on the Rifts.

all beak and feather-fluff blond hair. It was almost impossible to get angry at him, but irritation wasn't out of the question.

"Christ knows where he got the clearance." *Or if he did.* Maybe the canteen had something good today. Why couldn't the kid just announce what was for lunch and take his place at the screens? "There should have been a department memo about this."

As usual, Aleks missed the point. "Who cares? I tell you, he's got something *big* planned. There was a transport today. A prisoner. Some rifter the Rat recommended."

"The Rat." A moment of silence. Barko leaned back against a metal bookshelf stuffed with printouts, wires, bins of strange odds and ends, and dust. It groaned a little under his weight, a familiar, ignored voice. A moment of silence was a nice idea, but in practice, the world always intruded somehow. "I told Kope he needed a full team last time."

"Yeah, well, he's probably going to send you in now. Congratulations." The kid bounced up on his forefeet, a balloon full of a dizzying lack of proportion married to vast tracts of enthusiasm. His overalls and lab coat never fit him quite right.

Barko almost shuddered. The skeletons from last time—good scientists, men who deserved more—were deep in Bay 17, where all the stuff you didn't want to think about was jammed. Even Ashe, strange and nasty as she was, hadn't deserved *that* kind of death. "I'll stay out here, thanks. You go ahead."

"Right." Aleks's laugh had a jagged edge. His parents had struggled and scrimped to send him to uni, hoping a Rift sciences degree would pave the way for him to get a good corporate position and provide them with a comfortable retirement. Unfortunately, he'd been drafted into an ILAC quota, which meant a stipend and enough nondisclosure forms to choke the profit from any discovery he might make before it began. If he'd been sent to a smaller Rift, he might have been able to sell a few odds and ends on the side. As it was, he was low man on the totem pole here, without the contacts or the clearance to get his hands on anything worth selling.

No wonder he was such a bouncing basket case most of the time. Right now he showed his strong young crooked front teeth in an excited grin. "If I wanted to commit suicide, I would've during undergrad."

The older man grimaced slightly. "Don't say shit like that, kid." And, by extension: *Not so close to a Rift, it's bad luck.*

The skinny kid hopped from foot to foot. "Is he going to send us in, Bark? Come on, you can tell me." At first Barko had thought him addicted to something that made him so itchy and fidgety, before he figured out it was just…youth.

"Tench your springs."* Barko scratched behind his ear with one blunt finger. "He'll send in military and someone with research seniority, if he really wants to drag something good out."

"You mean Morov and Riggs. And probably Tremaine." Aleks made a sour face.

"Go ask them." Barko turned away from the bookshelf, heading back for the workstations. The computers were new, at least—say what you would of Kope's methods, at least he knew how to squeeze gear out of the bureaucracy. "I'll be over here doing some actual work before my lunch."

Aleks didn't bother responding to the sarcasm. He scraped

---

* Slang: Calm down, loosen up.

all his fingers through his corngold hair and headed past Barko for the other door. It was a little longer to get to the prime spaces, but he could go down the gallery hall and look at the thick opalescent edge of the Rift, shadows rippling in its depths. The curtain of energy shorted out any measuring device trained on it, and the rifters said it had a mind of its own. *It smells fear, Barko,* the Rat had said once, grinning her little ferret-smile. *That's why you're never going in with me.*

He found out he was rubbing his scalp again, polishing with his palm as if that would give him a solution, or get his work done. The kid wasn't bad, he was just ambitious. And so, so goddamn young. They got excited, being this close to a Rift. The source of all the stories, all the new myths humanity was telling itself. There were books about the Event now, scholarly and otherwise. Some of the early pulp ones were going for a pretty penny on the Bay.* The grainy footage, replayed over and over with hysterical or scholarly voiceovers, was burned into every head. First, the exodus—pets gone missing, the moving backs of rats swimming great rivers, fleeing the cities; the stampedes in wild places. Then, the ringing—who knows why some people reported that high-pitched grumble from the sky? Derided, called cranks, but few of them decided to leave their homes. Just as the apocalyptic fever began, just as other people were beginning to think nothing was happening...the Event.

There were even pornos about it. Fucking while the world ended had a certain appeal.

What did *not* appeal were the casualties. It wasn't just the first wave—people falling over, blood foaming from mouths

---

* One of many sites for purchasing merchandise from other private citizens.

and ears, clutching each other the way the doomed at Pompeii must have. Or the second wave, when the shimmer descended and all of a sudden there were blank spots on the world map. Some roughly circular, some jagged, scattered in the equatorial belt but thicker in the temperate regions. None above the temperate zones—whoever had visited didn't like the cold.

Barko had long ago decided it was the third wave that bothered him most. His grandmother's stories were full of the aftermath. Refugees fleeing, the apocalyptoids feeding their kids cyanide, petty warlords looking to make a buck or indulge in murderous dreams tamped down by civilization, hospitals overrun and death that had been easily preventable the day before suddenly inescapable now, dislocation and the disaster as the economy wobbled, toppled, crashed...

The screens glowed. Sequencing fluctuations from irradiated glaslime was boring, time-consuming, and the type of scientific scut work great discoveries were drowned in. Maybe someone would have a use for the vast mass of data, but since the Calgary Accords, no State-sanctioned rifters had gone in. Since last year, the ones on the payroll at QR-715 had been canned, and the deadzone patrols shot to kill every time even a rabbit moved out in the razed belt. They'd burned a good ten kilometers from the wall with acid flush—the smoke had lingered for weeks—and ripped up most of the train tracks or any other ingress.

It even made a politician's sort of sense. Put the resources into the smaller Rifts, try to map and mine them, contain the bigger ones until you knew exactly what you were dealing with. The Wild Era of rifters crawling into any goddamn energy wall they could find was supposedly over. Funding was being reallocated, corporations brought on board, and freelancers discouraged.

Or at least, that was the plan. The corporations, let alone the freelancers, had their own ideas.

Which made this interesting. If the expedition Kope was thinking about was sanctioned, it would have to be quiet. If it wasn't, it would *still* have to be quiet, and pulling a prisoner out of some deep hole—because the transport officer who had the shit kicked out of her on the tarmac this morning had worn a black pip on her cap, which meant international travel—was bound to make some noise.

So.

Barko found he was rubbing his head again and put his hand down, with a grimace. He should be watching the sequencing. It would be just his luck if a deviation spiked while he was busy shooting the shit with Aleks or during his own goddamn daydreaming. His stomach pinched itself and growled, but his appetite was minuscule at best.

Yeah, Ashe the Rat had told him he reeked of fear and that was poison in a Rift.

Kopelund had told him, this morning before the prisoner landed, that Barko had seniority, and was going in.

# 8
## CAGEY BASTARD

><|><

Midafternoon in the Rabak was a long, slow sleepy time. The two joyholes* on duty—a male-and-female pair of washed-out, rail-thin blonds—had the time to sit at the ancient, wheezing synthesizer and pick out limping tunes between heavy-footed clients. The barkeep, a widebeam piece of meat from Brest, spent his time polishing the bar to a high gloss and either nodding or shaking his head at a trickle of furtive, hurrying types with something to sell. The nod meant they were allowed to penetrate the shadows at the back of the long low room that was the bar proper; the shake either sent them back out the front door into the cold or, if they persisted, filled said shadows with two looming shapes known locally as Bric and Brac. The twin bouncers were part of what made the Rabak a watering hole for the slightly higher grade of corporate wet-whistlers.

The boy joyhole was attempting a wandering melody that

---

* Licensed sex workers.

jumped from key to key without warning. The door made its usual *squeak-thump*, announcing the newcomer was a regular since the squeak was short. You learned to lift the door slightly at just the right time, after a while. A blast of thin white winter sunlight scraped along the much-polished hardwood floor covered by a glittering mat of woven and knotted floxing-cable. Scuffing your soles on it produced a cascade of spitting sparks, and also temporarily shorted out any clipbugs* you might be carrying.

Zlofter shut the door, the pomade in his black hair glistening, and hurried off the mat. The bartender was already pouring his usual, and as soon as he had the tall glass holding precisely two inches of amber liquid in his hand, the corporate man headed for the right side of the room. Along the wall were the booths, separated from each other by carved wooden screens reinforced with wire netting. The screens, rescued from a pillaged, flaming country estate at the time of the Event, were the Rabak's major claim to a certain amount of fame and a small amount of class. The really high pay grades watered at the Zamszowe, and of course, the rifters had the Tumbledown. There were other bars—this close to a Rift, drinking was more of a necessity and a vocation than a pleasure—but none of them were quite the thing.

The Rabak was for ambition.

He slid into the booth, and the lean, knife-nosed man on the other side barely lifted his dark head. Zlofter settled his

---

* Small pieces of wearable tech meant to record conversations or track a person's movements. Often used by corporate spies, petty warlords, or ILAC and national law enforcement.

ample ass firmly, stuck his own pudgy nose in the tall glass, and inhaled deeply. Satisfied, he took a mouthful and grimaced after he swallowed. His silver earpiece glinted, and his wrist chrono flashed red once before it settled into a reboot.

The other man didn't speak, just measured his well-nursed beer with a soft, slitted gaze.

Finally, Zlofter leaned forward slightly. "I'm glad you could make it." There was nobody in the booths on either side, but he still half swallowed the words as if afraid of being overheard. Meeting here was a calculated risk—that bastard Kopelund could have a set of eyes in the neighborhood—but it was far better than venturing into the Tumbledown *or* breaking his usual routine.

A shrug was all the communication he received.

Zlofter's irritation showed itself in a single eyebrow-twitch. "Well, it worked. She's at the Institute right now."

That produced a reaction. The other man closed his eyes, leaning back a little. Something about that small fluid movement would have told any onlooker familiar with such things that they were looking at a rifter. When he finally spoke, he didn't bother keeping his voice down. "Shine."*

The corporate man winced, his chrono finishing its reboot and blinking a small green light twice. "It'll be a full team. He acts like he doesn't know what's in there."

"You act like you do." It was a mild enough observation.

"So do you." The corporate man's wide round face set itself in immobility. "I couldn't find out when they're going in. He's a cagey bastard."

---

* Slang: That's wonderful, that's great. Can also be sarcastic.

The rifter tilted his head slightly as the joyhole at the synthesizer switched keys again. The door opened again, *squeak-thump*ing, and another corporate man with slicked, shiny hair stepped in. This one was Yesil Inc., you could always tell those fuckers by their canary neckties and their brass-gleaming Aurovoxes.

"Don't matter," the rifter finally said. He took another swallow of his beer, appearing not to notice it was warm. The sleeves of his jacket matched the weak alcohol's color. "She won't wait."

"Well, as long as you're sure." Zlofter pursed his lips. "You have everything you require."

A brief nod.

"The rest of the payment on delivery."

Another one, even briefer. The rifter's pitted, scruffy cheeks flushed. He hadn't shaved, and his broad, capable hands were hard and callused. For all that, they were clean, and his dungarees were too. His corduroy coat moved stiffly, flexarmor patches inserted and broken in hard.

"Well, then." Zlofter almost made a dismissive movement, thought better of it. He glanced nervously at the Yesil man heading for the bar.

The rifter began to slide along the bench seat, obviously considering the conversation over. He stopped dead, though, in that creepy way they all did. Freezing wherever they happened to be, nostrils widening a little, ungainly posed as setters pointing at an unwary bird. "How'd she look?" This time, he almost whispered, so Zlofter had to lean in to catch the words.

For a moment, it made no sense. Why would he ask? Of course, rifters were cagey, too. Maybe this one was looking for an edge. Zlofter was a big believer in giving subordinates what they needed to perform efficiently. "Like shit," he said, finally. "Skinny, ugly, dirty. I was surprised she didn't need medical attention."

The rifter nodded. He slid out of the seat, unfolding to his true height, and his belt buckle gleamed. It was a piece of pig iron, too heavy for his lean hips, shaped in wavelike whorls. He headed across the Rabak's almost-empty interior, opened the door quietly as a regular, and vanished into the glare of white light beyond.

Zlofter shook his head, settled back in his seat, and eyed the joyhole at the synthesizer. He'd send the bill to the Institute, since he was technically "consulting." When you worked hard, you were entitled to a few perks.

He took another drink and allowed himself a wide, bright, unsettling smile.

# 9
## ANIMAL BODY
>+|+<

A real shower, from one of a row of chrome showerheads arching serpentine from the wall. Hot water. Not tepid, *hot*. Government-issue soap, orange and vile-caustic, but it cut the crust on her scalp and the greasy black mess between her long toes. She stayed under the spray until her fingers wrinkled and the tile was squeaky-warm underfoot, until the very last swirling thread of gray dirt in the water had gone down the drain with a throat-clearing gurgle. Svin might have stayed until the water turned cold, if it ever did, but there was a prospect of *food* as well. Even if it was colorless prison slop, it would be welcome.

Her ribs stood out starkly, her hipbones too, and her face was a gaunt ruin, bruise-puffy circles under her eyes and her lips turned to thin lines. There was a slice of mirror over the sink, and it showed her the gray-tinged pallor of sunless solitary confinement stretched tight over bone framing. She hadn't quite hated being cubed—other people were a distraction at best and dangerous at worst—but she'd been homely in a sort-of-fetching way when she still had the glow of youth. Not so much, now.

Ashe the Rat liked them young and worshipful. Not that it mattered now, did it. Svin hadn't expected letters, the Rat wasn't the epistolary type. Maybe she'd expected Svin to be too canny to get deezed.*

Kopelund had issued her a duffel packed with various clothes and oddments—anything she had on her had been incinerated or sold when she went into Guan. It was all right, though, a rifter learned early to never get too attached to anything you couldn't hide, in an orifice or otherwise. Live like a snake, wriggling out of a skin when it got too confining, or breaking off your tail to escape a trap.

She almost swam in the clothes. No panties, not that she wore them anyway, no bra. Not that she needed one, she was down to mousebites on her chest. Faded dungarees, a military-issue undershirt that had been washed so many times it wasn't scratchy anymore, a huge gray wool sweater with a wide neck and stretched hem, leather patches at its elbows. Everything in the world was too big for her, and always had been.

Except the Rift. At least there was a worn, thin leather belt to cinch the jeans around her hips. There was even a tube of unscented lotion in the bag, but she didn't want to grease herself.

No windows in the locker room. The lockers all stood closed, red paint chipping from corners and edges. Her prison jump-suit was filthy, so she stuffed it in one of the empty lockers.

---

* DZ'd. "Deadzoned." Murdered.

It would have been more satisfying to clog one of the toilets with it, but she didn't have anything in her bowels to really finish the job, so to speak. She hefted the dirt-colored duffel and headed for the door. There didn't seem to be cameras, either, but acting as if there were was good tactics.

No guard at the door. Stupid of that Kopelund asshole. But really, there was only one place for her to go, and it made sense to get a meal or two and maybe some supplies beforehand. So, maybe not so stupid. Maybe they didn't have the manpower to guard one skinny-ass felon rifter? Where were all the rifters who should have been on duty, watching the blur or scraping nootslime, or just sitting around bullshitting, drinking, and playing various games with the guards? She'd never worked an Institute, preferring to freelance, but she'd heard plenty about how to kill time in one.

Svin slid down the blue-flecked linoleum hall, peered cautiously into the left-hand turn at its end. *Canteen's down there. I think today's chicken day. After that, ask anyone where my office is, and they'll tell you.*

It was strange to walk without the shackles instead of shuffling, and strange to keep glancing around without seeing bulky armed guards with smoked-glass lenses over indifferent peepers. She didn't have to follow the painted line on the floor, or cross her wrists, or listen for the crackle of stimsticks. The doors to the canteen were open, and a soft murmur of conversation floated down the hall.

Svin stopped dead, as if she were in the Rift and sensed a change. Good or bad didn't matter, you simply waited until you could tell the difference. The new boots were military-issue too, but at least they fit, and there were even thick socks without holes. The duffel got heavier and heavier on her thin shoulder, the strap cutting, but she didn't shift it.

*People. Shoving food into their stupid faces. Probably men.* A cold, clammy shudder raced up from her heels; she clamped down every muscle she could, not even daring to sway.

In a Rift she wouldn't have the duffel. A backpack was best, with a mapbag at the hip, its strap diagonal over the chest. Sometimes they argued about how to hang it, under or over the backpack straps, and what exactly you wanted in the mapper other than strips-and-bobs.* You didn't look in another rifter's mapper, you could claim to have a scuttlesnake in yours and nobody would argue.

What exactly was the problem?

Well, after being in fucking solitary for a while, seeing other people was goddamn unpleasant. It was slightly better when you had no choice, you could fill your ears with static and just let your body do what it had to. *Deliberately* walking into a roomful of assholes chewing and laughing and smoking and metabolizing...

But there was food. She could smell it. Her mouth was full of thick spittle, her head a little woozy. After a certain point the animal body didn't care if the situation was dangerous, it wanted some fucking calories.

Even if the rest of her was paralyzed.

Svin stepped forward, boot-toe touching lightly, testing the linoleum. It looked ordinary, felt ordinary, *was* ordinary. She rolled through, set her heel down, and the floor didn't move.

---

* Strips of material tied to small heavy articles—nuts, bolts, etc.—thrown inside a Rift to discern the location and/or nature of invisible dangers.

It stayed right where it was, doing just what it should. Out here, treacherous ground was all inside the meatsacks moving around. Chewing. Breathing. Processing food and beer and harder fluids, sweating out nicotine and sour sugars.

She tested each of the next five steps, and after that, it got easier. Roast chicken, the faint gritty undertone of potatoes, a thread of coffee stitching it all together, a sinker pulling her in. Swallowing again and again, like a flucwasher* with top front teeth eaten away and the roof of the mouth gone too, the cavity filling up with grit and hardening mucus. Two maroon-painted doors, CANTEEN stenciled in white above them. They wouldn't move on their own, a human hand had to push them.

*Fuck them all. I'm hungry.*

With one last check of the empty hallway, Svin shook her damp, still string-knotted hair and hitched the duffel higher, then strode for the door as if her legs didn't remember metal cuffs and chains, as if she were about to meet Ashe for the first time again, her heart pounding high and hard and her skin alive with cleanliness and danger.

---

* Slang: someone addicted to fluc, a drug lozenge held against the roof of the mouth and worked at, producing several short periods of brief, intense high.

# 10
# FIELD EXPERIENCE

⋺╫⋵

hat's her." Aleks craned his skinny neck, hunching over his tray. His shoulders were sharp points under his lab coat, twin peaks almost touching his jug-handle ears. "Look—it's her."

The fluorescents in here turned him pasty, picked out every crack and divot in the round plywood tables. A clatter of trays and cutlery being washed warred with the hum of conversation from scientists on lunch breaks, sardies catching a bite before guard duty, sweeps, or tower watch, a few of the perennial coffee-swillers avoiding work. A greasy smell of communal boredom underlay the aroma of roasted chicken and garlicky paste-potatoes, cheap imitation butter and a bitter tang of alcohol sugars-and-sweats.

"Sure, stare like you're at the zoo." Captain Morov snorted, wiping his mouth with a napkin that rasped against dark stubble. A filthy-smelling cigar, half smoked and extinguished, laid neatly by his plate, waiting for him to finish shoveling potato paste. His boots were spit-shined, his uniform trousers pressed, and even sitting still his back was regulation-straight. He might have been mistaken for a martinet if amusement hadn't lurked behind his dark eyes, a sour cynical gleam.

"Never been to a zoo. Do they even have them anymore?" Aleks kept staring, sandy eyelashes all but quivering. The lump in his throat bobbed. "Shit. She's tiny. How old is she?"

"Why don't you go ask?" Curly-headed Riggs jabbed his fork into a plump, if somewhat rubbery, chicken breast with fat-rich, crispy skin. His hair was a little longer than regs allowed, but Kopelund had other things to hassle his sardies for. Which meant Morov allowed a little leeway in personal grooming if you kept other bits—nose, dick, and mouth-hole—reasonably within limits. "I hear she's a real winner."

"The Yarker T-dick had it coming." Morov speared a solidi-fied chunk of potato paste, chewed around the words. Small starch-crumbs escaped while he spoke, a sure sign of his own unsettled mood. "Don't fuck with rifters, man. Remember when the Rat stuck a fork in that guy's cheek?"

"I thought that was just a story." Aleks settled back in his seat, every bird-thin line of him jittering with the desire to turn around and stare again.

Fresh out of uni and spastic as a private before his first bor-dello call, Morov thought. Like a puppy, just aching to attach himself to any humpable boot and pee on every lilac bush. "No story. They get funny in the head, after a while. Just fine, and then all of a sudden, you say something and *whap!* Slit his cheek just like a bag of klish.* Could see his teeth." The amount of blood had been amazing, too, and the wet flapping noise as the

---

* A gelatinous drug, often transported in balloons sewn into the omen-tums of unwilling couriers.

man gurgle-howled could have starred in a nightmare or two, if you were prone to them.

"Well, what did he do?" With his eyes round like that, the kid looked about twelve himself. They were always starry when they arrived clutching their degrees and full of that crap about Science solving all problems. It took a while for the gloss to wear off and the desperation to set in.

"Asked her on a date." Riggs snorted at the memory. He dug below the table for his silver flask, added a healthy splash of colorless sliv* to his mug. Morov pretended not to notice.

"He *what*?" Aleks almost spluttered.

The kid was kind of fun sometimes. Pull the tail and hear the puppy squeak. "You're a dimshot," Morov announced. "I hear *this* one killed four cops when they dragged her in for running poppers."

"That wasn't all." Riggs washed the potato down with a swallow of hot coffee-plus-sliv, grimacing a little at the bite. "The Rat was mixed up in that, and some warboy. *I* heard the cops were moonlighting for the warboy, and they were after the Rat. She jumped in time, but this one didn't. Didn't say a single word at sentencing, either."

"Old-school." Morov grunted a little, a slight sound of approbation. You didn't see anything like that anymore—honor among thieves, and all that shit. The world was going downhill, just like it always had. "Stupid, more like."

"Why would she do that?" Aleks jabbed at his own chicken. The canteen was alive with whispers as the new rifter walked

---

* Transparent, high-octane alcohol, used as a solvent and for nearly odorless drinking.

slowly but surely for the counter. She moved strangely, like they all did, not committing her weight through the first half of the step then doing so all at once, with a queer fluid grace. She looked half starved, and the duffel slung on her shoulder—regulation sardie issue, excavated from some storeroom or another—was almost bigger than she was. Her hair was still damp, and stringy-colorless, hanging in clotted, tangled snake-ropes.

For all that, her dark eyes glittered with feral intensity, and fat gray-braided Manda behind the glass shield didn't hesitate to give her a tray. Sometimes the Canteen Queen, in her kerchief and rubber gloves, demanded to see a newcomer's meal card. Standing in front of the shield with a pained smile while she examined it like an ILAC MP* with a chain gorget and a severe case of furious constipation was a rite of passage.

Not this time. The Queen of the Canteen just nodded at the rifter, normal as you please, but took care to shove a battered red plastic tray at her with fingertips only.

"What's she gonna eat?" Aleks whispered. Each day he wore a freshly washed white lab coat, as if his barcode tag wouldn't convince people he was in the science division. Old Barko certainly had his hands full, with this little sausage-choker yapping at him all day.

Barko was all right, for a civilian. Morov made a mental note to get the old man alone and find out what *he* thought of this. It was bound to be interesting. Balding Barko didn't say a lot, but when he did open his mouth it was obvious there were

---

* Military police (officer).

actual wheels working behind his eyes and not just doped-up rats in the skullhouse like most of the scientists.

Dealing with Rift shit made you crazy. You caught it, like a disease.

"Food, just like the rest of us." Riggs set his coffee cup down, exactly on the ring it had made when he first placed it on the table. He picked up his fork, always left at a precise angle across a medium-sized chipped enamel plate.

"I think he's in love." Morov contemplated the remains of his chicken-and-paste. It was about time to pick up his cigar and have his post-lunch smoke. "Better not, kid. The radiation in there gives 'em mutations. She could have teeth in her vag."

"I saw some papers on that." It was Aleks's turn to sound dismissive. "No conclusive evidence, just a lot of conjecture—"

"Yeah, because the rifters won't let you guys poke at 'em." Riggs stabbed a callused finger at the kid. "I hear that at the Penta* they injected people with glaslime just to see what would happen."

"That's *unethical.*" Aleks's chair scraped back along the linoleum, with a long rancid squeak. "No scientist would ever—"

Morov couldn't decide whether he believed that or not. Either way, the kid was getting on his nerves. It was only mildly amusing to listen to brainless, youthful mouth-diarrhea, and no more. "What *did* happen, then?"

Riggs was more than happy to supply the gossip details. "Crazy shit. Bodies exploding, blood turning to glass, brains turned into beef—"

---

* A large slice of the American Pentagon was turned over to military research and Rift experimentation.

"Oh, come *on*, you don't believe that, do you?" Aleks's voice threatened to break. They were turning them out younger and younger these days, smart on the tests but dumb as rocks where it counted. This kid would have been given an exemption from frontline duty, one way or the other, especially fresh outta basic. You got to have a sense, after a few tours, of which ones would break and endanger the whole damn unit. It was a good thing he was civvie.

"Ever been in the Rift, kid?" Riggs knew perfectly well the little scientist hadn't. "After you go, you come back and tell me what you believe."

"Wonder if I can get in this time." Aleks rubbed at his cheek, almost bouncing in his seat. Too much wasted energy, it was about to give Morov a goddamn headache.

He pushed his plate away. It was enough to kill anyone's appetite. A smoke would help. "Kopelund's doing the roster. Talk to him. But between you and me, stay the fuck out of there, kid. Nothing good ever happens inside the blur."

"Yeah, well." The boy stood, gangly and self-important, and scooped up his tray, one of the newer blue ones. Manda probably liked him. "I'm not gonna be like Barko. Field experience is better." Coffee splashed inside his half-drained mug as he balanced it on his plate.

The new rifter chose a seat near the doors, her back to a wall and a good clear field of vision—oddly enough, right where the facility-employed rifters had sat before orders came to disemploy them. They never gathered at a table, though, just sat one apiece. One of the sardie wags had dubbed it the Experimental Section, but the rest just called it the Gallery.

One rickety crumb-laden table had just emptied, maybe a

little bit quickly, when she started walking steadily for it with her tray heaped high. She didn't appear to notice, just settled in a squeaking red plastic chair and began to carefully, methodically, chew and swallow. Three cups of coffee stood sentinel at the edge of her tray, and she didn't hunch over her food like they did in prisons, shoveling before it could be stolen.

Aleks headed for her table, head held confident-high and his lab coat—how many did the kid have, for Chrissake?—flapping just a little. It was a shade too big for him, but neatly pressed all the same. Maybe his mother had taught him how to iron.

"Young love," Riggs grinned, a few of his teeth mashed with canned, reheated peas.

Morov sighed, picking up his half-burnt cigar with blunt but delicate fingertips. "Kid's gonna get himself hurt." He shook his head, sadly, and began searching for his lighter. Manda hated it when you smoked in her canteen, but she could shove that preference right up her wide end. Ever since he was promoted, Morov figured he'd goddamn well earned a bit of cancer after lunch. And one after dinner, too. At least he didn't roll *makhorka*.* He hadn't since his last combat tour.

They watched as the kid approached the rifter's table. She didn't look up from her food. Her teeth were good—one of the first things a rifter of any brainpower did was pay for thermabond† and a shiny smile. There were so many different kinds of radiation inside a Rift, you didn't want to hit tolerance on one

---

* A rough, uncut bacca.
† A medical process whereby bones and teeth are reinforced with substrata Riftglaze.

that would turn your bones to sponge and your fangs to rotting stumps.

When the kid stepped over some invisible barrier of personal space, the rifter looked up. Those dark eyes were huge in her thin gray face, and between her long nose and her pointed chin, she looked almost feral. A creature in an iron cage, guarding a pile of meat, staring with bleary, hate-filled goggle eyes.

She lifted a drumstick to her mouth, slowly. Bit down, and the crunching sound of bone splintering was loud in the sudden hush. She sucked at the marrow, and when she had it her lips skinned back from those white, thermabonded teeth. Her irises were so dark her pupils vanished, and the effect was unsettling.

It didn't seem to faze the kid. He dragged out the chair across from her, and the clatter of his tray hitting the tabletop was very loud, since everyone in the canteen had decided now was a good time to see if the rifter was going to go crazy. The only murmur was of bets being placed, and the squeaking of chairs as men craned to look.

Aleks said something, lowering into the chair, and the rifter just stared at him. She kept eating, mechanically, even chewing the bones—the thermabonding would like the extra minerals. Her unnerving stare never wavered, even when the kid laughed, a high, nervous sound.

After a few minutes, in the middle of one of his sentences, the rifter unfolded, leaping to her feet. Her chair banged the wall, a harsh hollow sound, and she scooped up her tray, still half full. Coffee splashed. Three cups of it would probably wire her half the goddamn night. Prisoners and sardies both liked caffeine as strong as possible.

Morov was pretty sure that wasn't the only similarity between the two populations.

She took two steps to her left, and the kid had frozen. The rifter took another few paces, still with that queer, almost cat-like grace. The table next to the one she'd chosen had already, magically, cleared. She pulled a chair out, placed her tray with finicky precision, and settled down to eating again, just as slowly and carefully.

The kid sat there for a while, the back of his neck a deep crimson, before he got up and hurried out, leaving his own tray, a spot of fresh blue, lonely on the table.

# 11
# JUST ONCE

>⧓<

**C**lean." Hurrack showed his stump-teeth in a wide, pacifying grin. "Untraceable. Takes standard cartridges."

The rifter, in a dun corduroy coat full of flexarmor patches, considered the weapon. Finally, he put out one callused hand and accepted its weight. The dingy, crowded pawnshop was full of golden light for a few minutes, the sun blear-glaring red under a pall of formless gray cloud as it sank below the horizon. Alloy security bars in the display window almost vanished in the hazeglow, their shadows turned starving-thin. The light gleamed in the rifter's dark hair, picked out the pockmarks on his cheeks, and glinted dully on his belt buckle. "Ammo?" He sighted down the barrel, his finger laid alongside the trigger and the muzzle pointing at the floor. Raised it a little, still sighting, his hand bouncing a little to test the heft.

"How much you want?" The right side of Hurrack's grizzled face twitched, a neurological tic instead of a nervous one. His left shoulder was frozen, twisted high toward his ear; his ribs squashed down on the opposite side. His right leg, thick and muscle-corded, ended with a stack-heel boot that tried to keep him mostly even-keeled.

No answer. But Hurrack bobbed his head, understanding, and turned away from the weapons counter, shuffling for the ammo cases on shelves tucked far back from prying fingers. "All right, all right. Anything else?"

"Medikits," the rifter finally said. All around him, merchandise was stacked, arranged, displayed. Leather jackets. Small sealed boxes with techcoceds* stamped on their outsides. Glittering jewelry on faded velvet pads in a cube of solidified glaslime sheets, impervious to blunt force. "Two-three? Full."

That made the pawnshop proprietor stop with a swaying jerk, his right thumb hooked in his belt to keep his hand from swinging into a display case or the edge of a metal rack. "Gonna patch 'em after you pop 'em? That ain't like you, Vetch."

Whether it was or not, the rifter said nothing. He just waited, dark-gray gunmetal gleaming as it dangled at the end of his arm. His eyelids fell to half mast, and the momentary slackness of his face showed what he must have looked like when much younger. Sullen, unpretty but striking, a certain fineness to the long high nose and the thick dark lashes fringing hazel eyes— he could have been attractive, if not for the pitted scars and the cold, congested look of resentful pride so habitual it had settled on the bones and wouldn't leave.

When Hurrack came back, the ammo boxes stacked on a gray plastic tray and the two medikits hitched high on his frozen shoulder, he made a small *tut-tut* with his tongue. "Put it in the case, or I ent gonna bring you shit."

---

* Universal magnetic, UV, and chip inventory control tags.

Vetch did so, sliding the gun into a carrying pouch a little too big for it, obviously meant to cradle a cousin brand of death-spitter. He zipped the case up, sent it sliding along the counter with a single efficient flicking motion, and stepped back, not committing his weight until the very last moment. Hurrack's floor, jury-rigged from below to squeak and moan at the slightest movement, barely whispered under the rifter's heavy boots. Heavy silver stimtape crisscrossed the instep and held the top together, glittering dully with the last flash of bloody gold before the sun slid behind the Event-era tenements opposite, diving for its nightly bath.

The sudden cessation of floodlight made the shop owner blink and sneeze, a wet, juicy sound. He thumped the ammo down and began counting it out while Vetch opened the medikits and glanced over their contents. He pointed when Hurrack had counted out enough—about half of what the man had hauled so painfully across the groan-creaking floor behind the counter—and reached into a pocket. "Forty."

Hurrack laughed, a genuinely merry sound ending on a deep racking cough as he blinked the ghosts of sunset from behind his eyelids. "Fuck *you*, rifter. Two cent, and that's it."

"Kits are past their pulldate." Vetch's pupils swelled, adapting quickly to the sudden dimness.

"Like gauze is gonna go bad? And that piece is *clean*. No serial. No maggie-may-I* stuck up its ass. Two cent."

Vetch blew out between his strong, white, thermabonded teeth. "I'll go up a little, the piece is pretty sweet. Say, fifty-nine."

---

* A pinprick chip containing tracking and manufacturing information, required by law in every projectile weapon.

Hurrack brightened. "Two cent, you bastard, or you can go to Deegan and get a boompop* that'll blow your fucking hand off when it malfunctions." His smile suggested the thought pleased him; he drifted a fog of halitosis over the counter with each word. "As well as substandard slugs to choke it with and med supplies crawling with squiggles."†

"You're not my only stop tonight, Hurrack."

"Oh, I know. But I'm where your ass came *first*. Maybe I like that about you. Maybe we have a relationship, Vetch. So. One cent fifty."

Vetch considered this. "One thirty. That's it." A peculiar flatness to his tone, one a less-acute listener would have called disdain but Hurrack would no doubt hear as finality.

"All right, all right. You rob an old man." His right hand thrust out, and Vetch's closed over his wrist. They shook once, wrist to wrist, the salute one rifter gave when making a deal with another. Perhaps that was why Hurr would risk this kind of transaction in the daytime.

After all, it had been Vetch who carried Ol' Hurr pigaback out of the blur on his third and final trip, the one where a pressure-wave had gone overhead and the older man hadn't hit the ground fast enough. The sinewash dragged Hurrack a good ten meters, racking and twisting his body while he screamed, and finally dumped him just out of the reach of a tangle of hungry silversedge, waving its flat-tape ends yearningly in his direction as it scented meat.

Vetch could have just left him there. He never gave any

---

* Slang: a gun.
† Slang: germs.

reason for dragging him out, and Hurr—now called "the Cork"—never asked.

The younger man's mapper swallowed the piece in its carrying case; the ammo went into double paper bags with the medikits on top, the stiff almost-cardboard rolled down. Hurr the Cork pushed the bag across the counter, but his swollen left hand rested atop it for longer than usual.

"You goin' in?" The twitching in his right cheek intensified, a thin crimson moisture collecting at the inside corner of the watery pale blue eye on that side. He hadn't even made enough from his three trips to pay for thermabond on his teeth. It was maybe a blessing, maybe not—the bonding might have stopped his bones from warping, or it might have made them shatter under the stress.

Vetch raised his chin a little. Regarded the old man. The red drop thickened, traced a wandering path down Hurr's jumping cheek, a drop of oil skipping along the bottom of a hot pan.

Vetch shook his head, gently loosened Hurr's fingers, and took the bag. Set off across the shop, the stimtape on his boots creaking more loudly than the rigged floor.

"Just once," Hurr said. "All I need."

The younger man shook his head again and kept going. The bell on the door jingled sweetly, and he was gone.

Hurr didn't bother wiping away the bloody track on his bunching, pleating cheek. They all came to the Cork when they needed quality, and sooner or later, one of them would do what he asked. He had his mapper all packed, and he only had to pay for once over the blur. He could carry his own piece, a twin to the one just sold.

There was one bullet in his mapper, and it would be enough.

The Cork crippled across the shop, the noise louder as he reached the door and stamped, heavily, a perverse grin lighting his half-smashed face. He locked the door and turned the sign, peering out into the narrow, dusty street.

Vetch was nowhere in sight.

# 12
# HILLS AND CRACKS

⊃╫⊂

A bunk, a wooden chair, a gray metal locker bolted to the wall. A tiny, utilitarian bathroom, with government grime in the corners but only faintly sour-smelling. There was even a window. True, it had reinforced glass, but it faced the blur and she could break it if she really wanted to. It was large enough to let her scramble out without too many scrapes or contusions.

"It's not a hotel," Kopelund said, ponderously. He even stood back from the door, not crowding her. He'd dealt with rifters before, it was all in the little things. His shoes were mirror-shine, but already wearing on the sides from his bulk and heavy step. "But you can lock the door. Tomorrow you can look at the slugwall and see what you think."

Svin turned in a complete circle, studying every corner of the room. No apertures big enough for a fibercam, even. Not that it mattered. If poverty didn't cure you of needing a scrap of dignity, prison did. Best to be a self-contained marble sliding through their maze, so it didn't matter what the fuck they saw you doing. If you concentrated on the rolling noise, bumping against the sides of the corridor didn't matter.

When she finished, she looked him up and down. His uniform didn't look very wilted; maybe he kept his office cold so he didn't sweat. He was apparently waiting for an answer, or some fawning gratitude.

She gave him neither. "I need to go into town. Supplies."

"You want a guard?" As if she had a choice.

*So you're pretty sure I won't go running off.* Of course, if she did, she might get arrested again. She didn't know if her record was cleared or not. Not like it mattered, with what she had planned, and asking would just give him more satisfaction than she ever wanted anyone to feel in her direction. "Not unless Javu Henkell has eyes in town."

"Henkell? The warboy? He was executed two months ago. Murder and profiteering." So he'd anticipated she'd ask, or he'd made himself familiar with the circumstances of her arrest.

Either way, it was good news. Pity Ashe wasn't around to see it. Svin let the duffel dangle, leaning a little to offset its weight. "Then no."

"You need credits?" Another hard little bullet question. Like it pained him to even ask. Nobody liked giving up cash, but this puckered-up bloat probably cared less for it than most.

"Fifteen hundred." Might as well ask for more than she knew she'd get. If he was giving her cash for outfitting, he was *very* sure she wouldn't ditch.

"You'll get a kilo exactly. Don't spend it all on liquor."

Well, better than she'd hoped. "Rifters like getting drunk."

"So I've been told." A tense silence bloomed. Kopelund's dark eyes in their almost-bruised pouches narrowed a fraction, that was all. He was big enough to do some damage, if he caught you.

But all that meat would slow him down.

It would be easy, Svin decided. Let go of the duffel-straps. Two quick steps to gain momentum, launching herself, grabbing the top lip of the doorway and pistoning out a leg to hit him in the face, then the other leg thrown out to wrap around his neck. Letting go, that moment of freegrav as she swung, the crack of a neck breaking, orienting herself inside a smear of color and kinetic energy...

The moment passed, like they usually did. The point was being ready.

Being prepared.

"What are you really after, in there?" Svin dropped the duffel, let her hands dangle, loose and useless. Not crossed in front like they demanded in prison. It felt strange. You could get used to anything, consider it normal, habitual, common.

"You know damn well what's in there, Miss Pajari."

"Don't deadname a rifter, lundie."* Her chin dipped a little. Her hair was clean now, brittle and breaking but longer than she thought it would turn out to be. It fell in her eyes, and she was going to need a trim. Or a shave.

"Apologies." He smirked, looking not very apologetic at all. It was the expression of a government asshole who had everything lined up and liked to make everyone else sweat a bit, but only if he could avoid expending enough effort to get damp under the arms himself. An economy of stress-moisture.

She took one step forward. Two. Touched the doorknob.

---

* Rifter slang for non-rifters. Possibly derived from "Landser."

"Good night." Kopelund turned, and his footsteps echoed as he hauled his widening ass along. You could tell when someone had sat at a desk for a while. The hips became soft in a particular way; they swished just like a Brinkie manhole.* Especially inside red-piped sardie uniform trou.

The corridor could probably be locked at either end. The slice of ground outside the window was definitely in the enfilade of at least two sniper towers. But guard duty around the Institute itself was likely to be boring and sleepy. The rifters would try for ingress away from the hive, and the guards on their leavs would rabbit-hunt, hopped up on thick-boiled coffee and the prospect of bloodshed.

Svin pushed the door shut. Locked it, both knob and deadbolt. Dragged the chair across the worn linoleum floor and propped it just under the knob, not stepping back until she was sure it was perfectly placed. Then she prowled the space and the small washroom, flipping the light switches every time she passed them.

Light. Dark. Light. Dark. It was a luxury, to be in control of illumination. No guards to scream *LIGHTS OUT* or to plunge your small cubby into sheer blackness on a whim. She hadn't been jabbed in the kidneys since the landing that morning. She was clean, her stomach was full enough to make her sleepy, and there were no ratholes along the baseboards. It could have felt lonely, except for the glorious *freedom*.

Dark. Light-dark. Light. Dark again.

She was only a few feet from the slugwall, so close to the blur

---

* Male prostitute from the Brincolas.

she could taste it. She was going in, and Kopelund wanted her to bring out the Cormorant.

The silly fuck.

Finally, Svin pulled the thin mattress off the bolted-down bedstead, shoving it into the hole beneath the frame. The dingy taupe sheets and blankets were clean, the pillow lumpy but the case smelling of bleach and industrial soap. She stuffed the duffel between herself and the wall and curled up, staring across the flooring. Seen this close, it was all hills and cracks, and the dust under the bedstead tickled her nose. Svin ignored it, breathing past the maddening itch.

Her eyes itched too. The linoleum landscape blurred.

*The Cormorant*, Ashe whispered in her ear. *We're gonna get it, you and me. And we'll live forever.*

Now, at last, Svinga could let her eyes leak hot salt water. Silently, her nose getting full and finally trickling out onto the pillowcase, she stared until her body, twitching slightly every once in a while, decided it was safe enough to sleep.

# PART THREE

# BASE

# 13
# FEW ANSWERS

⊰╫⊱

*…Skorczeny takes another route, assembling what he calls a "constellation" of qualities rifters tend to share. Resistance to authority, paired with a high chart curve on the Faulkner free-association series, are matched with an equally high score on the Poulsbo critical-thinking scale (*Relics, *151– 212). Alcohol and caffeine use are almost universal, but the use of other drugs or substances is extremely low (*Relics, *89–103). Attachment disorders and paranoia are common, as are extremes of impulse control. Skorczeny cannot decide whether rifters have excellent capacity for delayed gratifica-tion (*Relics, *214–238) or none at all (*Into the Rift, *125– 146). Even the taciturn among them show a great deal of verbal aptitude and ability, and an overwhelming percent-age (hovering between 80 and 90 percent, depending on which factors you wish to adjust the numbers for) report they prefer traveling to staying in one place. Remarks such as "Got to visit all the Rifts," or "It don't matter which one you go in, they all the same," pepper the narrative.*

*Their casualty rate, habits of emigration, and the necessity for a certain secretive cast of mind make even so dedicated a data-gatherer as Skorczeny rely on a great deal of guesswork.*

*They are one of the few discrete subgroups that seem truly egalitarian—female rifters are as common as male (*Relics, *80–112). Promiscuity is higher among male rifters than female, with some notable exceptions, but most tend to be serially monogamous and indeed to prefer non-rifter partners (*Case Studies, vol. 3*). Despite this, the birth rate for these unions is very low, and further affected by what Skorczeny calls the Third Wave—various quasi-deformities or strange talents the children of rifters and their partners overwhelmingly display. The Third Wave will be treated later, in Chapter 8.*

*Most rifters are highly intelligent but resistant to school, unless it is for a trade or something similar. Mechanics seem to make good rifters, while scientists, no matter their drive to gather data, do not seem to fare nearly as well. Strugovsky, the father of Rift sciences, dismisses all rifters as criminals, but as pioneers in a highly lucrative and quasi-legal trade, it would be a wonder if none of them ever came into conflict with law enforcement. Their convictions, however, tend to cluster at the petty end of the enforcement spectrum—drunkenness, small theft, vagrancy, or vandalism. Copley's work suggests rifters are comfortable with interpersonal violence but strikingly reluctant to use it until other strategies to de-escalate a situation have failed (*Fights and Flights, *409–553).*

*The most intriguing assertion Skorczeny makes is that rifters can tell, with a high degree of accuracy, who else might survive regular trips inside what they call "the blur," if they're guided properly. The evidence for this is more anecdotal than many researchers would like, but even Skorczeny's detractor Morley agrees that they recognize potential rifters and that a successful rifter is usually right when he or she predicts the advent of another successful rifter. However, when pressed to answer why a certain person might succeed and another might not, very few answers are forthcoming.*

*—Who Are They: A Compilation of Current Research on the Phenomenon of "Rifters,"* by Garden, Horry, and Blake

# 14
# SPRAY OF PINE

⋊╫⋉

The Tumbledown had once been a barn. When the Event hit, far-flung suburbs and semi-rural slices were flooded with refugees; the shacks went up as fast as you could say "mother-fucking aliens." Dislocation, sudden concomitant poverty, and governmental crisis all tangled together; the biggest lifesavers were community organizers on the ground trying to get at least some of the people fed and sheltered. You could see it in the tired frames and lean-tos slumping against the more solid pre-Event structures. What was temporary in the smoking chaos had since become accretion, slowly solidifying. Near some of the more active Rifts, slum-clearings were beginning; the major cities that had been swallowed by larger Rift-pimples were still in prime geographic locations, with infrastructure built about them. New skyscrapers thrust upward, fingers raised in defiance of the interruption. If the rich survived, they grabbed the best of what was left; those who *became* rich helped. Within eighteen months of the Crash the social strata had firmed.

Humans are resilient.

A heavy old-fashioned neon sign in the shape of a fiery mythical bird stuttered over the Tumbledown's double doors, the upper story full of blind, darkened windows. None of the glass was broken anymore, not since the rifters had started drinking there. Nobody knew why they picked certain places, some close to the blurline and others on the other side of settlements or towns, as far away as they could get. The Tumbledown was about ten klicks from the base gates, and word was joyriders or nubas* used to juice up there before catching the railroad tracks a short distance away, following them straight into the Rift.

Most of them died on impact with the blurline, not knowing how to cross. Others vanished inside and didn't return. A few came back out, and either drank or drugged themselves to death—or apprenticed to a professional rifter. Though *professional* was a very loose term. If you survived going in without a guide, you were already lucky enough to make any other rifter nervous. Around here, with the Rift locked tight and sardies patrolling with flamethrowers as well as rifles, nubas no longer used the tracks.

The rifters, even though the slugwall was off-limits, stayed. If there were ways in past the deeze patrols, nobody was stupid enough to advertise them. New ones came into town, too, and sometimes one of the local rifters disappeared, either to another city or past the blur.

All part of the game.

Svinga stamped on an ancient, tattered mat woven of tak-fiber† and strips of ancient tires made almost obsolescent by the

---

* Amateur rifters.
† Thin, strong cable made from recycled plastic.

advent of leavs. The poor to middling still drove earthbound rigs, but more and more cars were coming standard with leav cells instead of wheels. *Man made the wheel, but* they *made the Rift*, the proverb ran.

She ducked her head a little, one eye closed as she hit the swinging doors then snapped open and the other closed so the sudden dimness didn't completely blind her. The lid-flicker, just like a lizard, turned her face into a mask, generous lips barely closed over her teeth. Outside, the shiny black leav from the base rocked slightly on its springs, its smoked-glass cockpit closed but the dillybotter* gun at its crest turning in lazy, random increments. A regular junker would be stripped to bones unless it was a known rifter's ride; an armored springer meant live ammunition just looking to take an arm off a petty ride-thief. There could even be a sardie driver in the temp-controlled cabin, bored but comfortable as he waited for his passenger—or for someone to give him an excuse to shoot.

Svin hopped down the half step, landing cat-light as if she had just gone over the blurline, braced for anything. A quick scan of the interior showed two occupied booths, an old, crack-faced Wurlitzer playing a pop-hissing anthem in a corner, a full table near the window with the shadow of the safety grille making a curling pattern over the tented-together inhabitants; there were two slumped forms at the bar and a 'tender the size of a Jukou '56, with just as much chrome in *his* grille. The teeth were a custom job, polished metal lit with tiny

---

* Slang: a type of poisonous flower grown in Rifts, harvested for its large hallucinogenic stamens.

speckles of thermaglit,* and they peeped between a black mustache attached to muttonchops that continued around the back of the skull, leaving the proud high dome of the scalp bare and oil-gleaming. Hard muscle padded with fat had not yet degenerated, and the white apron tied around the barkeep's capacious belly hadn't achieved a last-call state of spill and wipe.

The bartender's tiny coal-dark eyes fastened on the new arrival, and as Svinga eased across the rough lumber floor he visibly considered asking for ident. By the time she reached the tables, though, he was already reaching for a glass, polishing it with a snow-white expel cloth.

Bartenders got to know the look, and you didn't ask a rifter how old. It wasn't good business.

"Pine," she said, when she got close enough. "Two, full." She slapped a crisp fifty-mark onto the bar's glossy, afternoon-clean surface.

You *also* didn't ask if they were sure when they asked for borderline-illegal booze, or enough of it to knock four strong men down.

"Yes ma'am." The 'tender hurried along the bar, ducking into a small alcove behind a beaded curtain. One of the two lumps at the bar lifted his matted beer-blond head a little, peering through a haze strong enough to drop passing fruit flies with alcohol saturation. For all that, those eyes were gleaming, and unsettlingly lucid.

Even the purest ethyl couldn't take the Rift away. But it sure as hell blunted the edge.

---

* Glitter made from scrap thermabond.

The bartender came back, each step rumbling through the floorboards and communicating to Svin's boots. "Two pinc." He carried a bottle sloshing with venomous green, and his wide paw scooped up a second tumbler as he passed shining ranks of them arranged on gleaming wooden shelves. The mirror behind the liquor shelves was darkened just enough, so you didn't have to watch yourself drink if you didn't want to. If you *did* want to, you could peer at your own ghost.

Svin didn't look. Gray from prison, a monkey face and her huge teeth, it didn't matter. She nodded as the barkeep set the second tumbler down next to the first.

"Crystal?" he asked.

Svin shook her head. Neat, that was the only way to drink it. Hard and fast, without ice knocking at your teeth. He poured, and when he slid the first one her way, she dipped two fingers in the oily liquid and flicked them at the floor.

"Ah." The barkeeper nodded, a slow, ruminative movement. Svin couldn't decide whether he was more walrus or bovine. "You here for Rory?"

"Rory?" In other words, *no*.

"Headed down the tracks. Got past sentries, but the blur killed him on impact. Changed his nuts with his head, stupid kid. Chalke told him not to go."

"I'm not here for Rory." *Chalke? That sounds familiar.* She kept her left fingertips on the bill. "Chalke's got an ocular in his left, and a limp?"

"That's the one." The barkeep poured the second pine, a generous measure, and slid it toward her. Svinga lifted all but one finger off the fifty. "You lookin' for him?"

"No." She lifted the first glass, weighing it. Touched it to her lips. "I'm here for the Rat." Ashe wouldn't stand here and drink, she'd take it to a booth and settle where she could watch the door.

Even the static-wheezing Wurlitzer in the corner paused for breath. Svin took the first mouthful without exhaling, threw the second as far back as she could, did *not* gag on the third, and when she popped the glass down on the bar with a heavy, confident sound the 'tender's mouth closed with a snap.

"Pig?" His tone was low, confidential, and his eyebrows could have been braided into his muttonchops if he'd a mind for it.

Svinga suppressed a belch, nodded. Waited for her stomach to figure out what the fuck she'd just done. Pine was supposed to taste like an ancient industrial solvent, and it was a hell of an accelerant. There were stories of rifters fighting off scuttles or pinchoks* with a spray of pine and a spark.

The bartender nodded back. "I'm Rafello." His ham-hands rested, one on the counter, the other loosely clasping the bottle of pine. His knuckles held pads of scarring, boxer's mitts. A good one, if his skullmeat wasn't completely decoupled by repeated pounding. "Put your paper away. I got something for you."

Svin didn't argue. She whisked the fifty back into her pocket, a darting sideways glance daring the blond, watching rifter down the bar to add anything to the conversation. He just blinked, blearily, focusing not on her but past her, peering into memory or the mists of expectation.

---

* A flying animal, said to be Rift-mutated from vultures.

Her stomach exploded from the fierce warmth, a nova dropped into her middle, and she pulled the second, full tumbler toward the edge of the bar until its bottom peeked over. She swallowed pine-scented, burning saliva, hard, twice.

Ashe had left her something after all.

# 15
# IN HIS FAVOR

꘡

In a frigid wooden-walled room with a polished metal desk, a pen scratched against one of the endless requisition-and-report forms. The ancient black tetherphone, its cable snaking to the wall, buzzed viciously, and General Kopelund reached for it without looking up, his weary dark eyes peering from flesh-pouches.

"Uh, General, sir?" The voice on the other end of the patchy connection was familiar, but the note of hesitation was new. Bechter was not the indecisive type. "She's been in there for four hours."

"So?" *She's been in prison for years; of course she's going on a bender.* Kopelund glanced at the atomic clock attached to his office wall, a small blue marble rotating easily in its three-pronged cenestat setting. It would continue ticking when he was dead and gone, unless someone pried the popper out to use in something else.

As far as the scientists could tell, the energy from the little blue globes was clean and infinite, or so close as to be indistinguishable. They could even divide the goddamn things in a C-stat engine, each marble the same size, same weight, same mass, and emitting near-infinite energy in packets that adapted to whatever small appliance it was attached to. They couldn't make them bigger, couldn't run cars or large equipment off them, but the scientists were so fucking proud of themselves you'd think they'd solved time itself.

"So should I go in and get her? The place is filling up and it's getting dark."

Kopelund suppressed a sigh, leaning back in his wide, cushioned, very expensive Ygraat chair. His window was half open, and damp almost-spring chill stole in with the sound of parade drill in the courtyard, boots smacking and yells so familiar he barely heard them anymore. He liked his office cold, barely using the thermagrate in the winter but dialing up the frostweave in summer's swelter. You just thought better with a cool breeze or two. His uniform jacket was hung on the wrought-iron stand near the closed door, he was in his under-sleeve, and small curls of steam sometimes lifted from his hairy bare forearms when the draft from the window freshened. "Negative, Bechter."

"What if she slipped out the back?"

*Then I'll burn that fat fuck Rafello's place to the ground and send you to the front lines in fucking Guyana.* "She hasn't."

"...Sir?" Was that a *whine* in the man's voice?

What the fuck? Kope had chosen one of the real hardasses to go with her, just in case. Or, at least, he'd *thought* the man was a hardass. Looked like a drastic revision of Bechter's personnel file was in order. "*What*, for fuck's sake?"

"She just came out. She's got a...a bag with her, a big one. Sir, she's *drunk*."

Now *that* was interesting. The Tumbledown's owner would likely have a full report on whatever deal she'd made inside, but getting it out of him would likely call for more than Kopelund wanted to trade. It wasn't necessary, especially since Rafello refused to touch guns. For that, she'd need more than a kilo and a visit to the most visible rifter watering hole. "Well, it's a bar. What did you expect?"

"Sir...she just...she just *vomited*. On the leav."

"Well, get her inside with a bucket, soldier. What the blue fuckbuckle you calling *me* for?"

"I just..." Muffled thumps. "She's banging on the door."

"Then *let her in* and quit wasting my time!" Kopelund slammed the receiver down. He felt around on his desk for a small black notepad, flipped it open, and scribbled down a reminder to put the man on shithole-cleaning duty for the foreseeable future, as well as slip a note in his personnel file.

As for the rifter, well, if she stepped out of line before stepping into the blur, there was a hole back in Guan ready for her. Even if she *did* do the impossible, going in and returning with the one thing Kope wanted, it would be...impolitic...to keep her around for long. If she managed to bring out something profitable, the risk of keeping her for another run wasn't one he liked to take.

Kope's chair squeaked a little as he bent back over the paperwork. All he had to do was keep everything quiet for a few more days. Then the team would be in the Rift, and they could second-guess him all they wanted before this brat Svinga came out with the thing Ashe the Rat couldn't catch. If she didn't, he was laying his groundwork now to make it seem someone else's fault. There was never any shortage of patsies around.

Stacked in his favor, like a gamble should be. Kopelund kept working.

# 16
# LIGHT OR HEAVY

⊁╫⊰

Nightfall brought them into the Tumbledown, bright- or bleary-eyed, thin and quick or stolid-thick. A year ago there would have been a double score of them, but tonight there were only twenty-two, and their hush filled the entire bar with a strange, charged expectancy. The lundies who came in—a grupper* or four, some nubes, a few spinsoaks† the rifters could tolerate or had even adopted as mascots in their sideways way—were the only ones talking or laughing. A group of stick-thin, bright-haired pollyplecths‡ with gold-toned Aurovoxes in their pink ears and expensive Chaboflot trainers was downing a pitcher of mimosas in one of the booths, aghast and amused in their affected way by their own daring.

Sabby the Pooka was at the bar, sobering up after a long day spent nursing one smokzkey§ after another. He'd even napped

---

* Groupies, often attempting to attach themselves to a particular rifter.
† Bums.
‡ Slumming rich kids.
§ High-octane Belarus "golden" vodka.

at dusk, but as soon as the sun slid down, he began to wake up, just as usual. He unfolded like corktape grass after a hard rain, shoving dusty hands through his blond mane, and didn't look up when a familiar bulk settled on the stool just to his left.

Vetch nodded as Rafello, his apron beginning to show the spills and drops of a night that promised to be profitable, got out a bottle of imported Vat 69 and poured him two fingers.

Sabby blinked, his face slack but his eyes still wide with mad clarity. "Vetch." Sounded like his tongue was a little too big for his mouth. "Hey, dintchu used to know the Rat?"

Vetch watched the glass as Rafello slid it toward him. The barkeep raised his head, looking over the Tumbledown's interior as if scanning for an empty glass or a troublemaking sod.

Vetch hooked a finger around the bottom of the glass and drew it along, slowly, reeling the drink in. "Rat?"

"Ashe. Skorryna* year ago blockside."† Sabby blinked several times. "Wait, no. Was before you blew in."

"Heard about it." Vetch considered his drink.

A loud spray of laughter from the pollypleeths splashed against the walls. Rafello hefted the Vat 69 bottle slowly. Sabby turned back to his own glass, hunching and glancing at the mirror behind the shelves. When the barkeep finally lumbered away to the end of the long polished counter, Sabby didn't move, but his lips did. Just a little, a jailbird's whisper.

"You goin' in?"

Vetch lifted the glass, inhaled a good long breath of whiskey.

---

* Slang: "Bit it." Died. Passed on. Shuffled off the mortal coil.
† Slang: on the Institute side of a slugwall.

He said nothing, but his gaze met the ghost of Pooka's in the mirror.

The blond rifter closed his eyes, ran his fingers along the bottom curves of each glass lined up in front of him. One, two, three. "No. I ent gonna." Four. Five. "You know wha's in there."

"So do you." Vetch's lips didn't move much, either.

The unspoken addendum—*that's why you're here drinking on credit, you bastard*—hung between their shoulders. Vetch's steady gaze didn't alter, tracing the lines of Sabby's ghost in the mirror. Above their reflection-heads, the bottles gleamed and glowed, each one with a bastard promise of liquid surcease.

Wide-hipped, daze-eyed Cabra arrived on Vetch's other side. She hitched one of those glorious hips up onto a spinning barstool and set her half-full glass of pinara* down. Her braids, starred with blue, red, and yellow beads, were wrapped tightly around her round, heavy head. A fingerswiped glare of white greasepaint slashed across her left cheekbone, a hyphen looking for another half to join it.

Sabby's head dropped forward. Six. Seven. Eight. One for every hour he'd spent in here, feeling the tingle across his nerves, loathing and craving it at the same time. "When?"

"Soon. Poundside up."† Vetch downed his whiskey all in one shot, and Cabra made a face.

"You don't even respect it," she weighed in. No need to whisper now. "Light or heavy?"

"Heavy," Vetch said. Some of the other rifters in the bar

---

* Pineapple-scented alcohol with enzyme additives, also used as a cleaning fluid.
† A rifter expression. "At the usual place."

stirred, sensing the change in the current. Just like lions at a waterhole, when a bleeding piece of meat staggers by. "One, Cabra. No more."

She nodded, sharply.

"I ent gonna," Sabby repeated.

But Vetch dug in a pocket and flattened a battered, creased hundred-mark on the bar's shining surface. Rafello, catching the motion, began to lumber back. "For his tab," Vetch said, tipping his head in Sabby's direction. Cabra laughed, a short unamused bark caught halfway through and strangled by her lips, as generous as her hips and just as sought after.

She usually paid the Pooka's bill.

Vetch slid off his stool and stood, feet planted, his ghost behind the bar straight and tall until the shelves started at his deceptively lean shoulders. His ghost's expression, though, lumped and distorted by the bottles, was just as hard as the flesh's.

Rafello swept up the bill. "Anything else?" The bartender's eyes held avid little pinpricks in the center of the pupils, and there was a general movement for the bar.

Vetch shook his head. He glided for the door, and by the time he stepped out into an icy sleet that nonetheless betrayed spring's advent by splatting dully into mush instead of freezing solid, Cabra had already chosen the fourth rifter to make a team.

Profits were all you could carry, and the word was to come armed.

# 17
# JUST BY LOOKING

⋊╫⋉

A n exhausted, icefog-choked sun glared at the Institute, and the rifter looked just as rough-tracked. Barko watched the skinny woman as she stood, her freshly shaven head cocked and her hands on her hips. Her dark eyes were bloodshot and her clothes were baggy, with creases that suggested they'd been in storage for a while. It was the closest thing to a uniform rifters had—armor-patched dungarees, a wide leather belt, layers on top: thermal undershirt, two flannel button-downs, a woolen coat with flexarmor patches sewn in odd places. Over the coat, the rifter's hipbag—they all carried them, and all she was missing was a backpack. Since she wasn't wearing the latter, she probably wasn't planning on stepping right on in.

"Not today," she said, finally. Her thin, sharp-peaked shoulders came up, and she actually sounded *disappointed*. "Blur's going too fast."

"Too fast?" He couldn't help himself, repeating it stupidly. The breeze shifted, and he caught a whiff of metabolized alcohol, the fragrance of a pine bender. The stuff that made it taste like an intense but false memory of trees metabolized into sick-sweet sweat. Bechter had spent all night scrubbing out the leav, and was full of vengeance. *Wait for four fucking hours without even a piss, then she starts screaming halfway to base and fucking vomits everywhere.*

Well, what had the dead-eyed, by-the-book asshole expected? A woman just out of prison and drunk as a dead dog wasn't going to sing "Hello Piggies"* all the way home. Barko's lab coat flapped, and he wished he'd put on a parka. Spring was right around the corner, but the wind still cut right through everything. His hands were numb, and he couldn't help glancing nervously at the towers.

"Yeah." She pointed at the shimmering wall, flicking her finger back and forth, following a motion Barko couldn't track. Slugwalls moved like the surface of a soap bubble, curtains of energy that looked thread-thin until you tried to cross. The rifters could somehow sense gaps in the curtain, and even when you hooked them up to EEGs while they did so all you could see was a queer clustering of brainwaves, never the same twice.

You couldn't put a rifter in an MRI. At least, not sober. Even those who might have agreed to it before going in and signed releases and contracts flat-out refused when they came out—*if* they came out. Not a one of them would say *why*, either.

"You have to wait," she continued, in the same flat, colorless voice. Her shaven scalp gleamed white, and the demarcation between the paleness and the gray of prison was a line as thin as the slugwall. All in all, though, she looked better than she had

* A popular children's song.

100

yesterday. Hungover was bound to be better than just-released. "Go back and tell Kopelund."

*I'm a scientist, not a messenger.* "He'll figure it out when I don't call for the rest of the team." Barko realized he should have taken the excuse to walk away, and wondered why he hadn't.

It was an uncomfortable thing to wonder. It was also strange as fuck to be out here without the loudspeakers looping containment and dustdown protocols. Spending all your time inside the warren of the Institute, especially when you had a room in the scientist quarters instead of offbase, had gotten a lot quieter when the continual blaring admonishments had been switched off. Just plain shooting everything that came out didn't require a list of protocols.

A smaller Rift probably had that song playing constantly. Barko had more than once thought about putting in for a transfer, but always ended up deciding it was less hazardous to stay where he was.

"Team." A coughing scoff. The rifter's boots were wrapped with tarnished stimtape over the instep. It took a long time in storage for tape like that to begin to discolor. "Plenty of rifters in town. And he drags my ass out of Guan."

"You complaining?" Barko found himself polishing his own scalp, dropped his hand with an effort.

That got him a full thirty seconds of silence, and the rifter half turned, her dark eyes uncomfortably sharp. She studied Barko from his busted-heel wingtips to rumpled, flapping lab coat, indifferent shave, and bald head, then glanced at the sniper towers rising from the ends of the U-shaped complex.

*She's calculating.* He couldn't help himself—his mouth

twitched, and she noticed. At least, he hoped the slight tremor of her own chalky lips over protruding teeth wasn't just a sign of detox or psychosis.

"No," she said, finally. In this light you could see her irises, a shade or two lighter than her pupils, but it still made her gaze uncomfortably feral. "Just curious."

"Me too," he admitted, hunching his broad shoulders. Standing this close to the wall, even if you had clearance, was dangerous. You never knew when some asshole in the towers would get nervous. They got a ration of engine-cleaner for every "intruder" shot down—pine, sliv, vodka, harch, whatever was on tap. Shooting at shadows was one of the few ways to relieve the boredom.

Maybe that made her feel friendly. In any case, she spoke again. "You look like the curious type. Ever been in?"

"Prison? Or the Rift?" Why was she bothering to talk to him? Kopelund had just brought her down, and Barko looked up from his morning coffee with a shot of carefully rationed high-grade whiskey to see the rifter, small and childlike, looking at the screens of moving data with a line between her thin dark eyebrows, as if she could see the ebb and flow of the blurline in them. *Take her down there, get a time to go in.*

She made a soft plosive sound, as if his response was too stupid to be believed. "You haven't been in *there*." She jerked her chin at the slugwall.

"You can tell just by looking?" Another stupid question. Of course she could. "But no, I've never been to prison."

She nodded and sank down to a crouch, rocking back and forth slightly, exhaling a formless whistle from behind her strong white teeth. Barko, now the tallest thing in two thirds of the yard, found himself tempted to sit down too. Safety in numbers, and making himself a smaller target.

He waited, but the rifter didn't speak. Just made those small rocking movements and kept whistling a little. "What are you doing?"

"Watching." A flat, colorless word. "Thinking. Go away or shut up."

Later, it occurred to him that he should have chosen the first option. He should have just walked away and left her there, instead of standing like a huge lumbering idiot, freezing himself solid and eventually turning his gaze to the slugwall. He stared, wishing the soap-bubble swirls would make some sort of reasonable, rational pattern.

They did not, and the wind numbed every part of him it could reach so badly he needed a shot in his afternoon coffee, too.

# 18
# YOU WORKED FOR IT
⊰⊹⊱

Aleks might have hoped she'd notice how smoothly he piloted the leav once they left the guided tracks of the base, but she just slumped in the passenger seat and stared out the smoked window, her spidery fingers drumming randomly on the patch over one thin knee. She stayed that way for the entire way into town, other traffic—both wheeled and antigrav—parting in front of their obviously official craft. He set down in the government section of the square, and the whine of the leav's generator powering down was interrupted by the rifter throwing open the hatch on her side. She was almost out of sight by the time he finished cool-and-lockdown, heading for Deegan Alley where the black market had settled, a residue of stalls and hawkers pooling in the shadows between two rows of rotten-tooth pre-Event buildings. Small and quick, she darted into the crowd and if not for her pale shaved skull and distinctive bird-hop gait, Aleks would have lost her completely.

He had longer legs, and the hurrying buyers divided around

him like water. When he caught up to the rifter, she was in front of a blanket mounded with all sorts of showy metal—creamers claiming to be silver, brass dishes and implements polished to glow in the dimness, flatware pretending to be genuine. Her head down and slightly cocked, she stared at the glittering, and the seller crouched spraddle-kneed on the blanket drew his lips back, exposing all-natural crooked yellow teeth.

"You gon' check mah sheets?"* the seller sneered. "Or you just wan' li'l doshka?"†

"What?" Aleks was abruptly aware of his cadet jacket with its yellow-and-red piping, clearly marking him as a government employee. Maybe he should've worn a lab coat. Did they know the two slashes on the sleeve meant *scientist* and not *sardie*? Now the behavior of the crowd made sense. Maybe they thought he was a soldier, looking to provoke a response to shut some of the hawkers down. "No, I'm a—"

The rifter glanced over her shoulder, her dark gaze flicking over Aleks in that same swift contemptuous arc. "Blur it," she said, not very loudly. "He's just stupid."

Aleks opened his mouth to hotly dispute such an assessment, but someone bumped him from behind and hissed something suspiciously like *shitfucker*. It was a good thing he'd zipped and sealed his trouser pocket, or he might have lost his ident and whatever spare marks he was carrying. He'd heard the gossip about the pickpockets in the Alley, and just a month ago a sardie in full uniform had been found off one of the branching

---

* Slang: identification papers, licenses.
† A kid's pocket money, or a bribe to make a warboy refrain from burning your settlement.

byways, his throat perforated and half his internal organs excised.

There was a good market for meat, and Institute sardies could be assumed to be relatively clean. Except for their livers.

"Fuckin' reggers." The man on the blanket shook his greasy, graying head. A kerchief, rolled into a rope and tied at his nape, kept his hair back, and Aleks wondered if he ever took it out to wash. The owner of the cutrate* near his parents' ruthlessly clean flat in Kielce had looked enough like this guy to be his cousin. "You buying, or just scaring away all my custom?"

"Neither, now." Something in the way the rifter said it made the man drop his gaze, maybe because it was a good idea not to piss off anyone crazy enough to go past the slugwall. She turned, a military-smart movement, and pushed past Aleks, who was already hurrying to take his coat off. "Fuck that. They'll smell govvie all over you, idiot, and you'll lose your fur. Come on."

He hurried to keep up, pressing the seal-tab at his collar nervously. It was the first time she'd spoken directly to him. He searched for something to say that didn't sound stupid. *Govvie. Lose your fur.* Rifter slang, and even though she'd been in prison, she was using the same phrases he heard in the Tumbledown when he sneaked in to drink and listen to rifter talk. He could nurse a single stein of oily lo-alk pitsch† for hours, hearing that slurring mishmash of terms and tongues. The sheer number of them drinking on endweek evenings was the surest

---

* A quasi-legalized store providing small articles—snacks, porn, cigarettes—at a discount, usually because said articles are rejects or stolen.
† Very weak beer.

sign that the snipers and machine guns and floodlights weren't working to keep people out of QR-715.

The rifters had names for every bubble. They called this one *Cormorant Run.*

She plunged under an arch cobbled together out of collapsing rubble and into a twilit passageway where the real goods began to appear. Aleks hurried to keep up, but the rifter abruptly slowed and glanced back at him, again. "Stay behind me." Even and flat, like she didn't care if he heard her. "Don't look up, and don't open your fuckbuckle mouth."

Aleks clicked his teeth together so hard they sounded like poppers banging against each other on a tabletop, and nodded.

She waited another few seconds, her well-worn stimtaped boots picking out clear spaces in front of her while her head was turned sideways, hopping from cobble to cobble with weird, mechanical grace. She didn't even have to look down to walk, and Aleks's head hurt, a spike through his temples. His feet had always been too big, especially when he'd first arrived at uni and tripped over everything—stairs, paper, flat ground in the commons. What was it like to just *know* where to put your toes, to have a body that small and neat completely under control?

She finally made a clicking noise with her tongue and snapped her chin forward, and Aleks had to trot to keep up with her afterward. Raucous cries came from every side, hackers, jackers, and fences crying out in codes that changed from day to day, or even hour to hour, as hard marks changed hands and merchandise slid away tucked into pockets or waistbands, bags of cloth or leather, small boxes or hidden folds.

The sardies didn't come in here. Aleks's nape tingled, his

heart hammering and his cheeks aglow. He was following a *rifter* through the black heart of Deegan Alley. He wouldn't tell anyone about this back at the base, not even Barko. This was so much better than sifting through data on outdated tablets, or running seventy iterations of a Passek-Minor test on shit that came out of the Rift even before Kopelund brought Ashe the Rat on. It was supposed to be science, but it was piecework, and he couldn't transfer out for at least another three years.

This, though, was more like what he'd dreamed of. This was *real.*

The rifter slowed, changed direction, walked aimlessly past one or two small plywood stalls. Aleks didn't even realize they'd been followed until someone fell into step beside her, a heavy pair of boots with fresh silvery stimtape crisscrossed around the instep and holding the upper part together. They kept pace for a little while before the newcomer spoke.

"You fucking govvies now, or is this bait?" Male, a trace of an accent scrubbing the corners of every consonant.

"He's still got his daddy's runoff in his ears, Vetch." The rifter's tone hadn't changed. It wasn't even insulting, just a matter of fact. The tape on her shoes was tarnished, Aleks realized. He hadn't thought stimtape ever went dark. Maybe it was oxidation? No, the profile was all wrong.

A scoffing sound from the stranger. "Ashe liked 'em young, too."

"Easier to impress." The rifter's feet kept going, and Aleks began to try to step only where she did. He'd read that was how you were supposed to follow one of them inside a Rift. You had to even try to replicate their movement, the way they transferred their weight, just to be sure. "Surprised to see you here."

"Not mutual."

*Vetch.* Not a name Aleks knew; he stole small glances at the man's pants. Heavy denim with flexarmor patches, those boots much larger than hers but queerly similar, the dungarees fraying where the heels hit them, slightly too long. The newcomer walked differently, heel-first and rolling through, but both of them seemed to only step where the cobbles were clear of trash, mud, or other substances it was best to avoid stepping in.

These cobblestones were older than the Event. Were there any inside QR-715? Maybe he should ask her. He'd requested, in writing, that Kopelund put him on the team going in. Even if he didn't *officially*, if Aleks just showed up, maybe he could wriggle onto the team. He already had a brand-new backpack, better than the battered one he'd taken to uni.

The rifter—Svinga—stopped. Aleks almost ran into her.

"I'm letting it go." For the first time, she spoke above a flat, disinterested mumble. Now each word was enunciated clearly, and she actually had a very clean, sweet alto. "Old history, time done, blur gone."

The man spat, a juicy wad of saliva. No brown-tea in the splatter, which meant he didn't chew bacca. Maybe he had yellow teeth anyway, and probably a stubble-hard jaw. "Ha."

"Serious." As if she ever sounded anything else. Aleks was beginning to think this woman had never joked in her life, never laughed. *Vetch.* He hadn't heard the name, but something about the boots triggered a fuzzy memory. Had he seen this rifter in the Tumbledown before? Could he look up now?

"Come off it." The man jabbed one heel down on a clear cobble, as if he'd seen a bug that needed killing.

She was unimpressed. "I'm not going to shiv you, and you

110

can keep your part of the payoff. It's fucking spent already, if I know you."

"I invested. Fifty percent's yours, for the trouble." The stranger shifted a little, leaning subtly toward her.

The dim memory wouldn't surface, no matter how hard Aleks concentrated. She'd been in prison for two years, right? He hadn't heard that she'd ever been around QR-715 before. Rifters moved around a lot, though. Itchy feet, some said. Wanderlust. Others said they were all criminals anyway, hopping away when things got hot.

She didn't move, even to lean away. Just kept her weight balanced easily on those small, oddly delicate feet. "I don't want it." Slow and patient, as if speaking to a not-terribly-bright child.

"Don't be stupid."

There was a long pause, the chaos of sellers and buyers around them a dark surfroar. No sunlight got down here, the leaning buildings blocked out everything but a narrow slice of gray, drizzly cloud overhead. Aleks's cheeks felt hot and damp. Only another rifter would say something so insulting, right? And especially in that angry tone, the words sharp as a Harrison spike in a short-term measure of radiation fluctuations.

"Keep it." Svinga finally turned, neatly, her heels placed just so. She would be peering up into the man's face, if he was taller than her, and based on the size of his shoes and shadow, he was. "You worked for it. For once."

They stood like that, toe to toe, and Aleks burned with curiosity. He kept sneaking glances further and further up the man's legs. Thick, strong thighs, and a pair of callused hands hanging by his sides, opening and closing as if this man felt Svinga's throat against his palms.

Or someone else's.

"Bitch," the new man said, thickly. "Did she teach you that?"

"She didn't teach me anything I didn't already know." One step back, two, the small rifter hopping just like a tiny drab bird.

Aleks peeked a little further up. The man's belt buckle was a large round piece of pig iron, twisted in strange dollops and whorls like the slugwall itself. Yes, he knew that buckle—a dark-haired rifter with a big nose, thermabonded teeth, and a set, disdainful face. Aleks began trying to guess how one could make a buckle exactly like that. If he studied the contours, he could probably reproduce it, and—

"Come on, kid," Svinga said, and he moved to obey. There was a wet splorching, and something cold immediately seeped past the flexfoam on his trainers. He should have worn boots. Like her.

The other man just stood there, but he wasn't done yet. "Tani."

For some reason, the single word made the blood rise to Aleks's cheeks again. Like standing in front of the ancient pot-bellied oven at his grandmother's while his aunt made samda* the old-fashioned way. It was the caressing of the vowels, the way the man lingered over the name. Just two small syllables, but there was something in them—a poisonous longing, a strange possessive inflection.

"She's dead, Vetch," the small rifter replied. "Over the blur

---

* A dish made popular during the post-Event shortages, a thick stew of literally "whatever can be found."

and into the hole." Back to that small, colorless tone, but distant. Like a shout from a faraway hill.

She set off again, and Aleks followed in her wake, his palms sweating and his ears burning too, as if he had just heard his parents moaning in the middle of the night, their bed's springs creaking.

# 19
# HASSLED ANYMORE

⊰╫⊱

The canteen went quiet again as soon as Svin entered. Maybe the kid had been yammering that the rifter had business in Deegan Alley, and maybe not. In any case, Kopelund had to expect she would be making connections or picking up necessaries. If Ashe hadn't left all Svin's gear with Rafello, she wouldn't have let the kid trail her into the Alley. The little snot-nosed chaser had all the brains of a mipsik,* she should have left him in there to rot. It might even have been interesting to watch the predators circle him.

On the other hand, if he was all Kopelund had watching her, it was better to leave him in place. If forced, the older man might actually put someone competent on her tail, and in her current half-starved condition, that just sounded like too much trouble. A half-grown nube was only dangerous inside the blur.

---

* Creatures thought to perhaps be survivors of the initial Event, extremely hairy humanoids with very rudimentary language skills. They die if taken from the Rift, and are quite skilled at evading capture.

She glanced over the big empty space and decided she didn't like it. Too many eyes pointed her way, and the air didn't feel usual. Off to her right, in what was the blind spot for an ordinary person, there was...something. Svinga kept moving, but every fine hair on her body rose, her pulse spiking and settling into a hard thumping just below fight-or-flight. Her pupils dilated slightly, the room brightening.

He probably thought he was quiet. He also probably thought that, because he was bigger, he had the advantage.

Svin turned, very slowly, keeping her grav-sink* nice and low. Her knees were loose, her hands too, and the only surprise was that it was the sardie who had flown the leav out to the Tumbledown. She could barely remember the end of that ride, hugging the bag Ashe had left her and feeling the sawtooth metal in her chest spin and spin and spin, digging through meat and bone alike. What was his name?

She hadn't asked, or cared.

Svin exhaled softly, measuring him from toe to top. Yeah, regular off-duty sardie with a wheat-colored flattop. Grablee boots, with their soles capable of gripping the slickest of surfaces, fatigue bottoms, regulation-issue belt, and he'd probably chosen the T-shirt because his muscles showed through the thin blue cotton. Looked like he lifted, probably on the grav-flex machines standard in every installation built before the post-Crash budget crunch. His arms had the look—the biceps bulked and the triceps merely defined, not actually *used*.

He was posturing for someone. Did it matter who?

Her feet were already in the right place. She regarded him

---

* Center of gravity or a differential well on a heavy antigrav sled.

curiously, all of her loose and ready, her mapbag hitched further back on her hip and buckled to her belt. It wouldn't be moving while she fought, and everything inside was tamped down the way she liked it. A familiar friend, but it sat differently because she was skinnier these days. The sardie stood far enough away, for now, and his chest puffed up a little.

"Hey, rifter bitch." Loud enough to carry. He wanted this to be public. She hadn't pegged him as one of the big dogs, the ones you had to challenge immediately when you walked into the yard just to keep your ribs unshivved and your ass unpeddled.

"Hey, sardie scum." She didn't even have to think of the right insult. It was so stupidly easy. The only thing that puzzled her was *why*.

The ride back from the Tumbledown was a blur, her entire body rejecting the amount of pine she'd poured down her throat, and she hadn't been the one to tell him to stay in the leav while she drank anyway. That was Kopelund's order. It didn't look like this asshole cared. Tables full of sardies behind him—more than there should be, he'd been working himself up to this, and word had spread. Bored out of their minds, they would welcome a good bit of violence. One of those male communal rituals, like a Zeeland splash* or a chunnit.†

Why was this particular man the one, though?

Well, again, it didn't really matter. What *did* was getting out of this with as little damage as possible. There were few of the science staff around at this hour, and one of them was the

---

* A drink-until-you-pass-out game popular in warboy bands.
† A gang rape.

older bald man—Barko—who had stood next to her while she watched the slugwall that morning. His rumpled lab coat had pockets crammed with a paperback book and a couple anonymous bumps that were probably forgotten items, he had that distracted look. The nube who worked with him wasn't at late lunch, probably a good thing. Barko, in the canteen line with his tray half full, had turned to see what the whispers were.

"You fenched* all over my leav," the sardie said, this time *not* loudly enough to really carry. "You know what they do with dogs?" He grinned, his left top incisor glittering gold. Which was a waste of good thermabonding, but some went for flash like that. Mostly dumbass Tarnes† boys. He didn't look quick enough to be from that slice of the world, but she braced herself in case he was.

"I don't go outside my species." She made each word nice, and crisp, and clear. "Dogfucker."

He stopped dead, the confident smile falling so fast it was amazing it didn't shatter on the floor. It took a few seconds for reality to work through his ears and batter its way into the meat masquerading as brains between them.

*Wouldn't last long in the Rift.* She could even request him for the team and tip him into the blur, if she wanted. Easy as breathing.

"Bechter!" A short, commanding bark. "What's going on?" The bald scientist had left his tray; his heels made black marks on the floor as he hurried toward them. Svin tilted her head, considering this, watching the blond man. He was going to be

---

* Slang: any form of quickly expelled bodily fluid.
† A large slum near what used to be Marseilles.

118

trouble, no matter what, and if she didn't take care of it now the next thing might be an ambush somewhere else.

Or a shot from one of the towers while she watched the slugwall.

*Once you've made up your mind*, Ashe said, dimly, in the close steaming burrow of one of their many rented bedrooms, *don't give the motherfucker a moment more to breathe.*

It was academic anyway. Bechter lunged, arms spreading, probably meaning to get her in a bear hug. Svin held her ground, waiting, weight dropping into her right knee, and when he had plenty of momentum she pitched herself aside, landing hard enough to lose her own breath. Her left leg pulled up, then jackhammered out as soon as her right hip hit the battered, blue-and-yellow-flecked linoleum, and Bechter's knee gave sideways with a terrific splintering *crack*.

Svin rolled forward, gaining hands and knees with a quick catlike movement, monkeying after the falling meat on slapping palms and bootsoles, not bothering to stand up, just scrambling.

He didn't shout until he hit, and then it was the bellow of a wounded beast. Svin was on him in a moment, a tiny creature leaping onto the back of a downed buffalo, one boot grinding down on his outstretched wrist, the *pop* of an elbow dislocating as she grabbed his left arm and levered it up, back, and at precisely the right angle; and just as he finished screaming and was whooping in another breath to yell again she had her left arm across his throat and her free hand squirming around his face, fingers turned to sharp vicious claws even though her nails were bitten down. Getting so hungry you chewed your own fingertips robbed you of a lot of things, but it left you with the habit of nibbling. Not a fair trade, but what was, in this fucked-up world?

Screams. Chairs and tables falling, shoved aside. Svin's left arm tightened, a skinny iron bar across Bechter's throat while he choked on blood and snot and terror. This was *not* how he had expected the fight to go.

Her fingertips sank into something soft, and he screamed afresh. Everyone else was yelling, Bechter thrashed, they couldn't get close enough to pull her away with him moving that much. She made one last convulsive effort, wrist aching and her entire arm tensed, and when they could finally pull her off her bloody fist was clenched.

It was Barko who pulled the fire alarm to get reinforcements, and Barko who dragged Svin off Bechter despite getting a blow to the stomach that brought up his morning coffee in a hot acid rush after things had calmed down. The sardies might have clustered the rifter and stomped her with their own heavycatch boots—not grablees, they had only intended to be spectators—if she hadn't begun to laugh, a high-pitched crazy sound, and lifted what was in her right hand.

It was deflated but recognizable, a long tangle of nerve and bloodstrings widening into a pale orb slimed with blood.

Svin popped Bechter's right eye into her mouth and began to chew. Fluid spurted between her strong white teeth, and she lifted her lips in a blood-grimed snarl that forced the collective sardies back on their heels. One of them let out a little moan of disgust, and by the time Kopelund arrived shouting, "What the fuck is going on here?" Svin knew she wouldn't be hassled anymore at this facility.

It was a welcome thought, even if her lunch had to wait.

# 20
# STAMPED AND SIGNED

>╫⦂

For Christ's sake." Kopelund slammed his hand on the polished metal desk. His pen-cup rattled, and the molten ball of ammo he used for a paperweight—someone had fired into the slugwall with a machine gun—jumped a fraction of a millimeter. "Just like kids. I look away for *two goddamn seconds*."

Morov shrugged, his hands behind his back and his boots solidly planted in parade rest. At least Kope didn't have to deal with mothering the assholes daily, that was *his* job. And they wondered why he smoked. "She threw up in his leav, and he was pissed about it."

"So he decided to do a beat-down on a woman a quarter of his size?" Kope spread his ass more firmly in his squeaking, expensive chair. Sooner or later *that* piece of engineering was going to fail spectacularly, and anyone unlucky enough to witness it would get busted too, even if they kept a straight face. "And got his eye torn out? Help me out here, Morov."

There was no help to be had, and Morov knew it. He just shook his dark head, aware that as the commanding officer in the canteen he should have done something before Bechter got his ass handed to him by the rifter. As it was, only skinny-ass Barko'd had the brains to do anything.

The old man could move, when he had a mind to. Which was interesting. "Look, just tell me what to put on the paperwork."

"Industrial accident. Blurline duty's full of shit, we all know that. He'll go to Viflis and get an ocular. Then he's coming back here and I'm going to have him scrubbing toilets until the Return."

"Ocular'll disqualify him for frontline, sir." It was a faint defense, but all Morov could offer. He didn't like Bechter, never had, but still. Kope had a vicious streak in him, and he bit downward. There were precious few higher officers who didn't.

"I'll pull a string or two. I'm busting his rank down anyway, his goddamn stipend's going to be candy money by the time I get done." Kopelund sighed. His nose twitched once, twice, again. A bad sign. "Should have known better, rifters are fucking crazy."

"Yeah, well, this one's not making any friends. She *ate* his eye." Nobody would mess with her now. Which was, Morov suspected, the point. The bitch had some brains, first getting the transport 70 who brought her a beating, and now this. He longed for a fresh cigar, and for a nip of something strong enough to undo the way his neck was already throbbing with tension.

"What did they expect? Christ." Kopelund now massaged at his temples with one broad, spatulate hand. "He wasn't on your list to go in, was he?"

No use in lying. "Not now."

"Better rethink everyone else too, then. I don't want anyone trying to fuck with the cunt before she brings out something juicy."

Morov almost opened his mouth, thought better of it. Fortunately, Kopelund didn't notice. Instead, Morov looked at the half-open window. Dust grimed its corners and the thin late-winter sunshine had turned the frost on the glass into condensation, a spider-pattern of warming. It would freeze over again tonight, but not as hard as usual. The ground was softening, and there was even some greening in the packed dirt around the drillyard. It would turn to knee-deep mud soon, but that wasn't Morov's problem.

No, right now his problem was getting the paperwork right so Kope wasn't breathing down his neck all the damn time. Figuring out who he could take into the blur now who wouldn't try something funny with the rifter once they were offbase. And, not so incidentally, trying to find a way to get out of having to go past the blur himself.

*Well, fuck*, Morov decided. *Can't make him any madder than he is now.* "We're sitting on QR-715. Town's full of rifters. They have to be getting in somehow. Why not just put a few of *them* on payroll?"

Kopelund didn't stop rubbing at his temples. "Are you an idiot, Morov?"

"Not sure, sir." On a good day he would answer *yeah, it's why I got promoted*.

This was not a good day.

Kope's piggy little gaze flickered over him. "I never had you pegged for one. Don't act like it now."

"No, sir." Which made it obvious, since Morov was well

aware he was not the sharpest knife in existence, but he could work his way through some cutting if he had to. "So the stories are true. About *it.*"

"Not necessarily. But even if they're only fifty percent... even if they're only thirty, well, there's something to be said for getting in there. The Rat was no fool, and she wasn't a liar either, when you could get her to talk."

"And this little cunt was the Rat's buddy." The locals all had friends, too. Or at least, what passed for coworkers in their strange little circles. It would only take one getting curious about a disappearance to cut into Kope's expected profit margin.

"You're beginning to feel the drift. Now get out of my office and take care of the mess with that shit-for-brains." The general reached for a 7-17 report in his in-box, and the tetherphone at his elbow shrilled. "God fucking *damn* it."

"Yessir." Morov made his heel-clicking military turn, knowing it irritated the other man, and shut the door with a sound just short of a slam.

His transfer request was in his pocket, stamped and signed. He had a friend in the 59th Division's HR who had promised to fix the right kind of seal on it and get him out of this hole.

But maybe he could wait a little bit. Christ and the aliens, Kopelund was actually going for it.

He was chasing the Cormorant. Nobody knew just what that goddamn thing was, but rumor had it the rifters had a Holy Grail, somewhere in the biggest Rift on Earth. It was probably worth a pretty penny.

Morov was halfway back to his own small office—no high-up window for him, just a rectangle of wired-for-safety glass looking into the ass end of a spiny bush planted along the north side of the compound—before he carried the thought through to its logical conclusion.

The rifter was expendable. By extension, so was anyone else who went in looking for that mysterious object. He could count on casualties, and if he survived he'd have to make sure Kope didn't turn *him* into a Bechter.

Which meant, along with the paperwork for that sad, sorry sonuvabitch, Morov might have to fill out something else. Anonymously, of course.

No, today was not a good day. Morov sighed, and reached into his breast pocket for a half-burnt cigar.

He was, he suspected, going to need it.

# 21
# FINE FOR CROSSING

⋊⊦⊦⊂

In the middle of the concrete cube Kopelund had shown her to, Svinga sat on a blanket pulled from the bed and folded into a pad. Cross-legged, in a shirt she'd bought near the Birmingham Rift and a pair of Ashe the Rat's panties—too big for Svin, pale pink nylon, somehow stuffed into the bag of belongings Ashe had carted here and left with Rafello at the Tumbledown just in case. Dried blood made arcs under her ruthlessly short fingernails, and her legs were sticks. You could see the muscle attaching to bone, deep grooves on the inside of her thighs. Ashe would have laughed and pinched her. *Eat something, bitch. I like 'em round.*

The much-folded, dingy envelope had a cellophane window. Recycled, just like everything else between them. Ashe had taped it shut, not with stim or flex but plain old packing extrusion, and Svin's old pocketknife opened it easy as oil. Briefly Svin wondered how Ashe had stolen the blade from *politzei* evidence lockers, or who she had managed to bribe, but it was inconsequential.

Two sheets of coarse paper. Chunky, small, crude writing. Svin could almost *see* Ashe bending over this, pencil jutting from her left hand and her wrist awkwardly curled. The Rat got straight to the point, as usual.

> Bitch why you have to do that. Shoulda run we couda made it. Now you in prison and who gonna be my sweet thing?

Svin blinked, heavily. Gooseflesh spread across her shoulders, down her back, rippled across her thighs. The "arresting officers" had been so far in warboy Henkell's pocket it was a wonder they didn't smell his farts, and they'd laid ambush for Ashe on the way back to town. Didn't count on Svinga being there, didn't count on her going killcrazy, didn't count on one small rifter bitch with a bad wire in her head. When you had nothing to lose, you could tear open a man's cheek with your bare hands, or take a stimstick from a *politzei* and jam it almost through another one, even punching riot gear.

Ashe made it out, of course. She knew when to run, and Svin had pushed her down the hill before hopping on the closest man, the one with the gun instead of the stimstick. A stupid move, really. She should have run.

> I gon wait for you but if sommin happn I got this. You say I go on play but I aint gonna. I jus wan you.

When had she written this? The Rat wasn't known to be faithful when it came to her fucktoys. It had bothered Svin until she figured out she didn't have to be either, and there was Vetch just waiting in the wings. Some sticks liked it when their hole had another on the side. The fantasy of both at the same time got them off, and Vetch had been just rough enough. It'd been nice enough to occasionally feel...contained, to relax when he pinned her against the wall with his bulk. Or when she was jumpy after a return, all her senses dialed to maggie* and her body too survival-hoppy to be safe. Maybe he'd even liked her bad-wire moments.

Vetch had been part of the sting. Hid his share of the payout and went right to Henkell to sell their names, or maybe just Ashe's, figuring he could get Svin's part of the payout later. It had taken her a little while in solitary to piece it together, but she had. The only thing she felt, thinking about it now, was a weary revulsion. Anger might have burned itself out, or maybe she didn't like the percentage on revenge just yet.

I found it but imma keep it for you. Bossman here stupid thinks its somethin porty. You an me gonna catch the bird, I got him workin to get you out. If you reading this tho, I been erased. Dont cry. Imma wait for you catch the bird.

Svin's teeth made tiny oily squeaks of strain. She unclenched her jaw with an effort. Her eyes burned. Her neck ached. She'd put off reading this, knowing Ashe would have put *something* in the duffel, some message. What would have hurt more, Ashe

---

* Slang: mega. To the maximum.

saying *too bad so sad*, or . . . this? And the roll of marks—a full couple K of ready, and a string of numbers that was the code for the account Ashe had put Svin's part of the payoff in.

Probably every penny of it, too. Why hadn't Ashe just *taken* it? That would have been better.

It would have hurt less.

The second piece of paper, scribbled with cryptic marks, smoothed across Svin's knee. She traced parts of it, imagining sleek-haired button-nosed Ashe with her tongue poking out the corner of her mouth, wholly focused as she drew and shaded. There were a few *X*s drawn in puke-green crayon; it reminded Svinga of treasure and pirates, codes and spies. Another rifter might have been able to guess it was a map, but maybe not the whole value of it.

Besides, it was always best not to trust another rifter's map too completely. The Rift *changed*, and the rifters did too.

Kopelund probably was hoping Ashe had left some clue, a whisper in Svin's ear. Or that Svin herself could meld across Ashe's tracks inside the blur and somehow escape whatever had killed the Rat.

She spent a long time bent over, tracing and touching the different marks, occasionally mouthing a few jumbled words to fix something in memory.

When she straightened, she glanced at the door, then at the window. A curious expression crossed her face. Slack, thoughtful, and exhausted all at once, her dark eyes gleaming with the dull fury of a trapped animal.

The second sheet was heavy industrial paper, so it made a fine noise when she tore the map into strips. She chewed each one thoroughly into a colorless, flavorless wad, and washed them down with cupfuls of the mineral-tasting water from the sink. The small tin cup made a tiny clicking sound each time she set it down to stuff another strip in her mouth, like a key turning a lock and silence returning to a cell.

With that done, Svin got up, slid out of the panties, refolded them carefully, and put them in her backpack. She'd leave everything she didn't need in the duffels, and travel light.

It only took a few minutes to get dressed again. Ashe's letter, in its much-folded envelope, was tucked into her mapper, and Svin dragged the chair away from the door.

She went to tell Kopelund the blur would be fine for crossing tomorrow.

Early.

# PART FOUR

# RIFT

# 22
# INGRESS AND EGRESS

⊰⫢⊱

**INSTRUCTOR:** *Thorley, get your thumb out of your ass and pay attention. What's the most dangerous time in a Rift?*

**STUDENT A:** *Uh… any time you're not paying attention.*

**INSTRUCTOR:** *Goddamn right. Now, name the critical junctures where danger cannot be assessed.*

**STUDENT A:** *Uh… ah… Ingress and egress, sir.*

**INSTRUCTOR:** *So you were listening! It's a goddamn miracle. Now, everything about these fuckers is hazardous, but it's the wall itself that causes most casualties. You can't see what's on the other side, so you go in blind. You got to pick the one place that won't sizzle your tits off, that's why you hit the driftburn behind your guide, and once through, do exactly what your guide does. If he starts prancing around singing "Molly's Got a Boner," what do you do?*

**STUDENT B:** *Prance around and sing, sir?*

**INSTRUCTOR:** *Sing what, sardie? What precisely do you sing?*

**STUDENT B:** *"Molly's Got a Boner," sir.*

*[Laughter]*

**INSTRUCTOR:** *You laugh now, motherfuckers, but here's the thing: You don't know what's on the other side of that wall. The rifters go back and forth, and they stay alive, so you listen like you're in basic, you little bitches. You hear me, Makharov?*

**STUDENT C:** *Yes, sir.*

**INSTRUCTOR:** *The most dangerous times are going in or going out. Just like stickin' your cock in a joyhole. Or, in Igranova's case here, sticking your fingers.*

**STUDENT D:** *Strap-on, sir.*

*[More laughter]*

**INSTRUCTOR:** *I make the jokes here, Sergeant. Now get your asses over to that rigpole and we're gonna see if the wax is still in your ears or if you've heard a damn thing I've said. Move out!*

—Recording, Major Semyon Kalashnikov
Basic Rift Training for ILAC Ground Infantry, Day Four

# 23
# DRIFTBURN

⋊╂╀╉⋉

The sky had cleared, a night of black space and the hard cold points of stars draining off whatever heat the shivering earth managed to retain. Dawn shivered its way through the fog, a stinging rosette just beginning to boil up in the east. A thin tired frost coated the pavement, except for the long looping scorch left a year ago by the burning leav. The slugwall looked just the same, softly lambent in the predawn dimness, glitter-hard and thin as the ice on shallow puddles. Winter wasn't done yet, it still had a feeble punch or three to throw. The air was thick with exhaust—kliegs glared, harnessed to old gennies and filling the entire U with harsh eye-scouring light. There were a couple leavs, too, but the rifter had nixed those. *I don't drift that way*, she'd said, lifting her chin and daring anyone present to disagree.

Now they were lined up. Four hulk-shouldered sardies, Morov with his flattop in command making it five. The science side was bald Barko, prissy pursemouth Tremaine from Map Ops and lean, wander-eyed, bespectacled Eschkov, both weighed down with sampling equipment. Barko had his own complement of smaller scanners and data chips in his high-arched backpack. Aleks was nowhere in sight. Probably off sulking, since Barko had told him in no uncertain terms that he was *not* going into the Rift, and that was that.

The rifter eyed the slugwall, her hipbag over her peacoat but the strap under her backpack's harness to keep it precisely placed. A few days out had taken the edge off her gray prison tinge, and maybe eating Bechter's eye had agreed with her too, because she looked less skeletal. Her teeth were just as prominent, her eyes just as oddly placed, and her head was covered with dark stubble that would be peach fuzz soon. She didn't look cheerful, but neither did she look as apathetic or just-plain-exhausted as Barko expected.

Instead, she looked…intent. A laserlike focus, turning that sharp, unpretty face into a statue's, those big eyes lemurlike instead of froggy now. She didn't move when Kopelund stepped next to her, his broad bullish shoulders looming. One of the kliegs was behind him, and Kope's shadow lay over the small woman, a gravity well swallowing a tiny struggling star.

"You know what you're after." Kopelund tried to say it quietly, but the gennies were roaring. There were new quieter ones running off cenestat tickers* and Reslan coils,† but no space in the bony budget for them here at QR-715. Petrol was much cheaper, and the Institute scientists were agog at the idea of seeing another ingress—and maybe gathering data. You couldn't

---

* A field to keep poppers or another energy source in position.
† More reverse-engineered Rift tech, coils to amplify electricity or run anti-grav/lo-friction fields for larger machines.

do that in the dark. The rifter had been here since about 3 a.m., watching the energy flow. *Soon*, was all she'd say.

The rifter shook her head a fraction. "I know what *you're* after," she corrected, leaning forward. Her expression didn't change, utterly focused on the slugwall. "You coming in?"

"No, I have to—" For once, Kopelund sounded caught out.

"Then get out of my light and tell your boys to get ready. Almost driftburn." The rifters didn't call it *ingress*. She didn't even bother to wave one of her small, deft hands, but the general was effectively dismissed.

Barko watched the expressions sliding over Kopelund's wide, greasy face. They were small—a hint of exasperation, the pinprick to the paper-balloon ego of a pen-pushing man, the distaste of a martinet who couldn't punish an infraction just yet.

If Barko knew anything after being posted to QR-715 for nine years, it was that Kope could—and would—wait for the right time. The instant the rifter wasn't needed anymore, she was tipped into the drift, slagged out, or just simply sent back to Guan if Kope was in a charitable mood.

Which he hardly ever was. Today, the general's nose wasn't twitching at all. A bad, bad sign.

"Listen up," Morov was saying to the four clustering him. Senkin, Tolstoy, Mako, and Brood, all shoulder-wide and hip-lean in combat 'tigues. Two straight-up brawlers, one demo man, and Brood, whose pale gaze barely changed whether he was firing a gun or interrogating some poor shitbird they caught trying to sneak up to the slugwall and hadn't shot.

Brood was at least partly crazy, but he was also luckier than a cat and quiet as one, too. It was obvious what *he* was along

139

for. The only question was whether Morov could keep the leash tight enough on that particular feline.

Barko was considering bowing out, but if he did, he might as well consider himself a coward just like everyone else probably did. When would he get another chance? Next to him, Igor Eschkov bounced a little on his toes, his thick glasses sliding down his hawk nose with the motion. "Wait until you see," he said, leaning against Barko's shoulder. The equipment tied to his hiking backpack swayed, metal bits clattering against each other.

Igor had been in the Rift once, for about twenty-three seconds, in a haz suit and guided by two rifters, both rolling their eyes at his precautions. Back in the glory days of experimentation, back before the word had come down from on high that they were *mapping the smaller Rifts, leave the big ones alone until we know what we're dealing with.*

In other words, a committee had lost their balls looking at the casualty count, or a corporation had somehow achieved a stranglehold on all the others, including the government contract division, and was calling the shots.

Personally, Barko thought it was a combination of both.

"We go through after the rifter," Morov continued. "We go where she says and we do what she does—is that clear? The rifter calls the shots, and when she tells you to move, or to drop, or to bark like a fucking chicken *you do it*. I want all four of you assholes at our next dorm roll call, you hear me? Mako, Senkin, you go right behind me. Brood, you're at the ass end. Make sure our scientists don't get no wandering urges."

"Yes, Mother," Senkin, the shortest and widest of the sardies, piped up. "You already said that."

"I'm only repeating myself so your subnormal ass can understand, Tinkles. Form up, and be ready." Morov glanced at the rifter, evaluating, then past her as Kopelund stepped prissily away.

A shadow lingered at the base of one of the kliegs. Scientists were scurrying behind hastily arranged sensor arrays—an insert was the best time to get more data, and by noon that data would probably be sold on the black market even if Kopelund had the T1 line into the building chopped. Every single science-staff member was here, either watching from behind the yellow-painted crackline or attending to the arrays. Even the canteen staff was probably watching through a window somewhere, elbowing for a good view. Another cordon of sardies were at the back, keeping an eye on everything. None on the sidelines, though, and the ones in the towers had been sobriety-tested before going up there and given a dose of gramoxene so they wouldn't get all excited with a hip flask and ruin the moment shooting at the team as they went in.

*This used to be such a well-run installation.* Barko squinted at a flicker in his peripheral vision, movement where none should be. *What the fuck is that?*

"TIME!" the rifter bellowed, an amazing yell from such a small frame. She pitched forward, and the slugwall responded, its whorls becoming thicker, almost creamy. "TIMETIMETIME!"

"Shit!" Barko lumbered forward, the sardies fell into tac formation, and Senkin shoved past Eschkov, who rolled his wandering eyes and tripped, almost going down with a clatter, staggering to right himself.

The rifter didn't run flat-out, just jounced along in a weirdly graceful lope that slowed as she neared the shimmer. It was the movement of a swimmer eyeing the current and making plans for a dive, her hipbag bouncing and her booted feet side-skipping once, twice, finding the right angle. There was a scramble, a confusing double image as vibrations ran around her outline, she hit the slugwall...

...and vanished into its flow. A long dark streak showed where she'd went in, and now they all had to hit that streak or they'd bounce off at best. At worst the shimmering around it would flash-fry them, or transmute flesh and nerves to *something else*, or cut them cleanly in half—

"GO GO GO!" someone yelled in Barko's ear, a voice that shouldn't be there, and he almost tried to slow down as Morov and Mako vanished into the dark smear. The streak elongated, and something hit Barko from behind. He tripped, and it was the boy Aleks, pelting from behind the closest edge of a high-built sensor array, who grabbed Barko's backpack and shoved them both through the—

*Crunch.*

# 24
# THE REAL FUN

⊰╫⊱

She hit just right, thin slugwall breaking like a golden crust on a really well-fried meat pasty. On her toes, skipping sideways to give those behind her room to pop in, a hot flat bite of adrenaline to the back of her throat like a shot of burning pine. It was warmer, and golden early-morning sunshine lay butter-thick over a stretch of cracked pavement arrowing away, undulating gently in the distance. Small weeds had forced up through the fissures, and the stripes painted down either side and the middle of the concrete were blue-green because of the hexmoss* clustering old paint full of metal chips, chewing through in pillowy geometric patterns.

The first few seconds were the most dangerous. She took it all in, every hair on her body tingling, trying to rise. Her breath puffed out and she denied the urge to take a deep lungful until

---

* Small growths, possibly a lichen, native to the Rifts and feeding on certain metallic compounds.

she had cautiously sniffed, rolled the taste on her tongue, and decided it was okay.

Not just okay, but *wonderful*. Rich, heavy, beautiful air full of softness and a breeze much further along the curve to spring than the one on the other side of the shimmer. Dawning sunshine ran thick yellow over every surface, picked out small mica glitters in the pavement, edged the weeds with gold, sank into the hexmoss with a grateful murmur. Svinga's skin was alive again, a bath of delicious tiny bubbles sliding over every part of her. A shimmer bounced high up on her left, far enough away to be of little concern and heading north, rippling in puffs as dust found itself suddenly lighter by comparison.

Oh, yes. They had all sorts of stories about why rifters kept going back, even with the risks. All sorts of reasons why they drank when they weren't in, why they were different, strange, why they tapped on doorframes and tested each step even outside the shimmer. None of them were right, and no rifter would ever tell. It wasn't something you could put into words, anyway. It beat behind your heart and inflated your lungs, danced between your nerve endings and filled you out to fingertip, and even if you fucked another rifter, or God forbid *loved* one, you could not get at the heart of *their* mystery. The secret was just that: a secret, an excruciating loneliness you couldn't drink fast enough to escape.

The space inside you where the Rift lived.

The men piled through after her, and Svin crouched easily a few feet from her entry, watching. The slugwall, moving in its own slow, looping fashion, was already drawing away down the road, only temporarily touching this part of the Rift. To an observer inside, it would seem that Svin had just stepped out of thin air with a tearing sound, because the wall had already moved on.

Morov was the first, his noise of entry less crisp and more blundering than hers. His two prime goons appeared next, staggering into the sunshine and immediately spreading out to standard flanking. Right on their heels were the thin over-burdened pruneface scientist and the loud-breathing, bespectacled one.

Then the bald one—Barko—piled through with a limpet.* It was the boy Aleks, clinging to Barko's backpack and propelling them both to the left, for the edge of the road. The slugwall retreated, picking up speed as it rushed down the telescoping road.

*Shit.* Svinga unfolded, set her heels, and darted in, grabbing Barko's right arm. *"Stop!"* she yelled, and the last two sardie goons came piling through thin air with a long cloth-ripping noise, the pale-eyed one digging his toes in and going to one knee with his rifle coming up, as if he expected to be shot at.

She didn't even have time to consider him the idiot he was, because Barko had more mass and momentum than Svin could scrape together. Aleks was pushing from the other side, maybe maddened by the passage through the wall, maybe just exuberant. Stupid kid, she'd *specifically* told Kopelund he was a liability inside the blur, what in the fuck had—

A grassy verge rolled down at the edge of the paving. At its bottom, something that looked like water shimmered innocently blue, its surface ruffled perhaps by a breath of the

---

* A hanger-on, deadweight inside a Rift, a nubar attaching themselves to a more experienced rifter during driftburn.

pollen-laden breeze. Svin did the only thing she could, throwing herself down and thrusting a foot between Barko's. The bald man fell, a short cry forced out of him and choked off midway. He almost lost a chunk of tongue, too; the click of his teeth meeting was unnaturally loud.

Aleks yelled. Maybe it was sheer happiness, or maybe he realized he was about to run right off the paving. Svin tore her boot free of Barko's knees and scrambled to her feet, burning both palms on the concrete, lunging for the boy even though she knew it was too late.

The boy, blond hair glowing in the golden light, teetered on the edge in the middle of his victory cry. He'd scrounged a backpack, and it was hastily shut—a sock-toe flopped from the top where the zippers hadn't quite met. He was in a heavy dark parka and waved his arms wildly, his trainers slipping as the edge crumbled underneath them.

Just a little. Just enough.

He fell, careening head over heels, and landed with a sickening crackle instead of a splash.

The liquid, rippling quicksilver now, was not water. It flushed, crimson spiderthreads spreading from Aleks's point of impact. He twitched, and the pain must have set in then, because he began to scream as the corrosive semi-solid began digesting.

Sloslime. The only thing it wouldn't eat was ceramic. Outside the Rift it turned into a black, clinging mass of carbon they liked to use for growing industrial diamonds, but inside, it was deadly.

"Shit shit *shit*," Svin yelled, and got her feet under her. The sloslime rippled more, fringelike fingers now questing among the viciously green, overgrown grass at its edges, blindly seeking *uphill*. "Get back get back *get back*!" She had Barko's backpack now, and *hauled* on him as he thrashed, adrenaline singing coppery in her mouth. "Shitsucking fuckbuckle *shit*!"

Aleks's screams continued, and queer crunching noises began from the bottom of the hill. The pale-eyed sardie— Brood—moved forward, quick as a striking snake, and she threw out a hand as if to stop him, too. He paused, but didn't glance at Morov for orders, and pitched forward again.

"Christ." Morov had gone chalky-white. It made him look sickly next to the camouflage combat uniform. "Get him out of there! Help him!"

*"Don't fucking help!"* Svin snapped. "You want to stay alive you just *don't*!" She got her knees bent and her hips down, dragged Barko a few more feet. "If it's hungry enough it's coming up that slope, and your rifle won't do jackshit."

Brood slowed. He looked over the edge, half turned away. *"Fuck,"* he said, and hawked as if to spit, thought better of it. "Cap'n. You'll wanna see this."

Aleks's voice spiraled up in agony, the last cry of a hunted rabbit. Barko had shut his eyes, his feet moving weakly, trying to help her move him along. There was another shattering crack, a gurgle, and a low satisfied humming.

"It's eating him." Brood kept stealing glances, then snapped his chin forward. "Teeth? And...acid?"

"It extrudes chewers to break up organic matter. Back away before it decides you're next." Svin decided she wasn't going to tell him again, and further decided she and the bald scientist were at a safe distance. Sour sweat filled her armpits, soaking into the back of her waistband. "And you. Open your eyes. Get up. Come on. The rest of you, tighten up. We have a safe bubble here, but it's not a big one."

"Fuck," the thin walleyed scientist breathed, craning his neck to stare up. His glasses glittered. "Would you look at that."

"Don't!" Svin barked. "Eyes on the *ground*, fuckface!" The last thing she needed was for one of them to get sky-hypnotized and go wandering, too. Was there a slick up there? One could have been attracted by the commotion.

A hissing burble rose over the edge as Brood backed away, carefully, not feeling behind him with each foot like a rifter would but still doing all right.

"Shit," Barko moaned. "Not Aleks. Just a kid, for Chrissake."

"The young and weak casualty first," she told him. Why hadn't he learned as much yet? He was goddamn old enough. "Just ask your sardie buddies about that. Get on your feet, baldy, or I'll leave you here to rot."

He thrashed a little more, finally managed to achieve verticality. Svin dusted her hands off, ignoring the stinging. She glanced at the pale-eyed sardie, who was retreating from the edge step by step, his rifle trained down.

Maybe *that* asshole did have a sliver of brain. Even if he was probably the one Kopelund had sent in to kill her once she ID'd the Cormorant.

*They think it's something porty*, Ashe's letter whispered in her head. Oh, wasn't that amusing. She could almost hear the Rat's snuffling laughter, see Ashe's slow crooked smile. "All right," she said, finally. "Do not stare at the sky. Look at your feet, and tighten up. All of you. This way, toward me. One at a time. Nice and easy. Good. Very good."

The first few minutes were always the most dangerous. They'd gotten off lucky, with just the kid dead.

Svin stood for a few moments, her own head upflung, looking over the group of lundies. Big and brawny, or lean and nervous, and none of them with a lick of sense.

They were over the slugwall, now. After two years rotting in prison, she was right where she wanted to be. Over the blur and into the blue, out of *their* world and in hers.

Now the real fun began.

# 25
# BITCH FEELINGS

⋊╫⋉

Barko's head ached. He could still hear the screaming, for God's sake, and the glaring sunshine wasn't helping. All of them were sweating under their heavy packs, except the rifter. She probably wasn't big enough to sweat.

They walked in single file down the humpcracked road under a beautiful, deep-blue spring sky. The breeze wasn't quite enough to cool them under their clothes, but it ruffled the rolling grassy undulations on each side. The ditches were sometimes shallow, sometimes deeper, and the occasional sharp glitter on the horizon was probably an unbroken window in a pre-Event skyscraper throwing back the light with a vengeance.

So this had been the city, before the Event. There was no pall of exhaust hanging over it, the air was clear. They were too far away—they *should* have been about five miles from downtown, in a heavily built-up business district. Instead, they were, as far as Barko could judge, in the rural belt, a good twenty miles out. The sun was too high for when they had crossed the slugwall, and part of the disorientation was that somehow, coming through the wall had pointed them east instead of north.

He'd heard that the Rifts played havoc with distance and direction, but this made no sense unless the damn bubble was bigger inside than out. Which had been tossed around as a theory, but it was goddamn uncomfortable to be in the middle of.

The rifter kept going at a steady, ground-eating pace, sometimes stopping while she reached into her hipbag and brought out a small heavy washer or nut. A strip of cloth tied to the bit of metal fluttered as she tossed it, and sometimes she would consider its fall with her stubbled head cocked. Other times she would start moving as soon as she threw it. Warm, buttery sunlight gilded the dark fuzz on her head, and even Morov was quiet after what they'd witnessed.

The kid. He shouldn't have done that. The kid should *not* have done that.

*Young and weak first. Ask your sardie buddies about that.*

His mouth was still full of acid vomit-taste. The two men behind him moved quietly, and occasionally floppy-haired, muscle-heavy Tolstoy lit hand-rolled *makhorka* in a strip of cigarette paper. Each time, Eschkov in front of them jumped guiltily at the click of the sardie's popper-fed lighter.

On either side, grass spread in rolling waves, broken by stands of trashwood and bushes clumping between rows of pre-Event houses when they passed through a residential belt. Some windows here were intact, too, glittering sharply; the Institute's section of the shimmer faced almost precisely onto what had been a main artery running through a quiet residential section. The houses had been bigger then, and there were so many of them. Now, atonal birdsong rose instead of traffic noise, and the underbrush was full of slithering almost-sounds. Even the passage of the breeze against different surfaces sounded… wrong, somehow. Too heavy, or too light.

At each crossroads there were listing signposts. The signs would have held street names if hexmoss hadn't crawled over them, finding the paint and metal a very acceptable habitat. It didn't survive outside the Rift, for whatever reason, and there were stories—nobody knew how true—of amateur rifters going in to scrape the stuff and smoke it. The stories never agreed about the effects of such behavior, which was thought-provoking in and of itself.

The greenery surrounding the houses grew narrower and taller. Scraps of gardens long gone to seed, drunkenly leaning antique lamp-posts with shattered lenses. Sometimes there were sidewalks, sometimes not; the rifter turned seemingly at random, right or left, following curves and avoiding anything like a straight line for too long. Sometimes she took them off the road and between houses, or through fields of strange, sawblade-tooth grass that rasped against boots and trouser legs. Then it was back to the road for a little while, sometimes on the left side, sometimes on the right.

This particular intersection was slightly off-kilter, the roads meeting in an X instead of a cross. She stopped well before reaching it and sank into a crouch, which meant the rest of them hastily went down too, except for Barko. His entire body ached, and he'd seen her go down for just long enough to get everyone almost on their ass before rising again and continuing as if to spite them. His knees were already complaining. So he stayed upright, conscious of being taller, much older than anyone else, and probably the next one to get killed by something in here.

What a thought.

He scrubbed at his face. His beard wasn't thinning, even though his noggin was steadfastly naked. Would there be any water safe to shave with? Maybe one of the others had a popper-fed razor. Would there even be water to drink in here? They were carrying some, of course, but QR-715 was a fucking huge haystack and Barko was now aware of just how tiny-needle he and his fellow scientists were.

You could tell a lot about a man by how much quiet he could tolerate. Morov took about ten minutes, pretty much a record for a sardie. Which was probably why Barko liked him better than most of the others, too.

"What are you doing?" Morov finally whispered, shifting uneasily as he crouched. Sweat glistened on the shaven back of his head. He hadn't brought out a cigar yet, and that was a bad sign, too.

The rifter didn't respond at first. When she did, it was a familiar set of words. "Thinking. Shut up."

The sun beat down. The noise of bored, anxious men shifting intensified, under the moan and slither-rasp of wind through grassblades and between empty houses. Tremaine had already unlimbered a handheld thergo and was taking readings. Eschkov had a digicap and was snapping shots—the grass at the edge of the road, the hexmoss growing wherever paint and metal mixed, the weeds—they didn't look like native plants, for God's sake. Too angular, the yellow ones that should have been dandelions blowsy and nodding on too-strong stems, white seedheads on older plants sharper, burrs instead of parachutes. The grassblades were too thick or too spindly, most of them serrated; the daffodils and hyacinths stood in garish colors but with their flowers already elderly. It didn't feel like the cusp of a cold spring in here, and that was flat-out uncomfortable.

Even though the weather was mild, it was *wrong*. And for all Barko heard the noises in the grass, and the birds, he didn't see a damn one.

The rifter made small movements, rocking back and forth. It was probably to keep her muscles fresh, Barko realized, and decided he should probably try to get some data, too.

It was a struggle to get his pack off, but thankfully what he needed was at the top. Getting the backpack back on was a hideous cursing struggle as well, and by the time he'd finished the rifter had unfolded, slowly, swaying a bit. The spectra hummed as he powered it up and folded the keeper straps over his wrist and palm, and that familiar sound comforted him.

It didn't drive Aleks's screams out of his head, but it helped.

"Kid went straight in," Eschkov murmured, as if reading Barko's expression. Lank, graying hair clung close to his skull, and that wandering eyeball of his was disconcerting as fuck when magnified by the thick shatterproof lenses in their heavy black frame. "Shit. Kope ain't gonna be happy about that."

"Pension's automatic, and it doesn't come out of *his* budget." Blond, foreign Tremaine poked at his thergo. As usual, his accent made every word ponderous and unstable. He must have patted on aftershave this morning, because the sourness of his sweat was overlaid with a sweetish biscuity odor. "All sorts of different signatures. We're simmering."

"Anything fun?" Eschkov blinked, his pupils trying to float

in opposite directions. Every fifteen minutes he fished the rectangular gappa tracker out of his coat pocket and thumbed it, making sure it was taking in movement data and comparing it against the last session. It beggared belief, but he was the best cartographer in the country.

Just as Tremaine, for all his prissy foreign ways, was very good at departmental infighting—*and* had unlocked one or two new uses for poppers. "Well, there's something big over that way." Tremaine pointed to their right, where two ramshackle houses squeezed an alley between them. "I wonder if we could go in?"

"Will you all shut up?" Morov barked. "We're not here to follow your little fart fantasies, egghead."

"Then what precisely *are* we here for?" Tremaine kept his eyes on the thergo, deftly inserting a fresh memory chip now that everything was warmed up. "Someone else's fart fantasies?"

The rifter half turned. "Your boss wants the Cormorant." Half her mouth curled up, her generous lips barely covering those horseteeth. Her cheeks had flushed, and in this light, she didn't look prison-gray at all. Just so pale the vein-traceries under her skin showed. She would probably turn blue in cold water.

The instruments hummed. A collection of small birds in a tangle of slowly undulating thornvines a few meters to their left burst into peeping cacophony, and small bony clacking noises underscored their avian conversation.

"The *fuck*." The mouth of Brood's rifle, pointed down, swung a little as he made a small, contemplative moment. "That's the big secret? That piece-of-shit fairy tale?"

Tremaine's mouth hung half open. He visibly decided it was

a good thing to shut it, and did so with a snap. Tolstoy and Mako glanced at each other, the first with raised eyebrows, the second with a shrug. If the rifter had wanted to unsettle all of them even further, she'd done a pretty good job.

"That was supposed to be classified." Morov's knees creaked as he rose.

Barko surprised himself. "You think anyone here hasn't already guessed?" The spectra was going wild, but after a little bit of calibration it would probably start making sense of everything. It was best after dark, when the sun wasn't bouncing all sorts of energy toward the surface, but just the difference between day and night readings would be worth a pretty penny to one or two other research facilities. At least he'd get something out of this. Maybe he could even solve the riddle of how sunshine and air got through the slugwall...

He tried to focus on the spectra. There would be no Aleks chattering over the ancient coffeemaker in the morning. None of the kid's tripping over his own feet or isolating Manx variables in the data for fun. It had happened so fucking *fast*, too. Between one second and the next.

"Hey." Lazy-voiced, sleepy-eyed Senkin, who probably didn't give shit or Shinobi what they were after in here as long as he drew his hazard pay, pointed. "What the fuck's that?"

Everyone turned, and Eschkov let out an undignified squeak.

A queer black streak, like an oilslick, hovered around the roofs the next street over. It rippled, and the sheen on its surface was just like the slugwall—the same soap-bubble swirling, but as soon as the eyes decided it was one color or another, it changed. Red became blue, yellow became some shade there was no word for, and the whole thing made an uncomfortable sensation crawl lazily into the center of Barko's head.

"Just a slicker," the rifter said. "Don't look at it."

"But what *is* it?" Tremaine's accent had thickened. He lifted the thergo, dreamily, and fumbled for the knobs on the side.

"Form of plasma, near as anyone can figure." The rifter didn't turn around to look. "Comes out during the day when it's clear. Gets worse when you have a group, but it's harmless unless it hypnotizes some stupid asshole and they go wandering off. Or go killishok."*

"Eyes down, men." Morov was having none of that, thank you very much.

"How do they hypnotize you?" Barko tore his gaze away, took two steps forward and nudged Tremaine, whose blue eyes had widened as he stared, pupils dilating to eat the irises.

The rifter made a short, noncommittal sound. "Dunno."

"What exactly—" Eschkov began.

"Something like the northern lights. Radiation acting on particles in the air. That's what Ashe thought." The rifter sniffed a little, wiped at her nose with the back of her hand, and chose the left-hand road, heading away at an oblique angle. "Come on. Stay on this side of the intersection. I don't like how the other side feels."

"Shit," Senkin muttered. "Are we following your bitch feelings?"

The rifter didn't answer, just stepped carefully over the invisible boundary between "road" and "intersection," tapping her toes twice to test the pavement. Morov breathed a term of

---

* Slang: Rift-crazy and murderous.

surpassing obscenity and clapped Senkin on his meaty shoulder. Barko had to shake Tremaine to get his attention, and a funny feeling had started behind his breastbone. It was one thing to hear about the dangers inside a Rift.

It was another thing to feel the tickle of hypnosis inside his own head, and hear a kid's agonized, dying screams.

# 26
# ANYONE UNSTABLE

⟫╫⟪

Morov sighed as he popped the heating tab on a silvery packet of ration paste. It was probably spaghetti bolognese, which he hated but always seemed to get his first night out in the field, God's little joke played on a working soldier. "Nobody cares what you like, Tinkles."

God, Morov believed, was an NCO.

"I'm just saying, it ain't right." Senkin scratched at his cheek, glancing at the three scientists in their corner of the dark room. His nickname came from basic training—a certain incident involving a tin roof, a full bladder, and a couple of humorless MPs.

This abandoned building slumped on its foundations, a "landmark" according to the rifter, which apparently meant it was safe for the night. The sun was sinking fast, and the little bitch had already vanished twice, each time returning with a load of scavenged wood for the fire, which sat in a circle of cement excavated from moldering carpet and padding, strange opalescent rocks—again, gathered by the rifter—edging its merry crackle. Senkin continued with what they were probably all wondering. "What if she don't come back?"

"Then we go back the way we came." Mako slurped at his own ration paste. His round, flat face was set in its usual phlegmatic lines, but there was a strange gleam in his black, narrowed eyes. He let his hair get longer than regs, just like Riggs, and the stiff black mass was a halo.

For once, Brood spoke up. "Unless it changes." He stared at the fire while squeezing a little brown glue-paste out of his own ration packet, the feathering of bleached blond tips along his dark flattop glowing a little in the dimness. "*You* try rearguard tomorrow and look back a couple times."

"Makes my skin crawl," Tolstoy volunteered, baring nicotine-yellowed teeth in a grimace. "Road ahead of us, right? I look back and it's grass. Like it ate it, or something. Houses look all different too."

Morov's own scalp was crawling, but that could have been from sweat and dirt. Out in the field meant no time for a fucking shower. Which wouldn't have been that bad, but Mako smelled like rancid donkey balls even on the best day. Those demo motherfucks were always greasy, though, and it was only gonna get worse, especially if tomorrow was sunny again. The ration sleeve warmed against his fingers. Technically it was supposed to heat up the entire sachet of glop, but you'd get burning hot mixed with almost-frozen if you didn't mush it around a bit. If you mushed it, though, it became even more like baby pap.

The fire popped, and Morov almost twitched. The scientists were busy with excitable conjectures and setting up tripods and instruments, Barko's bald head rubbed with a couple charcoal fingerstreaks. The old man had worked with the kid; he was probably taking it hard.

Fuck, Morov supposed *he* wasn't taking it easy, either. The kid was always around, a buzzing annoyance, but Morov hadn't shooed him off. Riggs thought the kid was a hoot, all shiny eyes and Adam's apple, nagging with questions and burbling with conjecture.

Snuffed, just like that. Not even twenty seconds into the Rift, which from what Morov could see was just a bunch of dead buildings and weeds. Nothing very special at all.

Except for the way the weeds looked *wrong*. Except for the house they'd seen late in the afternoon, half of it afire with sunglow because it had somehow turned into glass. Walls, furniture, roof, just like a fucking greenhouse. The rifter had listened to the pleas of the scientists and taken them a little closer, and Morov saw the dividing line between glass and wood was seamless. Just *zap*, part of the fucking world turned into flat transparency, shivering a bit with a tiny singing noise as the wind stroked it. Sending a bullet through would probably make the whole thing fall down, and Tolstoy had looked damn tempted until Morov barked at him to get his mind back on the perimeter.

Yeah. Except for those tiny, little things, it was just a regular walk.

There were the rustlings in the grass, too, and the birds twittering. Except you never saw a single one. The sky held a few more of those oilslick things as it turned into afternoon, and the rifter had carefully *not* looked at them past a brief glance. It was goddamn hard to keep your eyes on the ground when you knew those fuckers were floating up top.

Brood's dark, thick eyebrows had drawn together, and he blinked owlishly at the fire. He looked troubled, which was *not* normal; he was Kopelund's pick for the team, and that made Morov... cautious. Tolstoy was a brick, and about as useful unless there was incoming fire. Mako hadn't blown himself— or anyone else—up yet, despite numerous chances to do so, which was what you were looking for in a demo man. He'd seen action in the Balkans, too, just like Brood. Senkin just plain did not give a shit, as solid as they came. Morov had figured he didn't want anyone unstable inside.

Or anyone who wouldn't obey an order.

*Don't you worry about the rifter. That's taken care of.* Kopelund with his hands behind his back, smugly contemplating his half-open office window like he saw cheering crowds outside the glass panes.

Well, now, that was all right, since Morov didn't like the little bitch much. He'd had to fill out triplicates for Bechter's eye, for Chrissake. Brood had Kopelund's orders for the rifter, but what was to stop him having orders for the rest of them? How much blowback was acceptable to Kopelund on this mission?

Morov had an idea, now that Brood had been attached, that the amount was uncomfortably high. At least Morov had sent off all the paperwork, including the anonymous stuff. He didn't like the idea that maybe he was plotkarz,* but there came a time when a man had to do *something*. It wasn't just Bechter's eye; the rifter had, after all, only her own crazy to fight off a group of soldiers with.

No, it was afterward, listening to Kope make his plans to

---

* Slang: a narc, a stool pigeon.

ruin the *rest* of Bechter's life, that left a sour taste in Morov's mouth. He'd seen Kope do the same thing before, but somehow, that was just the last straw.

A soft sliding sound was half buried under the fire's crackle and hiss; Mako was quickest, dropping his rations into his lap and reaching for his gun. The rifter, her dark eyes back to frog-huge in her wan face, melted through the doorway leading to what had been a garage before the Event. There was an antique petroleum-guzzling car-carcass in there, quietly moldering away under the blank greenish gaze of two overgrown windows. The house was partially covered with a drift of wiry, fleshy-leaved vines starred with weird tiny, triangular brownish flowers.

She halted, gazing at Mako like she knew what was going through his head, and for a moment her huge teeth, wide lips, and thin face made her a small animal eyeing the hunter and preparing to jump. Her wiry arms were full of dry wood, either torn from other houses or winter deadfall.

What kind of crazy went into the Rifts in the first place, let alone snuck around out there at *night*? Even if they did need the fuel?

"Fuck," Mako said. "Make some *noise*, shit." He picked his ration pouch back up.

"So you can aim better?" Brood elbowed him. "Dumbass."

The rifter picked her way forward and bent, her quick little hands moving this way and that as she stacked the wood, then pressed her knuckles to her lower back as she straightened, curving backward. Morov could remember his mother performing the same move, an unexpectedly feminine pose.

"Ms. Svinga?" The foreign scientist—Tremaine—bustled over,

carrying a small megboard. His hair was wildly mussed and the firelight showed high color on his cheeks. They were creaming themselves over there. "I wondered if we could get some equipment outside, because—"

"No." She didn't even wait for him to finish, just took two steps and sank into another crouch, staring at the fire. She made no move toward the bag of ration pouches set near the small blaze.

Did she have something in her backpack? Did she eat hunched over in a corner in the Rift, a prisoner or a malnourished child guiltily swallowing all she could? She hadn't seemed to mind in the canteen. Or were there secrets to surviving out here, caches of pre-Event food left miraculously untouched?

"Well, why? Is there something out there?" Tremaine looked just like a ruffled little golden dog with nothing outside the window to bark at. His accent got thicker when he was excited, and he was a prissy little fuck even at the best of times, but he wasn't a bad sort unless you were playing cards. He was a sore goddamn loser.

Foreigners usually were.

The rifter didn't say anything else. She just ignored him, and finally, awkwardly, the scientist shuffled back to his compatriots. He may have muttered something nasty under his breath, too, but it was in his native tongue. Wouldn't even call her a bitch to her face. What a skevvy.*

Morov mushed his pouch, almost angrily. It never failed— in barracks you were bored to death, out on maneuvers you just wanted to be back under a roof, when shit went down all you

---

* Slang: a sleazy coward, backstabber.

did was what you'd been trained to. You couldn't ever just be a happy asshole in your own damn living room. Not unless and until you retired, which was a long way off.

Well, he'd signed up for the ILAC Corps, and now he was in a Rift with three slaphappy scientists, the crazy motherfucker Brood, and a couple other nutsacks he had to return to base in original condition.

He took a mouthful of almost-hot ration paste. This time, of all times, it wasn't spagbol. The pouch had been mislabeled. Instead, it was chicken cordon bleu, which he hated just as much.

"Fuck," he muttered, with feeling, and took another gulp.

# 27
# FLAT COPPER

⋊┼┼⋉

Freezing fog had moved in with sundown, and thickened until a past-midnight soup of clotted white cloudcream lapped against the slugwall. A troika of leavs, rolling through cold clouds kissing frozen earth, stabbed around their moving perimeters with harsh white light. Their yellowish fog beams weren't supposed to reflect off water droplets as badly, but the patrol would be relying on thermascan anyway. The glare was enough to make a lookout's eyes water, safe inside a bulletproof bubble.

Vetch took point, loping along the slugwall's shellpearl glimmer, Cabra pacing him with one eye on the patrol. Therma would have trouble picking them up against the wall's stray energy flux, but if the leavs turned face-on instead of sideways there might be a glitterspike or two to give them away. The patrol began to turn, lazily, not expecting any trouble…and it was time, a rasp running across the nerves and a high flat copper taste in every mouth.

Sabby the Pooka, sweating a haze of exuded alcohol byproducts that steamed gently against the fog but bright-eyed and steady, kept his gaze fixed on Cabra's bead-starred braids. Behind him, the fourth rifter, covering the ground with a long shambling lollop, was Il Muto, his large knitted hat flopping gently and his big rawboned hands combing the air.

Cabra felt it first and didn't break stride, just skipped forward two steps and tapped Vetch on his left shoulder. He immediately veered, partly from her pressure and partly from instinct, and they both hit the slugwall at the same time, a dark rosette expanding against the shimmer. Sabby hit square between them and burst through with a jolt; last of all Il Muto. He landed a good four meters away from Sabby, who had gone down in a crouch and was craning his neck; the beads in Cabra's braids rattled and buzzed as she rolled. If she'd been just a little slower, her guts would have splattered the dirt.

A scuttlesnake loomed, rearing up from a nest of silvery tangletape, darting forward. Its snout struck where Cabra had been a split second before, and Vetch whistled, a high sharp noise meant to give it an aural profile to latch onto, a distraction from easy prey. Metal rasped and slid, a long jointed curve of gleaming segments, and the blunt wedge-shaped head separated, foxfire glittering on triangular teeth.

Il Muto made it to his knees, digging in his mapper; Cabra rolled again as the scuttlesnake buzzed another warning. Vetch whistled once more, a short sharp stutterburst, but it was Sabby who plunged his fist into his mapper and brought out a popper in a maglock. A brief flash of blue, the maglock whining as he thumbed it, and he tossed the palm-sized disc low and hard.

It smacked between two segments on the rearing scuttle's dappled belly. A flash, small booms of tiny thunder, a sharp whiff of ozone as the metal flanks closed a circuit. The popper pumped fatal electricity through the scuttle, which fell with a *crash-splat* and began twitching. Vetch darted in, grabbing Cabra's backpack, and Il Muto had a popper torch, playing the beam over the scuttle's twitch-thrashing length.

Sabby grabbed Cabra's hand, pulled her upright while Vetch hauled on the backpack, helping. Il Muto crouched in the middle of his safe bubble, and they crowded him, Cabra's breath coming high and hard, Sabby's teeth chattering, Vetch swearing once in a low, passionless tone. The popper torch flicked off and they huddled, a creature of eight eyes, eight hands, eight feet, four backpacks, and four pulses galloping in throat and wrist and gut.

The night on this side of the slugwall was clear and warmer than the other, though by no means balmy. Vetch raised his head first, testing the breeze. Night entries were dangerous, but getting past the patrols in the daytime was irritating as all fuck.

Finally, when it felt right, the rifters settled in standard formation—backs and backpacks propped against each other, leaning into the comfort of other human bodies. Il Muto's chin dropped to his sunken chest almost immediately, his breath turning to the slight sibilance of a deepening doze. The crackles from the downed scuttle had turned into formless white noise. The popper would keep working for a long time, until the scuttle's segments separated into harmless chunks. Someone might even happen on the corpse later and scoop up the maglock and its still-glowing popper, and maybe take the fanged scuttle's head, too.

Cabra had first watch, Sabby's damp blond head propped on her shoulder as he closed his eyes and dropped off.

They wouldn't move until dawn. Here, they were relatively

safe. The sentry would wake the others if the wind changed, or if the flat rustling grassland all around started to run with inky blackness, or if the half-seen shapes in the middle distance, full of swaying shagginess as they grazed, lifted their heads uneasily.

Vetch waited. His was second watch, and he should have been able to nap, at least. Cabra listened to him breathe, obviously still awake, but he said nothing.

None of them did. There was nothing to say.

# 28
# BOOGALOOS

>+|+<

They were all asleep but one. Svin sat cross-legged next to the banked fire, listening.

Two of the sardies snored, one in long gulping inhales and the other in short nasal bursts. Another lay on his side with his arm over his head; the fourth just breathed in the heavy satisfied way only a large well-fed man could. The fifth sardie— the ghost-eyed one with the blond tips, the one Kopelund had probably sent along to kill her, if he could, and take the Cormorant right before they came back out—was awake, staring at the ceiling, just the dim glitter of those pale irises reflecting what little stray light tiptoed his way.

The foreign scientist—Tremaine—whistled while he breathed. Sounded like something dry and hairy was stuck in that high-prowed nose of his. Eschkov had nodded off bent over a lap-board; he would wake to find a pool of spittle on the gleaming surface as it ran the data he had keyed in over and over, showing an adjusted result each time. Barko settled early and lay for a long time with his eyes closed, but he dropped off eventually. The bald man would probably have nightmares.

Outside, the Rift sang.

A low perpetual grumble lay at the very bottom of the auditory landscape. Tiny pinpricking scrapes needled up through the hum, and bushes rattled or stilled. An invisible rake clawed, snarling softly, through what had been pavement pressed by human boots just that afternoon, digging into the soft loam and juicy grass it had become. High, crystalline tinkling echoed overhead, oddly like the superstructure of a massive dome singing as wind brushed along its harp-tight beams. The night-hunting birds were out, owls with great baffle-silent wings and softly glowing excrescences around their mad, piercing eyes; the tall storklike stangers, their bills clacking softly every once in a while as toads and other things made ribbitcreaks along every rill of fluid, water or otherwise. Leather-winged bats, flapping with ponderous and ungainly agility, scooped at chitinous streams of night-flying insects with their shoveljaws, squeaking and crunching delicately. A few feral dogs circled the house the rifter had chosen, their yips and yaps vanishing in the distance.

Chances were, she wouldn't hear them again. Inside the Rift, humans were a liability, no matter how domesticated the creatures had been pre-Event. Sometimes they clocked a rifter team, sensing a chance at easy food. There were stories about dogs following a rifter out through the shimmer, but not many, and she'd never seen a rifter with a pet.

Most had enough trouble looking just after themselves.

The closest sound was the slide of fur along wall or rock or grass, and soft damp pod-paddings. The boogaloos were out, their cushioned, prowling feet feeling delicately along every surface, their bulging eyes sprinkled with phosphorescence. They were largely harmless, herbivores to boot, but if you startled them, their unsheathed claws could go straight through anything less than concrete and gut you on the other side. So you moved slowly, mimicking their own groping progress and looping paths. It was when their silver-furred bulks began to vanish and you realized you hadn't seen one in a while that the real danger started, between every patch of deeper darkness maybe holding a squeezer and every flicker at the corner of your vision a possible shimmer, and the other things as well. The air pressure might change as a wall moved through—in daytime you could see it coming, pushing down vegetation and scattering dust particles too light to be caught. Sometimes the wall would just roll over you and leave you bruised and shaken, but most of the time it was charged. You could get a nasty shock or flat-out electrocuted, for example.

If the wall held any other kind of radiation, you were fuckered up but good. Your flesh could be boiled dry in an instant, all your liquids evaporated out through your skin, or your bones reduced to splinters. The walls could generally be sensed after dark, but that didn't help. Put a foot wrong at night and you could end up in a puddle of Rift slime. The silvery almost-sentient sort only backed off when confronted with a spraycan of mass-produced glaslime, but there were streamlets and puddles of other sludges in every shape and size. Old Jervy, working the Birmingham Rift, had sworn there was a particular puddle-type that would turn whatever you dipped in it to gold.

Some corporation had taken an interest. Jervy didn't come back after one of his runs and for a while they were offering a bounty for a rifter to go in looking for that fabulous puddle. The corporate clone in charge of offering the bait money seemed to think it was like finding someone lost in regular mountains. Follow the footsteps and the broken branches, look for piles of the animal's shit, and run it to ground.

Svin almost smiled. Maybe Jervy's bones were gold-dipped now. It would please the old fucker to be plated.

So far Ashe's map held up. Svin's indirect probing at the edges of the Rift's whirl told her which way the current was going, and unless it reversed she was fairly sure she could edge closer and closer to the center. Her eyelids dropped to half mast. The fire was a sullen, nasty glare, but it was an old human trick, and it kept things...safer.

Or it could attract the attention of the things that preyed on boogaloo herds and the big shaggy grass-eaters out on the flat grasslands. You rarely saw the predators. Long sinuous catlike shapes prowled at night, their shoulders hip-high on a human and their teeth glowing ivory; there were long fat ribbonshapes with wedge-heads that the scuttles mimicked. Or maybe they were scuttles before they found metal armor, who knew? The small ones were venomous, the larger ones preferred to squeeze or take whole chunks out of their food. Then there were the *other* things, the ones you didn't dare look at. If the wrongness of their shapes didn't drive you howling-insane clawing your own eyes out, it might burst a vessel in your brain. Some of them had foxfire dangles on long whiplike tendrils, and those small lamps could hypnotize their next meal. Once, she'd seen them crawling over one of the grass-eaters at night, shadows and ripping sounds, those glowing dangles bobbing in time to the crunch of teeth splintering massive bones.

Much, *much* safer to find a bubble that felt reasonably tranquil as the sun began to go down, light a fire, and stay put. Ashe had sometimes wondered aloud if it was the *idea* of the flames instead of the actual light and heat that kept a slim margin of safety around a campsite. Svin had simply shaken her head, not really caring as long as the effect was the same.

The potzegs* stacked in a ring around the fire's concrete home could be thrown, if it came to that. They had secrets, too, leathery interiors under a hard crust. Jervy had shown her how to crack them, way back on her second run with him. You could use a bandanna as a sling, and anything that liked to snack on the silver-furred almost-mammal boogaloos, or the grass-eaters, would retreat in a hurry from a cracked potzeg. You could even drive off a scuttle with them, if you didn't have a maglock or a stimstick.

The light-eyed sardie kept very still. Did he suspect *she* suspected? He was the only one who walked the right way in here—test each step, test again, look and think. Maybe he wasn't a *complete* idiot; those who were almost cautious enough to be rifters were more dangerous than just plain lundies. She'd have to be careful.

*Ashe*, Svinga asked the quiet inside her own head, the space she'd done all the solitary time in. *Ashe, what do you think I should do?*

It was riddikulo-simple, really. *Take them up the Alley*, Ashe-not-Ashe, because Ashe was dead, replied.

Svinga's shorn head bobbed once, twice. She was technically

---

* Opalescent, stonelike growths with a leathery, volatile core. They are nonflammable but can explode if first cracked, then flung correctly.

on watch, as if it mattered. The thing that made her a rifter told her this place was safe for the night, and you learned when not to question. Just like you learned when you should go limp and let a transit guard push you, and when you should turn on a sardie with every inch of fury you could scrape together.

After a long while, Brood's breathing shifted. He was truly asleep now.

The rifter, utterly still, straight-backed and cross-legged by the fire, her eyes half open, slept as well. Smoke lifted, a curling serpentine ribbon, and collected near the ceiling. A soughing went overhead, not quite touching the structure's roof, and the smoke turned to thin fine ash, falling with a slight staticky noise.

None of them stirred, and the sighing vanished into the distance.

# 29
# MESSAGE RECEIVED

⟫╫╪⟪

A chilly gray morning filled the Rift from one wall to the other. Just how high the Rift domes extended was a matter of debate, since anything closer than a satellite going overhead got either fried if it was lucky or sucked in if not. The satellites themselves only showed glowing, puckered areas on the Earth's surface, every sensor array science could devise defeated by the slugwall. Each time someone wanted to point one of the fragile metal bugs in orbit at a Rift, a budget committee asked if it was *really* worth losing the bug and its instruments.

The rifter stood for a long moment in the doorway, balanced on the threshold, and listened, closing her eyes. Her peach-fuzzed head didn't glow today; the stubble growing in was almost-black and the gray light didn't help. Barko hunched his shoulders, half listening too as Tremaine burbled excitedly about data the thergo had collected overnight.

The spectra had been busy gathering, too. It was classic Rift signatures—high hard and fast for seven seconds, flattening out for three, spiking to max for two, then bubbling along at a high clip again for another random amount of time. When they stopped tonight, Tremaine and he would pop data into the collator Eschkov carried, and look for matches. One of the mysteries of the Rifts was the absolute noncorrelation between thergo and spectra readings. It was as if they willfully refused to match up properly.

You could almost think the Rift had a mind of its own, and delighted in fuckering about with human insects crawling inside it.

"How long is this going to take?" Mako, slurping another mouthful of boiled coffee, scratched the back of his neck at the same time. The man smelled like he lived on something fermented. Either that or it was his own sweat doing the fermenting.

Morov glanced at the rifter, who was busy ignoring all of them. "Don't know," he said, finally.

She didn't even glance at him. Just sniffed, deeply, peering outside while she grabbed the right-hand side of the doorway as if to steady herself. A small, pale, capable little paw, her palms scabbed from yesterday. She hadn't even stopped to disinfect the scrapes, and now it wouldn't do any good to bandage them. Barko had a hazy memory of waking during the night, seeing her next to the fire, upright and dreamy-eyed, licking at the wounds. A little pink tongue behind her protruding teeth, dabbing at torn flesh. There was more color in her face now, and her dark eyes snapped open, alive and alert. "Ready in five," she said, as if she expected them all to hustle.

"I ain't even brushed my teeth." Senkin heaved a long-suffering sigh, digging in a small canvas toiletries bag. "Shiiiiit."

"All right, pack up and fuckbuckle down." Morov's knees

popped as he levered himself up, jamming the usual half-smoked cigar into the corner of his mouth. "Mako, take care of the fire. Barko, get your eggheads together."

"Who nominated me?" Barko shot back, but not very loudly, as he heaved himself upright. That was the shitty thing about being a borderline responsible adult. You had to herd everyone else into doing their shitty-ass jobs.

Eschkov, his wandering eye rolling wildly, smacked a fist into his other palm to emphasize a point. "—if we could just get some equipment up *outside*. Why the hell didn't we bring a leav? We could have carried so much more." His hair stood up in graying tufts, and he looked like a rumpled, very upset bird bobbing its head over a dirtpatch where the worms refused to show.

"Yeah, if you wanted to end up like the last lot." Barko got his backpack settled on his aching shoulders. "Come on, guys. She says we're leaving."

That effectively canceled conversation. Tremaine didn't bother arguing, just folded up his already-filthy handkerchief and stuffed it in the breast pocket of the lab coat he'd insisted on wearing under his woolen peacoat. Eschkov gave Barko a dirty look, or it might just have been that excitable eye of his. Rumor had it he'd been the one to sell some of the specs on the alloy skeletons that had once been Ashe the Rat and the two scientists who had almost survived the trip into QR-715.

There had been a five-man sardie squad with *them*, too. Christ alone knew what had happened. Maybe they would run across some evidence?

Barko couldn't decide whether that was a comforting idea, or a terrifying one.

Outside, a heavy green reek could have been promising

rain. A pungent, burning metallic undertone coated the back of the throat and made the eyes sting; the rifter tied a faded, much-creased blue kerchief around the lower half of her face like a stickup warboy and the sardies hurried to do the same with their regulation nose-wipes. Eschkov had to make do with a thin cotton shirt, Barko hadn't packed anything applicable, and Tremaine just shook his leonine head.

The rifter, glancing at the sky every now and again, set off. This time, Mako and Senkin trailed her, the scientists were in the middle, and Morov trudged right after Tremaine, leaving Brood on rearguard again. Conversation sputtered along, Morov and Brood conferring in hushed tones, Eschkov muttering equations into a hand-record, and Mako occasionally snorting, hawking, and lifting his face-rag to send a wad of bacca-colored phlegm off to the side. Once, the rifter stopped just after he did that, turned around, and stared for a few moments, her now-bloodshot eyes narrowing.

He stared back, and Barko could tell from the set of his shoulders that he was probably smiling. It wouldn't be a friendly smile, either.

The corners of the rifter's eyes crinkled a bit, but she didn't say a word. When she set off again, it was slightly faster, but with no less finicky care about the placement of her feet.

Houses grew further apart, suburb turning back into quasi-rural. Huge saucerlike depressions began pocking the landscape, their inner surfaces scoured free of vegetation and threaded with parched cracks. Stamped flat with only faint shadows to show where structures had stood, the depressions clustered now in threes, now singly, and once the rifter led them counterclockwise around a group of five, their edges almost touching and starred with tough silvery sword-leaved weeds. The cracks inside the depressions were pressure-marks, and if he'd come across them outside the Rift he might have been fascinated, stopping to examine and conjecture.

Barko restrained the urge to look back to see how the ground behind them had shifted. It would only give him a squirming feeling deep in his guts, so he hitched his backpack straps higher and tried not to feel like they were going in circles, tending vaguely westward if the sun was any indication.

Apparently Morov felt the same way. "Bitch better know where she's going," he said once, softly, the words only floating to Barko's ears because Eschkov's coughing fit had just ended. Brood made a short noncommittal sound in reply.

Noonish found them on a long grassy slope down to a copse of spiny-looking bushes, working parallel to the ridgetop. The grass itself had turned yellow and moved strangely against boots and trousers, tiny serrations catching at cloth and leather both. The rifter pointed at a particular spot, no different from the rest of the slope. "Wait there."

"For what?" Morov piped up from the back of the line, flicking a popper-fed lighter and inhaling sharply to get his cigar to catch.

"Eat. Rest. I want to look around." She barely turned her head, tracking the chilly-raw breeze moaning along sharp grass. In the distance, a rhythmic tearing sound became audible, but the ridge blocked their view of whatever it was. "Long way to go before dark." The still, eerie light turned her sallow, picked out the weave of her dungarees, and leached the grass of any comforting green.

"Just where are we going?" Morov still didn't move, though

the others began trooping obediently for the patch she'd pointed at. Barko's eyes, irritated by whatever fume was lifting from the ground or—there was an unwelcome thought—descending from the cloud cover, watered, and when his vision blurred it did look a little…different than the rest of the hillside. Not darker, not lighter, but more…*there.*

More real. He couldn't quantify it, and it hurt his head to try. Or maybe it was just the bitch headache from whatever was in the air.

"Further in." She half turned, keeping an eye on the top of the ridge. Was she considering going toward the source of that rustling, booming sound?

"We've been going in loops, goddammit." Morov chuffed a little at his cigar. Maybe the smoke cut the heavy, caustic vapor. The sky was a featureless bowl, but at least those oilslick things had disappeared. Now there were just broad-winged shapes you could imagine were birds, even though their heads looked too heavy and their flapping too lethargic to keep them afloat.

*That's impossible*, Barko wanted to say, *because the landmarks keep changing.*

"You think anything in here ever goes in a straight line?" A short, contemptuous little laugh. "Don't go down the hill. Wait *right there.*"

With that, she took off for the crest with a long loping stride, amazingly fast for such a small woman.

"Crooked as the human heart." Tremaine eased his backpack straps off. "That's what they say at home about the Rifts."

"Poetic." Barko coughed, a deep dry sound. His throat was on fire, his eyes watering since morning and cutting salty tracks on his stubbled cheeks. "This shit stinks."

"Seems to be coming from those sinkholes back there." Eschkov, damn him, still sounded *excited*. His spectacle lenses were smudged, but he didn't seem to notice. His wandering eye rolled madly, and he seemed enchanted by the difficulty of mapping terrain that changed behind them instead of terrified at the notion. "You know, I wonder—"

"You think they're sinkholes?" Tremaine began digging in his backpack. "They looked like footprints to me."

Barko left them to argue about it and approached Morov, who still hadn't moved. Brood, behind the captain, stared down at the spiny-bush copse with a thoughtful line between his dark eyebrows. Their uniform pants stirred slightly in a thin, freshening breeze. Maybe the nasty, acrid air would begin to lighten up. He cleared his throat.

"What?" Morov watched the small figure of the rifter vanish over the top of the hill, heading at an oblique angle instead of straight on. Just like everything else here.

"Just checking in." Barko carefully didn't study the man's face, looking instead at the bushes. They were moving just a fraction too energetically under the dim, caustic breeze. "How we doing?"

"Shit." Morov shook his bullet-shaped head, digging in his breast pocket for another half-smoked cigar, which he examined critically. Why he didn't just smoke whole ones all the way down was one of the mysteries of life. "You don't want to know. You guys getting what you need?"

"Pretty much." *Not that it'll make any sense.* "Been thinking."

"Shit, again?" But at least Morov would listen. Brood, right behind him, was probably all ears as well.

"We haven't seen a single bit of scavenge this whole time.

Not even poppers or a lamper."* Barko found himself scrubbing at his head with his palm again, put his hand down with an effort. "That seem odd to you?"

"No stranger than anything else." Morov's eyes narrowed a bit above the snot-rag, that was all. "Don't you have a rag, for fucksake?"

Barko shook his head. Of all the things to head out the door without, he'd chosen a bandanna or a handkerchief. His mother would have scolded him, if she'd still been alive. "I'm gonna go back up before they get carried away. I just thought, you know."

"Yeah." *Message received,* Morov's eyes flashed, and Barko trudged back uphill, to the patch that did, despite all his efforts to ignore the fact, look more solid than the surrounding ground.

He just couldn't figure out how it did, and his headache mounted another notch.

---

* A small metal cylinder with an almost-perpetual light source at the end, similar to a flashlight but much lighter and without a switch.

# 30
## YOU WITH ME?

⊱╫⊰

Vetch kept them just below the top of the hillside, working vaguely northwest. The semi-rural houses were slim pickings, but their packs were already half full of loot. Poppers found in groups of three or five in the middle of small rooms or chasing each other in circles across counters, dried happa rosettes* carefully scraped from dark corners and sealed in plastic baggies, sheets of crumpleglass rolled up and stowed—now *those* were worth a few marks in Deegan Alley. You could spread it over barred windows and run a popper current, and immediately, *zappo*, you had a nice little hole to reach through. Snatch-and-grabs or loosening a latch, and at least thirty days if you were searched with some on you during a routine checkpoint.

It clouded up as afternoon approached, and Sabby the Pooka kept an eye up. Pinchoks circled lazily, not in tightening spirals

---

* Mineral excrescences found in damp, dark Rift corners, looking like crystalline flowers.

that would mean hunger or in the sharp banking turns that would mean curiosity. Instead, the birds just drifted, and that was a good sign.

Less good was the thickening acridity as Vetch led them past a few untouched neighborhoods. Cabra put up with it for a while, but when they finally halted just after the sun reached its zenith, crouching near the mouth of a concrete culvert that felt safe enough should a pinchok dive or a wall go over, she chewed on a protein bar and eyed Vetch narrowly.

"Went past good loot," she said, finally. Mildly enough. Her hair glowed, a few thermaglit beads glittering sharply among the plastic and glass. "You got a line?"

Sabby tipped his head back, still scanning the sky. Under his undershirt, button-down, and two jackets, his right shoulder bore long ropy scars. A long time ago, only Cabra's extra weight and refusal to let go had torn him out of the bird's claws, and sometimes he rubbed under his backpack strap, massaging the bunched-up, well-healed flesh. Il Muto nudged him every once in a while, reminding him to keep eating; the tall thin sunken-chested rifter glanced from Cabra to Vetch with all the interest of a spatterjunkie* watching a tennis match.

"Got business," Vetch finally said. His stubbled chin lifted a little, stubborn scowling pride bringing his mouth down at the corners and his eyebrows together. He examined the horizon, shifting his weight inside the crouch to keep his muscles loose and ready. "Welcome if you wanna, burn if you ent."

"Business." Cabra's teeth gleamed. She chewed, nice and

---

* Person addicted to a mildly hallucinogenic drug discovered by Bernard Blanco during the Crash.

slow, until the protein bar turned to mush in her mouth. A conservative swallow from her battered red canteen wrapped with stimtape, and she cleaned her teeth with a quick swipe of her tongue, pushing her lips out a little. "Anything to do with Pol Mavery?" He had ambitions of being a warboy, that four-eyed lundie, and word had it Vetch had stepped on his toes.

Vetch had a cold meat pasty, wrapped in greasy paper. He took small bites, masticated thoroughly, and swallowed before he spoke. "Dead business."

"Lot of that going around." Cabra's dark eyes hooded themselves. "Rafello says lots of people asking about Ashe Rajtnik, for example."

Vetch barely grunted. Sabby's shoulders hunched. Il Muto went still, his gaze arrested somewhere between Cabra and Vetch, held in stasis just like a shimmer.

There was a line between Cabra's eyebrows, a sure sign of unease. "Had herself a hole, I heard. Institute fuckers brought her out of deepfreeze."

"Saw her," Sabby said, surprising everyone, including himself. "Skinny. Hard time."

"What else you see?" Cabra took another hit from her canteen.

"Pine bender. Threw every second for Ashe." Sabby shifted uncomfortably. "I dunno." Meaning he wasn't willing to add whatever else he'd witnessed, or what he guessed.

"Now why they defrost Rajtnik's old hole?" Cabra wondered aloud. "Got me curious."

Il Muto made a soft sound, not quite a whistle. They all looked up, a pinchok's shadow floating unsteadily over them. They finished in a hurry, Sabby shaking his head when Cabra offered him another protein bar. Vetch took point again, uphill on an acute angle this time. They all dropped, a synchronized motion, before their heads could be seen poking over the hill-line, and muscled up on elbows and knees.

A pressure cup lay between them and the city's dusty spires. Today the skyscrapers of what had been downtown were the color of sandstone, filtered through a thick haze gathered in a ragged dome. The edges of the cup were breaking up, its miasma shredding on an eddy in the Rift's flow. Pleated ridges fell down from the height Vetch and his team occupied, and moving lazily along their sides were streams of thornback. It would look like a stand of spindly, scrawny, spiky young trees, but get too close and those branches would start to shake. Mostly, if you left them alone, they'd clear out in a day or so, moving along in their slow ropelike fashion, leaving scars of black churned-up earth behind them. That dirt was probably worth a fortune, but no rifter wanted to haul it out. It was heavy, and if you took it outside the blur anything dropped into it grew like mad. Rub it on your hand, and you might wake up with a tumor crawling between your fingers.

Crossing the wall was bad enough, but crossing it with a load of thornback drag on your back was just asking to be mutated into something hideous. Sometimes a rifter took the risk and brought back a sealed jar, but not often.

"Fuckbuckle," Cabra breathed. "Whazzat?"

There was movement on a slope in the middle distance, near an isolated stand of young thornback that had not yet begun to drag a black streak behind it. The spines shook violently, and the stand began to move, dragging itself uphill. Popping noises filtered through the edges of the pressure cup, distorted by time and distance. The pinchoks took notice, veering close to the edge of the pressure cup and away when the vapor got too thick.

"Sardie cracks." Sabby the Pooka ducked a little further, pulling his blond head back turtle-like as if a stray bullet might come all this way to smack him. "What the fuck?"

Vetch stared, his eyes narrowing, his fingers driving into the dirt. His lips twitched a little, and under his stubble, his cheeks had paled. A flash pierced the pressure cup; the cough-burr of a grenade reached them.

"Fuck*buckle*." Cabra squirmed down, away from the hilltop. "Institute sent *sardies* in? That's why we came carrying. You bastard."

Il Muto, his entire long face creased with worry, plucked at Vetch's coatsleeve. All four of them flinched a split second before a smear of greasy orange and yellow rose. The thornback's bark-rubbing scream rolled across the ridges, and the pressure cup shivered, its edges shredding even faster. A thin point of blue appeared, took a breath, expanded like a star.

A potzeg, cracked and flung.

"It's *her*." Maybe Sabby had just figured it out. He rubbed at his bloodshot eyes. "Ashe's girl on a pine bender. In with sardies."

"Blur your fucknozzle," Vetch said, finally. "Got a payday from an interested party. Big enough to send us all broadside."

"The *fuck* you do." Cabra was having none of this. "Sardies shoulda been the first line, not in the fine print."

"You wanna burn off, go 'head." In other words, Vetch didn't *need* them. Not now, not when he was past the patrols and actually in the Rift.

"Oh, man." Sabby grabbed Cabra's elbow. She had her knees under her and her fist raised, ready to fall on Vetch's back. Sabby wrestled her away, and they rolled down the gentle rise, neither her fury nor his attempt at soothing loud enough to cause problems outside their bubble. Professionals, both of them.

Well, as far as the term applied to rifters.

Vetch's mouth, thin and hard, didn't relax. He finally turned his head slightly, studying Il Muto, who still had his sleeve, long spidery fingers plucking at tough cloth over a flexarmor patch. He'd left Cabra to choose a fourth, guessing exactly who out of the crowd would get her stamp.

"I knew it would be you," Vetch muttered. "You know what they're after."

The lean, mournful face turned sadder, if that was possible. Il Muto nodded, lips parted as if he would break his silence. Rafello said Il Muto *could* talk, he just didn't see any need when people were fucking fools.

Rafello was an ass. But a smart one.

"You with me?" For a moment the past turned over against him. Outside the blur two and a half years ago. Svin right before they went into the sting, her dark thoughtful eyes huge and her hair pulled back, her lips relaxed and glossed with cherrybalm.

*You with me?* she'd asked. *All the way*, Ashe had said, not turning around, and Svin had shaken her head a little, ruefully amused as she moved out, not giving Vetch time to answer, too.

*To the end of the line*, he'd wanted to say, which was stupid. You didn't give a hole that kind of promise, even if she was a rifter too. It could easily end up bad all through you, like when you heard she'd been there when the warboy's crew made their move on the Rat.

Lying on the floor of a Rift with roaring and gunfire in the distance, Il Muto nodded. A spark had lit, far back in the man's dusty eyes, mirrored by the dull, sick, caged heat in Vetch's own.

"Good," Vetch said. Sabby would calm Cabra down. After all, they were in the Rift, and the odds got better if they tailed another group. They could slide along the disturbance the lundies were making, the stupid shit a rifter knew better than to do making waves.

Sooner or later, one of the sardies was going to try to tangle Svin, and Vetch would be there. Zlofter's promised payday was enough to tempt anyone.

Maybe she'd even be grateful, if he showed up at the right time. And if she wasn't, well . . . he had a plan for that, too.

# 31
# WHO WAS GONE

⋈⫟⋉

Geeorge Tremaine was having the time of his professional life. It was a huge opportunity to get in and get actual field data, and his only problem was that the rifter wouldn't let him gather enough of it.

Take, for example, the shrubs down the hill. The thergo went crazy whenever it was pointed at them, but he had to get closer to get a good reading. It was the first time a signature had seemed identifiable, and his heart raced at the prospect of classifying a flora mutation. Perhaps even one that would be named after him. He could publish, and Molly would maybe stop complaining about being posted to this horrid place with no proper tea, no proper shops, and no hope of advancement since it was a bigger Rift, meant only to be monitored from *outside*.

Thinking of Molly dampened his mood a bit. He could make a case for a pay raise if he discovered and published, not through that parsimonious bastard Kopelund but higher up at regional level. That would ease the bitter lines around her mouth and maybe, just maybe, she wouldn't push his hands impatiently away when he crept timidly into bed each night. Maybe she was even missing him, though sometimes he suspected... well, no self-respecting woman would go about with any of the locals. It was silly to think otherwise.

Still, she was so much younger.

That was another uncomfortable thought, so he drifted to the edge of the group. Eschkov was nattering on about one of his pet theories, that the Rifts were the product of some kind of natural disaster, and Barko was making listening noises as he nodded his bald, empty head. The old man was nearly useless; he was of the *old* generation and more inclined to view the Rifts as acts of God or some such foolishness. Tremaine suspected Aleksander had paid Barko to carry him through the energy wall or something. George himself had always snubbed the young blond nuisance, mostly because the boy's English was so poor. Barko's wasn't any better, but he had seniority, and that counted. Rank gave even a foreigner an element of respectability.

Tremaine placed his boots fussily as he took another few steps down the slope. One of the guards—the one with the light eyes and the close-cropped dark hair with bleached tips—was too busy lighting one of their foul-smelling, very strong cigarettes to care. The reek of that tobacco got everywhere, even inside Tremaine's own house. Molly didn't appear to notice, but she always wrinkled her little snub nose whenever they passed a smoking local on the street. *Filthy habit, that*, George would say, and she would hasten to agree.

He glanced back, hearing a small commotion. The rifter had come back, wiping at her bloodless, too-large mouth. Maybe she just didn't like eating with them around to see. She was an odd one, her froggy eyes and her horseteeth, and Tremaine had almost made some sort of overture.

*Hear you were in Birmingham*, he could have said, breezily. *Very close to home, that. What did you think of it?*

In the end, though, he hadn't.

The light-eyed guard had turned toward the group. George saw his chance and stepped a little more quickly downhill, training the thergo at the stand of bushes and small trees. They were very close together in a mass, what his mother would have called *not quite a bit of woods*, with one of her slight but devastating little sniffs. The thergo fuzzed a bit and he adjusted the knob on the side two clicks, waiting until it settled to take another step, then another.

Yes, there was a definite signature. When he got close enough he would hold the scan button, and who knew— maybe a paper. Maybe just a bonus for identification. He could buy Molly something small and shiny.

Perhaps that would shutter her complaints. His mother had warned him not to marry the little bint, but there had been the scare with the urine test. He had to do what was right, and she was so pretty, with her golden curls and her snub nose. A real blush-cheeked English rose, especially when she sat so nicely with her ankles crossed. He had told her—in the spirit of honesty, really—that her ankles were one of her best features, and given her a pamphlet his mother had recommended on how to keep oneself trim for the old husband.

She had seemed grateful, even though the stapled paper had vanished.

George found he had drawn much nearer the bit of woods,

and the thergo was flashing happily along. He had never seen this particular signature before—plateaus in the top third of the array, a quickening pattern of spikes in the middle, and a slow rise in the bottom. If he could gather enough, it might be just the breakthrough his career needed.

Imagine Molly's adoring expression when he told her of the pay raise! Mother was dead, of course, but imagine her finally wearing a faint look of approval, lipstick feathering into the cracks around her aged mouth and her dim eyes blinking nice and moist. Sometimes he thought he had married Molly because he detected a hint of familiar sourness in her expression every once in a while. A shade of disappointment, well hidden but still there.

The bit of woods was making an odd creaking noise. The breeze must be up, though he didn't feel it. His eyes watered a bit, but he concentrated on the thergo. Really, there was no reason to stay out of the Rift. It stank, certainly, and little Aleksander had a bit of bad luck falling into a puddle of some nasty waste, but—

*"Hey!"* someone yelled in the distance. *"Hey!"*

He didn't look back. The thergo fuzzed again and he let out a harsh breath with a term his mother would *not* have approved of. A man sometimes just had to use a bit of strong language, really—

Something curled around his ankle. George glanced down, irritated, and his eyes widened.

It was a long cable of plant matter, somewhat like a blackberry vine. Juicy, green, fat, and furred with small serrations; he had perhaps stepped into its curve? But no, he had been a fair bit away from the bit of woods. The thergo had a good range, and he hadn't meant to get *really* close, just down the hill a bit and—

*"Forget it!"* someone else yelled. *"He's gone! Fucking forget it!"*

Who was gone? George had only a moment to wonder before the cable around his ankle gave a terrific yank, dragging him into the copse that was not, after all, very far away. His shirt came untucked, the toothy grass tearing at pale tender skin beneath, and the thergo went flying. His head bounced against a rock, the world turned over and a starry pain filled his skull, and he was thankfully, blessedly unconscious when the final *crunch* reverberated through the whip-moving shrubs and slim, violently shaking trunks. There was a dense mat of wriggling roots and quasi foliage near the bottom, and he vanished into its embrace without a scream.

# 32
# MIGHT BE ME

⟫╫⟨

Mako yelled, letting off a burst of fire at the stand of spindly trees and thick underbrush. Tremaine vanished into its maw, and the rifter grabbed the back of Barko's jacket, hauling him backward again. The bald scientist went down hard, the sound of his teeth clicking together almost audible over a rifle's stuttering barks—projectile instead of plasma, because you couldn't ever tell what plasma would do in a Rift. It wasn't worth it, so the plas-switches on the Currago5K rifles had been disabled. The pin on the Suray Naga submachine the demo man carried had been fused, too.

"He's gone!" she yelled. "Fucking forget it!"

Morov, his knees digging into the grass, swore viciously. *"Cease fire! Cease fire, you fuckbuckle motherfucker! Hold your fire!"* Behind him, Brood had prudently hit the ground, and bullets plowed into the shrubs and shaking, spindly trees. They were plo-rounds, and anything flammable should have gone up in seconds. Certainly anything woodlike should have burst into greasy orange flames.

Instead, the trees writhed with queer rubbery shivers and the shrubs ran like ink on an oiled plate, extending long thorn-liquid runners up the hill. Dust puffed up, the serrated grass whipping wildly, and the rifter uncoiled over Barko in an amazing leap. She hit Mako squarely, and even though she was much smaller the unexpected impact threw the man sideways, into Tolstoy, who went down hard as well. Bullets spattered overhead, and Brood punched Morov on the closest thing he could reach, to get his commander's attention.

That just happened to be Morov's left buttock. Which cramped, viciously, because Brood had a helluva windup.

*"Motherfucker!"* Morov howled, but he knew exactly *why* the sonofabitch had done it. When you were being drowned out by combat noise, you were forced to other measures.

The thing was heading up the hill, sending out its shrub-tentacles, clawing against grass and earth. The rifter screamed, a high hawklike cry, lost under the gunfire and hideous crunching. Mako stopped firing, and Brood was on his back, fumbling at his chest while the thing heaved itself another few feet up the slope.

It looked angry, and it was making a *sound*. A low grumbling roar, gathering strength. The trees were less trees now, and more spinelike, the greenery suddenly little fleshy pods and tabs crusting their edges. The "leaves" crawled over the spines, and as the thing scrabbled closer, Morov could swear he saw them scurrying along, nuzzling at the scars bullets had torn. Lapping at them, swarming like white blood cells gathering to form an angry pus-filled pocket.

Morov lurched to his feet. Mako was no longer making noise; Barko was, a hoarse cry of despair. Eschkov, his backpack left behind, stumbled down the slope toward them, hands out-stretched and his spectacles askew. A lonely flash jetted off one lens, and he almost ran into Morov, his soft skinny hands closing with desperate strength on the officer's pack straps. He began pulling, hauling Morov up the hill.

Brood's hand finally came away from his chest, full of the sour metal apple of a barker.* *"Clear!"* he screamed, pulling the pin, and tossed it at the thing. He rolled over and scrab-bled, getting his legs inelegantly but efficiently under him, and almost ran into Morov, who stared at the goddamn thing as the grenade bounced once, vanishing into its quivering depths.

*You dumbass,* Morov had time to think.

*"Get down!"* the rifter yelled, and kicked Senkin's feet from under him. She threw herself on top of Barko, and Morov had a brief second to think *oh shit* before the grenade popped and the noise exploded outward.

A gigantic warm hand cupped every inch of his back, legs, head, neck, everything. He *flew,* weightless for a moment.

*Crunch.* The impact snapped something in his left leg and knocked all the sense out of him for a brief gentle second before the pain began. The world spun away, came back on a greased leaf full of tearing edges. He hung between Senkin and Brood as they slid down the other side of the hill, and the rifter was bellowing at them to *move you cocksuckers move!* She had some-thing in her hands—one of those queer opalescent rocks, and as she ran she twisted at it, tendons standing out under pale skin. It cracked, a thin thread of darkness appearing at its

---

* Concussion grenade.

heart. She had another snot-rag, a faded red one, and popped the rock into it as she ran.

Then she whirled, digging her heels in, and skidded to a stop, the twin furrows plowed by her boots glaring against the matted grass. The noise behind them spiraled up into a boulder-rubbing screech.

The thing was fucking *pissed*.

Tolstoy was on his knee at the top of the hill, firing at the thing. It crested the rise in a humpback wave, shedding those fleshy leaf-bits, whatever wet sound they made lost in the roaring. They fell, bloodsick knobs of tissue, and when they hit the grass small puffs of caustic smoke belched up. The rifter raised the fist with the red snot-rag, and began to whirl the trapped rock inside.

The thing heaved itself fully atop the rise, tentacles shooting out and dragging Tolstoy into its maw, which closed with a wet crunch lost under the roaring. Brood was down on one knee, shooting at it too, wasting ammo. Morov tried to shake the noise out of his head, tried to *think*. The roar turned everything inside him to jelly, knocked his head back on the smallish stem his neck had become, and the pain came again, diamondtooth ants biting down his back and legs, red-hot iron shoved into his left thigh.

The rifter's face was alive, bright color high on her cheeks. Her eyes weren't bulging so much as *shining*, and she whirled the makeshift sling just like the illustration of King David Morov could remember in one of his battered childhood books. His mother would read them, if she wasn't too bone-tired after a long day of slinging other people's wet laundry, and she would tell him the stories behind the stories—how David even then was a king, and his bloodline would bring the Messiah when it was time for God to call His chosen people home. How King Solomon had built his palace with demons as his slaves, the great ring glinting on his finger, how the wise rebbes made massive men of clay and breathed life into them to protect the ghetto.

There were other stories, but all Morov was seeing was the Goliath coming down the hill, gaining speed, and Brood screaming as he emptied one clip, then another at it. The bullets tore into it without effect, and the rifter let out another high keening screech. A snap of her arm, and the white, faintly glowing rock described a high arc.

For a moment it looked like she'd miscalculated, but the impossible happened. The rock *curved*, and the dark thread along its middle peeled open, a single spark buried in its depths dilating.

The rifter turned on her heel and launched herself at Senkin, who was holding Morov up because Brood had gone fucking killcrazy. She hit with a crunch and yelled something he couldn't hear. His head rang, and there was a soft, ridiculous *whoosh* before the flung rock exploded.

Fallen sideways, his head bouncing against the serrated grass, Morov stared.

The flame was blue, and it didn't act like it should. It spread like liquid while it leapt and danced, and a cloying, feverish heat blasted down the hillside as the spine-backed thing writhed, throwing even more of those tiny gobbets everywhere. One landed near Morov's nose. He watched, dreamily, as the round mouth on its end, ringed with concentric rows of inward-slanting, triangular teeth, opened and closed.

*Fuck of a sphincter.* The thought was very far away. Everything grayed out.

When he came back, touching down in his body like a dropped popper into a cenestat catch, he was on his back and Eschkov was finishing a very capable field-splint on his left lower leg. Senkin had an emergency kit open and Morov's sleeve pushed up; he smoothed a red painpatch onto his commander's biceps. The narcotic would begin spreading immediately. Senkin's mouth moved, but the words were only a faint fuzzy faraway buzz.

*Shock. I'm in shock.*

Barko, on his other side, held up a field-syringe of amber liquid. He tapped it, twice, and cleared any air before bending over Morov's arm, which had a tourniquet around it he couldn't feel. Barko's lips were moving, but maybe the man wasn't talking. It looked, instead, an awful lot like he was praying.

Morov's head tipped back. There was Brood, at a weird angle because his field of vision was sliding, standing watch. Mako, his head wrapped in a bandage already bearing a spreading clusterpatch of blood leaking through, was watching the other way.

The rifter crouched in the middle distance, stubble slicked to her scalp with grime and blood. Had she run her hands back over her head, like Barko was always doing? Her hollow cheeks were striped with weird, greasy soot. She wasn't looking at Morov.

Instead, she was studying Brood's back, and her expression wasn't quite unguarded, but it was...thoughtful.

*She knows he's Kopelund's fail-safe. I wonder if she'll...*

The thought spun away, replaced by other slow-moving

mental fish, a flock of them. It was dangerous in here. More dangerous than they had ever imagined. The thing had looked like *trees*, for fucksake. Had the rifter left them there knowing one of the scientists would be unable to resist the temptation? Or had Tremaine just been that stupid?

One more thought came circling back before the warmth of the painpatch crept up his shoulder to his neck and made everything seem just-fucking-fine-and-dandy.

*Someone else is going to die.*

*I'm hurt bad.*

*It might be me.*

# 33
# RIDE THIS WITH ME

⟩╫⟨

"[F]ine." Cabra's jaw had set itself hard as chaxalloy. She had calmed down, and made the decision he'd known she would. "We ride it, then."

Sabby, the left side of his face puffing already as his eye swelled shut, shook his head. His hair ground into the dirt, but at least she'd stopped hitting him. His arms, wrapped around her so tight they ached, hurt almost as much as his ribs. He settled his wrist against one of her backpack straps, his fist securely anchored in the tough material. "Ent gonna." Not like it mattered.

"You say that all the damn time," Cabra hissed. An angry flush suffused her dark cheeks, and her beaded braids glittered angrily as the sun westered. "*Ent gonna, ent gonna*, then you go ahead anyway."

"How much longer, huh? How much longer 'fore you drop me 'cause I don't wanna?"

"Don' wanna *what*?" She spread her pink-palmed hands. Every line on her was a taut curve, from those much-in-demand hips to the sculpted division of her lips. Even her eyelashes were thick, matted arcs. She was a Rift all in herself, though Sabby would never have been able to articulate such a thing. He *felt* it, and that was enough. Sometimes being with her scratched the loneliness like driftburn.

Other times, it hurt. Like now. Deep in the guts where nothing but the worst hunger settled.

"We got enough," he said, desperately. "Don' need no shady, no bullets. Go back along our line, hit cache or two, and get *out*." Oh, she wasn't going to fall for *that*, but if this turned out bad he could say *I told you so*. Or not say it, but she'd know he was thinking it loudly.

"Then what?" Frustration made her sharp. Her chin was up, the pulse in her throat beating quick and hot. "You drink it up? No, Pooka. I want off." A thin white line of evaporated sweat clung along the side of her neck, and his lips ached to brush it. Hangovers gave you the salt-craving.

"Off what? Off me?" Of course she would. Who wouldn't? He tightened his arms, clinging. She was going to have to scrape harder to get him away.

"You fucking mipsik." Her face crumpled. "Don't."

"We got enough," he repeated. "I won't drink it." He was lying, she knew he was lying, the entire goddamn Rift probably knew he was lying. Her decision was already made, and he was just whistling at a wall.

Her temper was all spent. "Imma hang and see what Vetch's line is." Cabra went limp. Her knees braced on either side of his hips, her weight atop him the only thing holding him to the ground. "You wanna driftburn out, you go ahead. But I am *done* pennying, Pook. Imma go home, and if you ride this out you come with me."

God *damn* it. Behind her head the sky was blue, and deep. The aching, marvelous blue you never saw *outside*, this was a sky stripped of pollution, of haze, of greed and wanting. When the pinchoks came back, they would drift like thoughts through a satisfied mind, barely flapping.

Up at the top of the hill, Vetch and Il Muto were probably ignoring them. It wouldn't matter to Vetch one way or another. The bastard probably knew Sabby wouldn't be going back to the wall alone. He never rifted solo anymore. Not since his shoulder, and the screaming, and the buffeting of huge dark wings.

Not since he'd felt the cold, loose, liquid relief of *well, that's over; don't have to live anymore.* Finding out he was still alive, stitched up, antibiotics and an expensive jolt of triphase fighting off the sepsis from pinchok claws, almost made him want to weep.

He'd thought he was *done* with all this. Of course, you were never done with the Rift. Like Cabra, *it* decided when things were over, not you, not a second before.

And not a split second after.

"You promise?" Christ, but he hated hearing himself whine. His shoulder was on fire, and his left eye was almost closed now. Maybe when they stopped tonight she'd regret whapping him with her elbow, and be soft again. Soft or furious, though, she was the only tenuous good thing he had left.

"I ent *promising*, Pook. I'm *telling* you. You ride this with me, and we get the fuckin' payday and go home."

"What if there ent no payday?" It had to be asked.

"There *better* be," was all Cabra would say. She untangled herself from him, and Sabby let her. She was calm enough now. "What you drag me off for, huh?"

"Dunno." But he did. Cabra liked to wrestle, and if she got her arms around Vetch, who knew? She might decide she liked being held down instead of doing the holding, and that would mean...

No, it was better if Sabby was the voice of reason, even if she roll-tangled on him like a scuttle taking down a grass-eater on the rim of the Rift. You could find the big swaying shaggy beasts in any bubble that had a little grass, though you could never get close enough to see their real shapes under the fur. They spooked easy.

Sabby didn't blame them.

Cabra smoothed her braids, settled her backpack. Bent her knees and offered one pink-palmed hand, her cheeks and beads gleaming. Sabby took it, let her pull him up. She put her arms around him, and he leaned on her, resting his chin atop her head. She was soft under the flexarmor and the stiffness every woman had before they decided you weren't going to hurt them, and the tension went out of her bit by bit. He couldn't close his eyes—they were in the Rift.

But his vision blurred and he held her, the feeling that he had just barely escaped the abyss running through him again, scalp to toes. She hadn't realized what a huge mistake he was. Not yet.

It was good enough.

# 34
# WHAT WE'RE AFTER

>+⊦+<

How much longer do we have to haul this fucker?" Mako's neck ached. His legs were sore. His fucking head had stopped bleeding, but the bandage was itching like fuck because of the crust of dried red human-juice. His back was singing the song of got-to-carry-your-buddy blues, because Morov hung between him and Senkin like wet laundry. It wasn't the captain's fault, he was high on painpatch and stuffed full of antibiotics and warmers to stave off shock. The old man had been the last one down, probably making sure all his boys were under cover, and wasn't that just like him? One of these days Captain Zus Petrovitch Morov was going to end up a dead hero, and Mako was going to lose the only motherfucker at Institute QR-715 he actually respected.

On either side, warehouses loomed. The rifter had taken them onto a road for a bit, working steadily uphill, then through a network of alleys in what had been industrial-zoned before the Event. The burnt shells of warehouses alternated with flattened husks, and she turned east again to plunge them through a wilderness of rusting pre-Event junkyard. The cranes and crushers rearing overhead were corkscrew-twisted, as if dipped in some unimaginable heat.

"If it was you I woulda dropped you a klick and a half ago." Senkin, from the sound of it, wasn't feeling too fresh either. "Yo, rifter! How much longer?"

"Stop yelling." She barely turned her head. Behind her, Eschkov pressed close and Barko limped; Brood was on rearguard again.

"How much longer?" Senkin persisted. "He's not getting any lighter, or any better."

Her small fuzzy scalp bobbed a bit, a soft nod. "Maybe another hour."

"Shit." Mako's patience was at the fast end of the fuse. "Can't we just camp?" There was plenty of cover here, for Chrissake. Maybe even something to burn.

"If you want to lose another half of the group by morning, sure." She stopped, and Eschkov nearly ran into her. The rifter paid no attention, just dug in her hipbag and produced another one of those heavy washers with a strip of cloth slipknotted on. Whirled it once, twice, testing, then tossed it in the general direction they were going, down a long hallway with stacks of cars crushed into jagged metal cubes on either side. The washer hit its apex—then there was a crackling sound, a *pop*, and the washer exploded, the cloth tail shredding itself violently from prow to stern. "Fuck." She let out a long, frustrated breath.

She hadn't flinched, but Eschkov damn sure had.

"Where the fuck we *going*, anyway?" Senkin wanted to know. He was pale, sucking at his bottom lip while he took most of the captain's weight to give Mako a rest.

"Further in. It's near the center." Her lips bulged—running

her tongue over her teeth. Oddly, it didn't make her look any uglier, maybe because she was the only woman around. She tossed another washer, this time to her left, and that one fell normally. She set off again, and Eschkov hurried behind her like a waddling cygnet after its mama. The stacks of mutilated metal drew away, and she scooped up the washer, wrapping the cloth tail with quick habitual motions before plunging her hand back into her bag and bringing out yet another. This one fell normally too, and she aimed them for a squatting, deformed building and—thank whatever god you prayed to—a gap in the cyclone fencing barely keeping the junkyard contained.

"The center? Of the Rift?" Mako heard the disbelieving bafflement in his own voice, and heaved his side of Morov up over a shattered window. The entire thing, frame and glass, had been blown out of the building to their right, which proclaimed, in faded signage, the name of the company owning the junkyard. It could have had an apartment up top for whoever had to watch the damn place during the day, back before the Event. You couldn't tell for sure because a helicopter had smashed into it from the top and the thing's back rotor poked up from the roof, a rusted flower.

Tremaine and Tolstoy, both eaten by something that looked like overgrown bushes. It was going to be a long time, Mako suspected, before he could look at even a ruthlessly clipped ornamental shrubbery and not feel queasy.

"This just gets better." Senkin coughed. "Shit, at least let us stop for a second."

She shrugged and froze, her boots fixed as if nailed to the ground. Eschkov was near enough to smell her nonexistent hair. "Fine. But be ready to jump."

"Sure, I'll jump," Mako grumbled. "Carrying five hundred pounds of Morov. Uh-huh."

"Cormorant's in the center." Her chin dropped, slid from side to side as she scanned in front of them. The gap in the fence led out into an alley, or what had been one. About two meters away from the fence, it opened onto two square blocks of wasteland—something had flattened the buildings, reducing them to splinters and shivers. The damage was confined to just those blocks, and the crack-starred streets at the boundary were curiously free of weeds. Come to think of it, the junkyard had no plant life, either. Not even hexmoss, which Barko told him grew on metal.

That probably meant some new danger. Mako almost shuddered as he and Senkin lowered Morov carefully. At least their commander wasn't complete deadweight, he was soupy-conscious enough to try to help his carriers.

Mako straightened with a sigh his grandmother would have been proud of, peering at their surroundings. The cloud cover had not eased, but the weird throat-burning fume had gone away by degrees. He stripped his rag away from his face with a grateful sigh, mopping at the sweat on his forehead and the back of his neck. It was always too warm here, except in the winter. Did it ever snow in the Rift? At home, they would call a treacherous stretch of wilderness by its proper name.

That halted him for a full thirty seconds. He couldn't remember the right word. He could see his grandmother's round face, her eyes crinkled with fans of both severity and laughter at the edges, and the fur-lined hood of her ancient sheepskin coat glazed with ice. But he couldn't, for the life of him, remember the right word.

She'd told him not to sign up with the military. *Stay here and hunt*, she said. Well, it was all hunting, wherever you were. Tracks in snow or litter on a township street, blood on ice or barbed wire, it was all the same. All you had to do was shut your blowhole and open your eyes, and everything was clear as day.

Right now he was looking at the wreckage, and at how the rifter moved—or didn't move. Some of the traditional hunters would do that—stay in one position, tensing and releasing muscles to keep them fresh, eating snow to keep their breath from showing. She disappeared at mealtimes, like one or two of the old folks who remembered the Thin Days, after the Event had fucked up everything and they had fallen back on the old ways for two generations. The elders absented themselves at mealtimes once they grew too frail, so as not to drag the rest of the family down.

*How much was lost*, his grandmother had sung, staring into the fire. But the rifter had stuffed her face in the canteen just like the rest of them. It would be a mistake to think of her, however grudgingly, as one of the People.

How many were left, anyway? When the infrastructure contracted, nobody wanted to take a vacation in Siberia, for fuck's sake. Mining wasn't as goddamn important when you couldn't truck out what you dug up, and there was failing need for it anyway because the population still hadn't reached pre-Event levels. Single mothers even got government pay for producing new little consumers in all the ILAC countries. In the warlord territories, harems and rape were endemic. It was a wonder any women survived at all.

Mako had been on the front lines twice. He had no desire to ever go back. Institute duty was *way* better. Then Kope got a burr up his ass about this bird in the middle of the Rift. What the fuck was he going to do? Put it in a cage and sell tickets?

Captain Morov, breathing shallowly, blinked several times. He looked like he wanted to get up, moving a little and wincing as his splinted leg tried to bend and was arrested. His color was bad, his dark buzzcut wet with sweat. He'd taken a nasty hit, a hole in the thigh from either shrapnel or a ricochet, and his shin was probably cracked from the grenade blast. He looked younger without half a cigar stuck in his mouth, or maybe it was just that his eyes were at low mast and his damp cheeks were slack.

"Fucking Cormorant." Mako said it a little louder than he probably should have. "Don't even know what the fuck it is, only that someone wants it."

"Welcome to rifting." The rifter made a small, unamused sound. "You don't even know what it is?"

"Someone has to know, or they wouldn't have sent our asses in. Can we smoke now?" Senkin yanked out his *makhorka* pouch, which reminded Mako it was time for a smoke, too.

"Should be okay." She still didn't move.

"Hey, Esch." Barko, his head gleaming where soot had been wiped or sweated away, took the thinner scientist's arm. "Come on. Sit down for a bit."

"He was gone just like that," Eschkov said in a thin querulous tone. The scientist's loose eye was drifting everywhere but in front of him. It was a wonder the motherfucker could walk in a straight line. "The thergo. We should have rescued the thergo."

"I know." Barko guided the little guy down to perch on a small flat patch of bare dirt. "Science has setbacks, Igor."

The rifter finally moved a bit, folding down increment by increment until she rested in an easy crouch. She must have been doing it for years, to look so comfortable all doubled up like that. Mako's grandmother had crouched like that, before her hips got bad.

"Maybe we should know exactly what we're after." Mako rolled his own cigarette. For a moment he wished he were back in the township, maybe in Molly's chintzy, overstuffed bed-room. *He never fucks me right*, she would say, and Mako would only grunt. She was an excellent little piece, but with Tremaine eaten by a bunch of fucking trees—and he was *not* going to be the one to break that to her, no sir—she was likely to get… clingy.

His lighter refused to snap on the first try, or the second. Finally, on the third, it caught, and he inhaled with relief.

It was a bad omen, for it to take more than three. The new popper lighters were supposed to catch even during a hur-ricane, but this was an ancient one full of flammable liquid; the wicks were getting harder and harder to find. He'd picked it up during his second tour, in Colombia. Or what *used* to be Colombia. The motherfucking warboys there cut out your internal organs while you were still breathing if they caught you. No prisoners taken. Not like in Romania.

Romania had been almost goddamn civilized, in comparison.

"Maybe you should shut your fucknozzle, soldier." Brood's pleasant tone was all the warning in the world. "If they wanted us to know *what*, they would have told us." Apparently, he was taking his single-stripe-higher-than seriously.

Senkin surprised them both, weighing in with a series of flat, unimpressed words. "I don't even think Morov knows."

That put an end to discussion. The rough reek of *makhorka* rose in veils, and the familiar nicotine hit soothed Mako's nerves.

There weren't even any real stories. Just the name. *The Cormorant.* It was a type of bird, but what kind of fucked-up avian would live *here*? The rifter said nothing, her face set but somehow avid. Maybe *she* didn't know, either. But she had to know something, for Kope to pull her halfway across the world and into this.

Pretty soon it was time to go again. Morov, breathing shallowly, was heaved up—not ungently—and the rifter moved out into the wasteland, tossing another one of her metal-and-cloth tails. Mako eyed the clouds overhead. The sun was going to set soon, and goddammit, he hadn't taken a crap since they'd come through the slugwall. He didn't feel like he could now, either, but when he eventually wanted to, what were the chances something was going to bite his ass while he squatted?

Mako sighed, hitched his belt with his free hand, and lifted Captain Morov a little higher.

# 35
# HIS BUSINESS

⟩╫⟨

An hour after dusk found them in another rancid, hunchback building—an apartment complex before the Event, now a collection of listing two-story hulks peppered with irregular, star-pointed holes. One or two seemed structurally sound, though, and the rifter had selected a ground-floor apartment near the center, with a view of what had been a circular drive-way in front of what used to be the rental office. There was even a bone-dry fountain crawling with hexmoss and long, clinging, silvery strands of something that fluttered in the uncertain, flirting breeze.

Morov wasn't doing so well—he'd gone even paler, and his breathing had turned shallow and labored. He'd sweated through his uniform, and soon they were going to have to divide his gear up for carrying. The rifter stood near a shattered window, peering out into the bruise-purple dimness. Brood approached her, stepping deliberately hard on the squeaking, rotting floorboard, but she didn't even turn her head. Her hair-stubble had turned to soft dark babyfuzz, and her swelling lips, stretched over those horseteeth, were a straight line.

Barko, swabbing a skinstrip across Morov's forehead, kept an ear perked. The strip absorbed beaded sweat on the commander's skin, and Barko was hoping it wouldn't turn bright red. Blue would be best. Yellow he could work with. Even deep yellow with red specks would be okay.

He wasn't a religious man, but the longer he was in here, the more he thought praying might be an option. It probably couldn't hurt.

"We can light a fire, right?" Brood stopped a respectful distance from her, but he kept a callused, dirty hand near his sidearm. His blond tips glowed, and for a moment he looked ridiculous, dirty-faced with his well-cared-for hair standing up in spikes.

"Yeah. Holes in the roof." Her voice was no longer a toneless mumble, or maybe Barko had just gotten used to it. She sounded a little tired, and faintly irritated.

Barko took a deep breath. It was fine. They were relatively safe if she said so. The floor was a little squishy, but not bad, and this building wasn't festooned with the weird silver strands, either.

"How come nothing attacks us at night?" Brood scratched at his grimy neck with blunt fingers. His right hand, resting on the butt of his Galprin semiautomatic, tapped its longest finger once, twice. One of his nails was torn, a semicircle of dried blood capping it.

"Because I pick places that smell bad to whatever might jump us." Just the faintest edge of disdain coloring the sentence, maybe. Or maybe it was just tiredness. "You got any ammo left?"

"Some. Not that it does any good."

"Not against the shit you waste it on."

Amazingly, Brood let that pass. That middle finger, tapping on his gun, sped up a little. "What was that? The tree-thing."

"Thornback. They make black dirt." She shrugged, thin shoulders rising, dropping with a small jerk. "Just know not to go near it. Looks wrong, smells worse." In three-quarter profile, her eyes were merely large and oddly luminous, her long nose was almost regal, and that mouth looked determined and resolutely lush, instead of misshapen.

"But what *was* it?" There wasn't a tremor in Brood's stance. He wasn't a querulous child asking an adult after a scare.

But, Barko thought, it was damn close. The skinstrip was deepening in color, and Barko didn't like that. He couldn't quite see *what* color; he'd have to use a lamper or bring it to the fire. If it was blue, well and good. If it was yellow, okay, he could work with that. He had to, he was the closest thing to a medic they had. He'd only taken the field training because it meant a raise, for God's sake.

Red meant infection had taken hold. What kind of antibiotics did they have? Just a field kit's worth. Christ. Was anything else in there, anything more useful?

Brood's finger kept up its steady tapping. One, two, three, one two, three, one two three, one, two, three.

The rifter was staring out the window, but Barko would have bet everything in his pack and his hope of getting back home too that she was paying a lot of attention to Brood's tiptapping phalanx.

"Rift's got a mind of its own," she said, finally. "Sometimes things that were before get a mind, too. Each one's like a body, and we're invading. It's gotta ID us."

Barko peered at the strip. Now it was fading. They were supposed to be proof against industrial contamination. In here, though...was that caustic fume earlier part of the Rift's defense mechanism? Then what were the Rift equivalent of white blood cells? Things like the tree-creature, or the silvery goo that had...eaten...Aleks?

Now he knew what a virus felt like, hunted through the body's secret chambers.

"Shit." The pale-eyed sardie's finger slowed. After a short while, he finally said what everyone in here was likely to be thinking. "Can you get us back to the insertion point?"

That made her head turn a fraction. The attractiveness of her almost-profile vanished as the angle made her nose too bony again, her mouth too wide for the rest of her, the skin under her eyes discolored by dusk or exhaustion. "With a limper, who knows? Plus the goggles, he's about to crack."

Barko couldn't help himself. He glanced at Eschkov, who was in the corner furthest from the window. Only his spectacles glinted, betraying his position. Had he shuddered?

Senkin and Mako hunched at a ring of those strange opalescent stones, Mako flicking his lighter now that they had the go-ahead for a fire. When it caught, they were all going to look like cavemen. Huddling, dirty, and afraid of the dark.

An orange flower bloomed, danced into yellow at the edges. Senkin gave a relieved sigh, and Mako muttered something in what had to be his native tongue. Maybe it was even a prayer. Did Siberians pray? What a research question. He should have gone into social sciences, studying the effects of Rift dislocation. History and dusty stacks of primary sources would be so much better than this.

Brood turned, a little awkwardly. Or maybe it just seemed that way, because he kept his right side—the side with the holstered gun—pointed at her. He glanced at the newborn fire, those pale eyes slitted and the shadows turning his face into a skull-grimace for a moment.

The rifter eyed him, and Barko could have sworn her own thin face momentarily leered. It wasn't anger, or even sadness. It was the face of a person who knew she was going to have to kill to get out of this alive, and who didn't mind the thought much.

Barko rubbed at his bald skull with his left hand, polishing the dome with a grit-dirty palm. His head should have been cold, but all he felt was damp, uncomfortable, and slightly constipated. He made sure Morov was propped up well enough on the stack of moldering carpets covered by the commander's own bedroll, and settled a crackle-thin foiler* over the man.

The rifter turned sharply, strode away from the window. Brood almost twitched, and Barko braced himself. But she just took the few strides to reach Morov's side and dropped into her habitual crouch—her hip joints had to have adapted to that from an early age. Maybe she took dance? He tried to imagine her in a leotard. Failed miserably, tried to imagine her as a child, and failed again.

He couldn't imagine Kopelund as a kid either. Or himself, anymore.

"What's it say?" She studied Morov's sweat-shining face, with the same set thoughtfulness she used outside.

---

* Space blanket.

Barko looked down at the skinstrip. "Don't know yet. Got a lamper?"

She shook her head. He hauled himself up and headed for the fire. Brood trailed in his wake. He'd stopped tapping at his gun, but whether that was a good sign or not Barko found himself too tired to care.

Uncertain firelight didn't help, but Mako had a lamper, and shone it directly on the strip. It lingered somewhere between deep yellow with pink spots, and a band of bright crimson in the center along the crease from its packaging. At least, Barko was going to blame it on the packaging.

Barko cleared his throat. "He needs rest, and another antibiotic jump. How long can we stay here?"

All eyes on the rifter. She had the back of one small pale hand to Morov's wet forehead, her long thin capable fingers close together. It was an unexpectedly feminine movement from such a thin, homely specimen. She looked up, those protuberant, dark eyes moving from one of them to the next. Armed sardies and scientists, all looking to her—a civilian, a felon—for an answer.

Barko didn't like the way that chain of thought was tending. Had she guessed Tremaine—or someone else—would be incapable of leaving the goddamn bushes alone? Or had she just, simply, gone off to eat in private, like a half-domesticated animal? She was never around at mealtimes in here, though she'd eaten in the canteen with the rest of them.

The most chilling prospect was that she had gone off to lunch somewhere safer, serene in the knowledge that someone, sooner or later, would be stupid enough to trigger some kind of immune response in the Rift. It was *dangerous* in here. All it took was a single misstep. Everything happened so fucking *fast*.

226

"Dawn," she said, finally. "Eat. Get some rest."

"About fucking time," Senkin murmured, and he and Mako began digging in their packs. Brood began feeding the fire bits of scavenged wood, and Barko approached Eschkov, who was studying the damp-spotted wall with every appearance of rapt attention.

"Look," Eschkov said, when the floor groaned a bit under Barko's feet. "It's not hexmoss. Maybe a type of lichen?"

Barko couldn't help himself. He glanced back at the rifter, who had straightened, her right hand low and heavy.

She held his gaze while she slipped Morov's sidearm and a couple clips of ammo into her goddamn hipbag. As if daring him to say something, anything, especially since Brood was right there, tossing a chunk of what might have once been part of a wicker chair into the fire.

The pale-eyed sardie's cheeks ballooned as he blew on the flames. Not very necessary, but maybe it made him feel better. Any caveman would be glad of light and heat when the darkness came. The Rift was crammed full of usable technology, but if you had to go through this to get it, was it really worth the goddamn trouble?

Barko turned away. Laid a hand on Eschkov's bony shoulder. "Come on, Igor. Let's get some food. Science needs fuel."

After all, he told himself, if Brood was looming over him or Igor, and tapping his fingers like that, he'd want a weapon, too. It wasn't Barko's business. What *was* his business was caring for Morov, and somehow getting Eschkov to eat something.

Not to mention staying on the rifter's good side, if she had one.

# 36
# DIRECTIVE

⋊⫞⋉

*A* piece of paper, angrily crumpled but then smoothed, found on General Timor Kopelund's desk:

## ILAC DIRECTIVE 3708-B (a)

Following the recommendation of the Anomaly Research Committee, the following has been found and warranted:

THAT the Anomalies are throughout ILAC territories, and are varying in size;

THAT the current piecemeal exploration and exploitation of the Anomalies is inefficient;

THAT standardization of exploration and exploitation is mandatory;

THAT avoidable casualties and loss of materiel can no longer be allowed.

Following the recommendation of the Appropriations Committee, the following has been put forward, voted upon, passed, and confirmed:

THAT the Anomalies under a certain diameter [see 3708-B (a) (1)] shall be explored, processed, and exploited first;

THAT said exploration, processing, and exploitation shall be under the guidance, control, and sole command of the ILAC ARC;

THAT unauthorized entry or exit to or from an Anomaly shall be a Class D Felony;

THAT unauthorized possession or sale of Anomaly Artifacts shall be a Class D Felony;

THAT all Anomaly Institutes be recertified by ILAC RC;

THAT all Anomaly Institutes be placed under direct civilian (ILAC RC) control;

THAT all persons possessing the requisite skills and capacities for Anomaly entry, navigation, and exit (RIFTERS) be licensed under the ILAC RC within the next four (4) years...

# 37
# GOT MY REASONS

⊶⋕⊷

The junkyard wasn't safe, but a cavernous, half-crumpled warehouse with its back to the fence was. Finding a tiny crack and burrowing in like ticks was how you survived when night fell. Not so different from in the city, really.

Cabra settled herself cross-legged near the small fire ringed with potzegs, its smoke rising in a soft column. Half this building was gone, an amphitheater of decay with a tiny spark deep in its well-throat. Beams and walls were sheared cleanly, as if a smaller Rift had come down inside this one. A little baby Rift, cutting through human structures like a hot wire through congealed fat.

Sabby lay, his back propped against a concrete pad holding up the wreck of some kind of pre-Event machine. He'd passed out pretty hard, and shivered in his sleep, both from detox and from memory. He'd been raised by Yarkers, and what little he said of his childhood was enough to turn even *her* stomach. Maybe that was why she put up with all of it. Or maybe because he was so grateful for her there was little chance of him running around after another hole, joy or otherwise. The men who wanted care instead of just-plain-poke were better.

More manageable.

Il Muto nodded on the other side of the fire, his pointed, blond-stubbled chin almost touching his chest. Vetch sat with his knees drawn up and his arms around them, a curious pose for a grown man. Cabra wondered if it was uncomfortable, with that belt buckle of his. He'd blown into town just before Ashe's last run, and had attended her wake. Good rifter, always with something to sell, popping in and out of this bubble like the patrols weren't even there. Careful, and always had money in his pocket. Crewing with him was generally good, but this time... well, to be fair, she should have twigged when he said *come in armed*. The only thing you really *needed* a gun for in the Rift was first-timers.

Regular rifters weren't stupid. They'd work something out over the payday, or if they got the drop* it would be evasion instead of a pitched battle, a race to the slugwall. Sardies, though... fucking lundies with guns and tiny little pokers to prop up. Nothing reasonable about them. They were, mostly, what you went into the fucking Rifts to escape.

So they'd pulled Ashe's hole out of deepfreeze. The Institute had sent a full team in, and they were working deeper and deeper into the Rift. Then there was Vetch, trailing in the wake, telling them to come armed.

"You think it's true?" She stared at the fire, orange and yellow

---

* Slang: to reach a particular objective before another team, to steal something.

eating scavenged, worm-eaten wood. Sabby exhaled softly, and his twitching eased a bit.

That was another thing to cautiously like about Vetch. He didn't pretend not to know what the fuck she was talking about. "Seems someone did."

In other words, the bastard running the Institute, enough to send Ashe in. Then pull this other rifter out of a hard freeze a year later. A sardie jackhammer-head wouldn't do that unless he thought there was a good chance of a return on the investment, now would he.

"So you thinking to get the drop."

"Maybe." He hunched even further, and Cabra looked up from the fire, studying him closely. Flames reflected in his pupils gleamed, little liquid fires, and his expression was... well, not familiar, but certainly one she'd seen before. A man didn't look that haggard unless there was something he was aching for, and maybe it was the thing rumored to be in the deep end of QR-715.

The Cormorant itself.

But maybe it was something else. So Cabra sucked on her lower lip a little, thinking it over, before she nodded, slowly. "What's her name? Ashe's hole?"

His expression changed fractionally. "Svinga."

The satisfaction of having a good guess confirmed was short-lived. "You doing all this for another rifter's hole? And they call *me* sentimental." They didn't say it very loudly, but she knew plenty who muttered she was dragging Sabby like a thornback dragged black earth behind it. If he wanted to stay in the Tumbledown and drink himself to death, who was she to stop him? What did she see in that junked-up pinchok-mauled wreck, anyway?

Vetch also didn't bother to deny the obvious. "Ashe wasn't too faithful."

"Was *she*?" This was the most interesting conversation she'd had in weeks. There was no shortage of lundie holes—or even other rifters—who would jump at the chance to swing with Vetch, not least because he always had a ready dosh.

He uncurled enough to select a broken bit of silver-weathered pallet, tossing it on the fire with a small, accurate motion. "Sort of. I ent doing this for her."

She bit back the urge to say *blur it, you ent.*

He must have seen it, though, because his lips stretched bitterly, twin lines bracketing his mouth. "Why you with the Pooka, huh?"

Well, one pry with a crowbar deserved another, she guessed. On the other hand, it wasn't his business, since she hadn't asked *him* to come jumping in the Rift after sardies with itchy trigger fingers. She asked herself that, sometimes, and never came up with the same reason twice. "I got my reasons."

Vetch nodded, making a slow not-quite-whistle as his mouth relaxed. "Yeah."

That was that. Cabra waited a few more minutes, tipping her head back to look at the half roof. Past the edge, a slice of velvet darkness full of diamond pinpricks and pebbles, clustered in streams and rivers, poured over the Rift. In here, there was no light pollution, except for the moon's cold, uninterested glare. Boogaloos wouldn't come into the junkyard, it didn't feel right. Scuttles might slide through, and it felt unsettled enough that a squeezer or a shimmer might spawn among the stacks of rusting metal and shattered glass. Or something else.

For right now, though, in this particular little hole, the ticks could doze and digest. Cabra finally settled next to Sabby, scooching her backside against him. He didn't wake, but his body moved sleepily, his arm threading itself over her waist and his face settling in her beaded hair.

Maybe that was why she hauled him along. Cabra closed her eyes, and like any soldier who has learned the value of unconsciousness, she dropped quickly into slumber.

# 38
# LITTLE GRISHA

Sergei Sergeyevitch Senkinistov was no coward. With a name like that, he couldn't have survived school if he was. *Toughen up*, Sergei the father always snarled, especially at the younger brother Grigory. *Fuck the crying. It get you nowhere.*

Grigory couldn't help it, though. His eyes were on a whole different circuit than the rest of him, and a little etched chip turned on the salt water every fucking time an emotion rose. Happy? He leaked. Sad? He leaked. Angry, hurt, disgusted? Leakage.

Senkin rubbed at his own hot, grainy eyes. The fire made small merry sounds, and Barko was snoring. Eschkov made little sip-sucking noises in his sleep, his hands twitching every once in a while. The two scientists had managed to dry out a patch of flooring with a heat lamp run off twelve poppers, and they'd played the lamp's beam over the pile of moldering carpet Captain Morov was propped against, little skittering things fleeing from the heap before the steam killed them all, puffing out for a good five minutes before Barko decided it was dry enough.

Morov was breathing shallowly as well. The sweat had stopped, and maybe his color was a little better.

Maybe.

Hell of a thing. It was always the good ones who got it in the neck.

Senkin shifted his weight. First watch was his preferred option. Exhaustion could always be pushed off a little longer, and the more tired you got the less you cared what you were lying on when you were finally relieved. Besides, it was time to do some thinking, and he liked to take it slow. He wasn't the sharpest tool in the drawer—his father had kept reminding him, adding thoughtfully *but at least you're better than Grisha*—but he could usually figure out which mouthful was the most useful, given enough time to chew.

Morov had asked, once, why Sergei never went in for promotion, even the automatic long-timer's stripe. *Because I like to know what to shoot at*, was Sergei's phlegmatic reply, and Morov had nodded as if he understood.

Maybe he even had.

That was twice he'd thought about Grigory, which usually meant nothing good. Carrying Morov reminded him of dragging his brother's limp weight through endless spindly-naked birch trees, their branches rattling under the force of a hideous, cold wind. Even semiconscious, his little brother had been sniveling, his nose chapped and cheeks raw from the slow drip.

Senkin sighed, very softly, and decided on a smoke. His lighter wasn't as good as Mako's. It took five tries, here where everything was upside-down and fuckered-up, before he got a steady flame. It could have been the way his hands were shaking.

Remembering was bad for a man. You couldn't do anything about the past except drown it in engine degreaser. He was on frontline duty, but not in any pissant warboy spitting contest. Some assholes thought this was an easy job, a *federal* job with a shiny badge for nothing but sitting around and waiting, cleaning barracks and eating from a canteen a few grades higher than a public co-op's but nowhere as nice as a corporation's. All you had to do was watch the slugwall or say *yessir-nosir.*

It wasn't the routine that got to you. It was that damn wall, the curtain of soap-bubble energy, currents sliding through colors there were no names for. You could almost feel the strangeness leaking out, silent-lethal radiation, turning everyone around you into question marks at best and downright motherfucking howlers* at worst. Kopelund was the biggest howler of them all, sending all of them into this deathtrap with only a goggle-eyed felon bitch for a guide.

The thought that they'd already lasted longer than Ashe the Rat's final ride wasn't really comforting. What the fuck had happened in here with the Rat and her crew? Ashe had been a medium-tall, rawboned and snub-nosed, perpetually smiling woman, her nickname coming from her ability to squeeze through tight spaces. Or so someone had said. Someone else whispered it was because she was a stool pigeon for some federal agency, and that was why she never seemed to get busted for any salvage, though she always had cash in her pocket. With rifters, you could never tell.

You just never knew. Kopelund had to have a sweet deal working with some corporation or another, or he wouldn't have

---

* A derogatory term for people driven insane by proximity to a Rift.

bestirred himself to send anyone in. The bastard was an old, cautious one, kind of like Sergei senior with his close-set eyes and flint-hard mouth.

*Fuck the crying. It get you nowhere.*

If he was going to think about the past, he might as well get it over with.

Sergei junior had dragged Grisha home that long-ago night, and as bad luck would have it, their father was drunk and had locked the door. The brothers shiver-slept on the porch, propped against each other, and when morning came Grisha's face was bone-white, his lips livid blue, and the tears had turned to frost on his cheeks. Sergei had only lost a bit of one ear to frostbite, since Grisha had awakened enough to wrap his own coat around his brother.

A faint brushing noise broke the memory. Senkin took another deep drag off the cigarette. The old man hadn't been able to stand the crying boy, but once Grigory was laid in the earth, he became a martyred saint and suddenly, inexplicably, teenage Sergei was to blame. *Stole his coat and left him to freeze,* Sergei the elder roared, when he got drunk again. *You're no son of mine!*

The sound was...strange. Like a paintbrush—or many paintbrushes—drawn ever so lightly over the outside walls of the buildings. One, ten, or fifty of them would be silent, but thousands and thousands? A soft, persistent susurration you couldn't get out of your ears once you'd noticed its whisper-clinging presence.

What the fuck *was* it? Senkin cocked his head, the neatly rolled cylinder in his right hand sending up a thin trail of nicotine smoke.

If he was going to think about Grisha, little Grisha who tagged along everywhere and never told his big brother's secrets, he should also think about the rest of it. It had been easy, really. Just waiting until the big fur-bearded bastard bought straight pine to get drunk on, and slipping antifreeze in. Senkin's father had been proud of his ability to withstand prodigious amounts of alcohol, and before the blindness struck he'd remarked that pine was starting to taste better than it ever had.

And after he was blind, it was time for straight methanol. They all thought Sergei senior had drunk himself to death with fatherly sorrow, and little Sergei Sergeyevitch was thought very brave for his stern expression at the graveside.

Right after that, he'd visited the recruiter, the only way out of that shitty little hole. Basic training was easy after years of dodging his father.

Senkin hissed a little, shaking his burnt fingers. The cigarette was done, and fell, the glowing coal at its tip winking out before it hit the ground. He still covered it with his boot, just to make sure, and cursed himself for wasting good *makhorka*. Who knew when he'd get another ration?

The sound kept going. Brushstrokes, all around. Or tiny wings, fluttering by the millions. It made his skin crawl, so he edged to the window, his rifle useless on his back since Brood had all but two clips of the ammo. A lowly guard had to make do with his sidearm, and you bet that fucker Brood had him and Mako doing the watch instead of his own creepy-ass self.

A silvery glow that could have been moonlight turned every shadow in the driveway into a paper shape with razor-cut edges. The bony lacework of the dry fountain was wrong, and Senkin had to blink rapidly before he realized what he was seeing.

The shining stuff on the buildings was fluttering. Maybe the sound was coming from that, or from the furred things moving slowly up and down the walls. Their shape was all wrong, joints moving in ways they weren't supposed to. Cupped paw-hands with starfish fingers gripped the walls, and the creatures' pale fur cowled sleek dark faces with long doglike snouts. They moved slowly, with terrible grace, and those long noses dipped and browsed as they munched.

He was cold all over. They were good targets. His hand was at his sidearm even now, fingertips caressing the ends of the etching on the grip. His palms were clammy, and his mouth dry. Either the brushing was louder, or he was sensitized to it now. There was another sound underneath it. A murmuring, like a sleepy little boy. A familiar voice, if he could just listen hard enough.

They'd spent time bracing the door earlier that evening, but they needed the ventilation from the shattered hole that used to be a window. The rifter just shrugged. *Set a watch*, she said, and hunkered down next to the fire.

Senkin tore his gaze away from the light-and-shadow play. The dank cave they were roosting in was even darker, and his pupils expanded. Everyone right where they should be, even Brood asleep. The rifter, curled in a far corner on top of a square of oilcloth, looked unconscious and limp. The pale smear of her face contorted a bit, as if she was dreaming of something unpleasant.

He set his rifle down, carefully, its stock against the rotting carpet and its muzzle braced between an ancient, moldering chair and the wall.

A few moments later, he had shimmied outside the window, breathing the soft fragrance of a night without internal-combustion fumes or the close fug of a dank, slowly decomposing building. His boots left dark prints in the rank, moisture-heavy grass, and after a few steps he was damp to the knees. He watched the fountain, its draperies glittering under the light that *definitely* wasn't coming from a moon. Instead, it came from the strands themselves, and from the fur of the pale creatures who were *everywhere*, climbing the buildings and making that soft, impenetrable brushing sound. They ignored him, and after a while his hand fell away from his gun while he watched the light finger their soft, blurring shapes.

*"Seryozha!"* A familiar shout in the distance, just a whisper on the wind, with the half sob in the middle. Just as Grisha had called him that winter afternoon, flailing because the trap had bitten his ankle, lucky not to lose the whole foot, lucky, lucky...

He turned toward that distant cry, the light and shadow soothing. Throbbing, almost, a hypnotic swirl. The boogaloos stilled as one, their fur rising powder-puff, but it was not his presence they sensed.

Sergei Sergeyevitch Senkinistov did not notice when they vanished, the furred things suddenly swallow-swift. He was too busy moving through the thigh-high grass, his sidearm dropping from one nerveless hand as green vegetation turned into fine, lacelike silver strands. He did not look back, chasing a faint voice from the echoing well of the past.

A flashing lure in water shimmering-silver had drawn in prey for the night, and after a long while, the boogaloos returned to serenely graze upon the silver tape festooning the rotting buildings once more.

# 39
# ON THE MEND

⇥‖‖⇤

"But where did he *go*?" Eschkov repeated, querulously. His thick, black-rimmed glasses were smudged but he made no move to clean them, and that was disturbing. His whitening hair stuck up in wild tufts, too, and his hands, while not overly filthy, were none too clean either.

"Tracks lead away," Brood said, heaving himself back in the window-hole with a grunt. "Left his rifle. Found his Tormund. That's all we know." His mouth pulled against itself, a thin rat-tail line of a scar digging down at one end; the rifter, standing right there, didn't move to help him struggle through.

The first indication of something wrong had been Mako waking up at dawn, well past the time he should have been shaken to begin his watch. At least everyone had a solid night's sleep.

The rifter, last to wake, peered out the hole that had served them as a window once Brood cleared it, and her thin shoulders slumped. "Probably heard someone calling him." She shook her dark-fuzzed head. "Ran off, and *pop*." Her thin fingers snapped, producing an amazingly large, crisp noise.

Brood, his pants wet to the knee with dew, had leapt out the damn hole to follow the tracks, and only came back when he visibly realized it was probably suicidal to keep going. He glowered at the rifter, who didn't even glance at him. "Who the fuck is out there?" He hefted Senkin's Tormund service sidearm, checking the clip with a practiced, efficient motion.

"Only thing that got close was boogaloos." She pointed at the five-pointed, strangely graceful marks pocking the softened ground outside. They had come very close to the window. "See those? Starfish feet. They don't eat meat, ever. He probably heard someone and went running."

*Jesus Christ.* Barko shook his head. He couldn't decide which was worse, losing someone right in front of you, or waking up and finding another man gone.

"Who?" Brood's pale eyes narrowed. His dark stubble was getting ferocious, and his blond tips were dingy. There was a glint to those gray-blue irises Barko wasn't sure he liked. Brood's left cheek twitched a little, the flesh jumping with reflexive speed. It didn't look as if he was aware of it, and that couldn't be a good sign.

The rifter shook her head. A faint ring of gray had settled at her neck, dust and sweat mixing and collecting in the creases. "Dunno just *what*. Just know you never follow a voice at night, in here. That's how they get you."

"How *who* gets you?" Brood was having a little trouble with this. The whipsaw of fear and aggression under his voice had hardened.

"Don't matter." She turned away, the bright morning sunlight giving her a momentary halo. "Just know not to go following the voices at night."

"Could Kopelund have sent another team in?" Mako wanted to know.

The rifter stuck her head out the window and inhaled, deeply. Maybe she'd track Senkin down like a bloodhound? She'd survived trips into the Rifts before, goddammit, and now Barko was uncomfortably aware that all she had to do was leave them here. It would take a miracle if any of them made it without her guidance. Every time she stepped away or went to sleep, some-damn-thing else happened. Her mapbag dangled at her side—she even slept with it on, hugging her backpack to her skinny chest.

Brood ran his hand back through close-cropped hair, dew-damp fingers cleaning streaks on his forehead. "Where'd he find another crazy-ass rifter?"

"Town's crawling with them." Mako, on his knees beside Morov, peered into the commander's face. "I think he's coming to."

Morov's eyes opened, slowly. He groaned a bit, shifting on the pile of carpet. The fire, stirred up to provide brief heat, snapped as it munched on a silver-wrapped worm-eaten piece of what had once been a table leg. The stuff festooning the other buildings curled up as it clung to the fuel, bursting with bright-blue flames and small popping noises. "Fuuuuuuck," he groaned.

Barko couldn't help himself. A braying laugh broke free, and even the rifter looked at him as it bounced off the lichen-spotted walls. He shook his bald, condensation-starred head, chuckling helplessly. "Speaking for us all." The chuckle still bubbled inside his chest, and Eschkov gave him a blurred, tremulous smile. It felt goddamn good to laugh, even if he heard the panic in his own voice.

"Hello, you old bastard." Mako sounded reasonably happy, all things considered. He'd taken off his jacket, and his uniform button-down was damp all down the back and under his thick arms, too. "How the hell are you?"

"Fine," Morov croaked. One of his hands came up, patted at his breast pocket, probably searching for one of his cigars. "Shit. Where the fuck are we?"

"Still in bumfuck and no end in sight." Mako's round face split with a very wide grin. His shoulders came down a bit, relaxing.

"Grand." Morov blinked a few more times. He stopped, his expression changing, and rubbed at the crust on his eyelashes. "Roll call?"

Mako's thin eyes shone with the relief of an enlisted man with a clear-cut job. "We're out Senkin, Tolstoy, and that foreign bastard. Brood's here, and me. We still have Barko and the goggles."

Morov nodded, slowly. "Rifter?"

"I'm here." She stepped, quick and light, and parts of the decaying carpet squished under her boots. They were a lot more supple now, much better broken in. There was some color in her cheeks now, and her lips rested much more easily over those large thermabonded teeth.

"Well, that's good." Morov coughed a little, and Barko scooped up the two open medikits. "There was a grenade."

"Yeah." She halted near the fire, carefully keeping Brood in her peripheral. "Your leg might be broken."

"It's splinted," Barko amended. "We don't know if it *is* broken, but just to be safe. You also caught a splinter through the thigh, it missed the artery. You're one lucky-ass soldier, Morov."

"Great." Morov coughed again. "Leg hurts. What's our supply situation?"

"Casualties are gone with their loads, except Senkin. We were just about to divvy up his, and what you're carrying." The rifter's expression turned placid, her eyes half-lidding and their muddy darkness impenetrable. "Fellow over there took command." Her head tipped in Brood's direction. She scratched dreamily at the side of her neck.

The pale-eyed soldier hadn't moved from the window. "Sir."

"Good job, soldier." Morov shifted again, uncomfortably. "Gonna put you all in for vacation *and* promotion when we get back."

Barko decided to err on the side of diplomacy, opening another skinstrip. "That's a nice thought."

Morov glanced at him, a ghost of the old familiar sharpness lurking in his pupils. "Optimism, baldy. It's a virtue."

Barko swiped the strip over the captain's forehead, collecting sweat and cells for the chemical-treated paper to taste. "I'd say I prefer science, but that's what got us into this mess."

"No, Kopelund got us into this mess," Brood immediately objected. "This Cormorant thing better be worth it. I better get at least a month of paid time off, or I'm going to bomb the motherfucker's office."

"For a month off, I'd bomb anyone's office." Mako turned his stretch into an upward-rising movement, gaining his feet with a lurch. The firelight painted his face with a clammy-grease sheen, turning him to an oiled icon.

"Senkin," Eschkov piped up, plaintive and hollow-sounding. "Where did he go? I don't understand."

"Goggles is cracking," the rifter said, very softly, examining Morov's face. "Smells like a wall coming. We need to move."

A wall? Barko decided he didn't want to know. "Senkin went to take a leak." He shook his head, glaring meaningfully at her. "Igor, can you get rations for everyone? We could all use some breakfast. And coffee." Giving him a task would settle him down. Or at least, so Barko hoped.

Morov's eyebrows rose. "How bad is it?" he mumbled.

Barko didn't reply, just let his expression do it for him. The rifter kept her mouth shut, but her small eyeroll spoke too. Morov closed his eyes and swallowed, and Barko took the opportunity to peer at the skinstrip.

"What's it say?" Brood wanted to know, and suddenly, Barko was very sure he didn't want to tell the man.

"Piss-yellow," Barko lied. "Our captain here is on the mend."

He crushed the bright-red crinkle of chemically treated paper in his damp palm, and Igor dropped a few packets of rations, scattering them far and wide. Mako, with a spitting sound of annoyance, rose to help.

The rifter said nothing. Her head was turning just as Barko glanced at her, and she studied Brood intently, with a placid, deceptively peaceful expression.

Brood hawked, spitting a gobbet of dry phlegm out the window. "Okay, everyone. Mouth some chow and get your bladders busted, I want us moving in fifteen."

Morov, his eyes still closed, said nothing.

# 40
# HEARTBEAT

>‖‹

Midmorning found Sabby crouching at the edge of the half-shattered building, his head up, testing the wind. "Dunno," he said, finally. "Don't smell right."

That made it unanimous. Il Muto was pale, two spots of hectic color high on his knifeblade-sharp cheekbones. He bent his knees, folding down like a grasshopper, and pointed.

Little darting smears of movement in the junkyard, popping from here to there. The fine hairs on Sabby's arms rose, his skin tightening. Cabra sucked in a breath, and they all tensed. Vetch's eyelids flicked like a lizard's; he squinted. His hands curled into loose fists, scarred knuckles broadening.

In the Tumbledown, there would be a general movement away from a rifter who did that. Here, the group pressed closer.

Il Muto pointed at the western horizon. Clouds raced and boiled, high-piled streaks of cottonwool bulging behind an invisible film. Underneath, coruscating dapples fell to earth. The wave was riding at them, not at lightning speed, but still quickly enough to cause concern.

"Metal in there make me twitchy," Sabby said.

"Yeah." Vetch's agreement, soft and total, still carried an edge. "Scuttles?"

"Too small." Cabra, looking the other direction, made a soft whistling sound through her teeth. "Mipsiks."

"Fuckbuckle." Vetch rocked back on his heels slightly. "Never seen 'em do this."

"Hiding?" Sabby glanced again at the wall in the distance. Those glitters falling to earth underneath could be harmless, but nobody here thought so. Danger scraped along the nerves, shortened the breath, and slid over the body in successive waves. "Which way we jump?"

Il Muto unfolded, digging in his mapper, probably to pull out a strip-and-bob. He didn't get the chance. A low throbbing noise slid toward them and away, lifting and rattling everything in the junkyard, making dust puff from the ground and dance and rattling the half cavern they'd spent the night in. The building groaned as it leaned even further into itself, its sides crumbling into great sloping jaws.

"Can't stay here." Sabby straightened, too, grabbing his backpack—none of them had left their gear near the potzeg-ringed ashes.

The mipsiks flitted between the avenues of junked metal, working closer. Their soft, throaty chuffing might have been mistaken for words. They milled, obviously uncertain, tiny dark eyes ringed with white, their matted, hairy heads rolling on short flexible necks, powerful chests and thick arms giving them an advantage when they dropped to all fours. Some said they were humans who had somehow survived the Event, but

Sabby didn't give a fuck. They weren't dangerous—they fled rifters and lundies alike, between one blink and the next.

Right now they were apparently weighing whether to dart past the rifters or further into the junkyard. Another thumping grumble came, the wall in the distance pushing air and solid matter in front of it.

"Shit," Vetch said. "Back up. *Back up!*"

They did, the four of them moving as a unit, and that decided the mipsiks. The furred creatures, human-sized but much heavier from the muscle rolling on their upper trunks, flowed into the beaten-dirt alleyways between cubes of shattered, stacked metal. They ran past the small group in their tiny bubble of safety, and the rifters all hitched their backpacks on, needing no explanation.

Vetch chose the moment, just like aiming them for the slug-wall. Near the end of the long flow, the herd streaming past with foaming mouths and white-rolling eyes, stamping and raising a cloud of choking yellow dust. They screamed, their usual two-part *mip-sik, mip-sik* lost in a high ribbon of wailing that could have echoed from the shattered walls of any war-bitten or disaster-chewed city.

The rifters plunged into the stampede's tide, legs pumping, the wall coming behind them. If there was a safe route away, the mipsiks would find it. They ran, Cabra's beads glittering and the sweat starting on her dark face, Il Muto's skinny legs almost blurring, Vetch's head down and his fists pistoning as if he were a child again, and Sabby stumble-trotting until he found his speed, the sourness of terror flushing away the last iota of metabolizing alcohol. He kept his gaze fixed on Cabra's bright bobbing head, wished he'd eaten something in the last twelve hours, and cursed at the way his lungs immediately began to burn.

The mipsiks cut across the edge of the junkyard, the first ones scaling an ancient wooden fence along one edge. The pressure of numbers was too great for the weathered wood, and splinter-cracking was lost in the noise as the pressure wall, having decided it was time to stop playing, swept straight for them.

A long string of hairy backs—brown, blond, black, reddish-gray—curved as the creatures blindly followed instinct, a thin line of safety under their bare, horn-callused feet. Maddened, they sped up, and the rifters followed, the pressure of the furred river bearing them along. Sabby picked up his feet and the hairy shoulders pressing against his hips and chest carried him. Il Muto, tall and thin, was shaken this way and that by the tide, his head shoved back and forth like a bobble-doll's. Sabby lost sight of Il Muto as the tide separated around a parked pre-Event car quietly rusting into oblivion.

The mipsiks screamed. Sabby's feet didn't touch the ground. It was like swimming, only the current threatened to crack his ribs.

Unwillingly, unhappily, Sabby the Pooka began to laugh, a high breathless screamy sound, a bright thread above the rumbling and roaring.

He was still laughing when the mipsik next to him, smelling of grass, cloves, sweat, and the broad oily funk of a hairy, healthy creature, foundered. Perhaps its heart had stuttered under the strain, perhaps one of its limbs had trembled at the wrong time, perhaps the ground underfoot had pitched with another one of those thump-rolling waves as the wall bore down.

The momentary gap swallowed Sabby. He went down hard, his ankle creak-snapping as it was caught between the terrified mipsik's legs. His knee gave too, and his scream—pained this time—was lost in the pounding of hands and knuckles slapping dirt and pavement, throwing up chunks of sod or strange Rift-native plants.

The world turned over and over, light and dark flashing, and the third crack was Sabby's neck. There was a brief merciless moment of agony, then blackness, and the pounding splintered bone and flesh alike. A red smear, a raw rag of broken bones and lacerated flesh, almost liquid by the time the stragglers of the mipsik herd galloped over him. The weak, the too-young, the too-old mingled bloodstreaks and a heavy reek of shit from terrified sphincters getting rid of every particle weighing the body down. A few minutes later the pressure wall arrived, flooding over the dead and dying, those soft golden glimmers turning out to be crackles of stray energy that popped between grassblades, hard surfaces, ends of broken and exposed bone. The thumping sound was a gigantic fist of some invisible radiation slamming down every few seconds, the golden spackles yelping like distressed metal as it pounded the earth.

Who knows what made the pressure wall turn sharply, veering for the south? The mipsik herd had guessed correctly, or simply known, and veered north to escape, toward the sharp high glitters of downtown under a slice of blue sky smeared with purple streaks, the clouds reacting to the pressure wall further away, catching stray particles. The herd ran for two further klicks before beginning to peel off and melt away, individual bands reasserting themselves and taking smaller rivulets of safety toward hiding places, leaving only two daze-stumbling rifters staggering at the end of a long dark oil-streak of shapeless bodies and splashed, bloody offal. Where the wall had sheared away, there were long fluttering strands of flat golden tape, lifted by the uncertain, flirting breeze. Thin threads of glitter poured through the blood-slick, crawling over the humped, flattened rags of flesh with a soft musical whispering.

The rifters didn't pause. They kept staggering, as fast as their aching, pummeled bodies would allow. Beads clacked in the hair of one, and the other kept opening and closing his fists, as if he longed to turn and fight.

# 41
# SALVAGE

⊁╫く

Igor Eschkov scrubbed at his spectacle lenses with the micro-cloth, and when he slipped his glasses back on, everything came into focus again. Immediately, he wished he hadn't done it. The world was in crisp detail now, from the juicy, too-sharp leaves of the yellow-flowered weeds forcing up through the concrete to the thin violet clouds streaking an otherwise innocent baby blue spring sky. The sun was blazing, and if they had still been on the outskirts no doubt birds would have been chirping merrily.

Or things that wanted you to think they were birds.

A strange rhythmic thumping echoed in the distance, a heartbeat drawing closer as the rifter hurried them along, her shoulders drawing up and her cheeks paling. Something happened an hour later, though, and the thumping drew away in an arc. It was a relief when that beat finally stuttered and died. The rifter didn't slow down, though, and the steady song of cursing from the men had dwindled as well.

There wasn't enough breath to fuel it.

Eschkov's hands were chapped, but he couldn't stop rubbing them against each other. Precious dollops of industrial-grade sanitizer had eaten at his skin, but he still doled it out whenever he had to touch anything in this godforsaken place. Not that it would help—the air was freighted with spores and bacteria. The thergo hadn't picked up killing radiation while Tremaine was carrying it, or he would have yelled. Now it was gone, and the spectra would only pick up massive overdoses of harmful emissions. Barko didn't even have the spectra *out*, he just walked with his head down, every once in a while glancing to either side with quick jerks of his once-shining head, now grimed with dull gray. Not a hair on his dome, but his beard was coming in like an old-fashioned patriarch's.

Once again the landscape had changed. Office buildings rose on either side of them, a streamer flung out from what had once been downtown, along the artery of an old highway. The buildings were slowly melting, bulging at their corners, brick and metal and concrete looking strangely elastic. The worst part was the windows—all intact, blank eyes rippling and frogging out as they watched the survivors' parade.

First the rifter, stopping every so often to toss one of her weighted handkerchiefs. She collected the ones that fell as they should and returned them to her bag, never using the same one twice in a row. There was probably a reason, but it did not seem *scientific*. Ritual or habit, probably, benighted superstition. That was the thing about the Rifts—nothing that came out of them made any *sense*. Humans were clever monkeys playing with toys they didn't understand. Like the poppers. The little blue things could be harnessed, of course, but the monkeys had no idea how they were *made*.

It was maddening. The corporations, of course, had moved in. Real science was forgotten when there was a profit to be had.

Igor shuffled along. It was too hot, but then they plunged into the shade of the buildings and the sweat turned clammy on you. His pack was too heavy, and it clanked as he moved. *Why not leave some of that stuff here?* Barko had asked that very morning.

Because *science*, that's why. Igor had merely shaken his head, though. It was all very well for Tremaine to slip up—his part of the funding would now go to Igor's own department, and while he regretted the loss of any colleague, the snotty little prick had it coming to him. He was a thieving little sod, really. As if Eschkov didn't know the foreign bastard been selling research supplies in town.

Which had cut into Igor's own profits from doing so quite a bit. Science was science, and sometimes certain...gray areas were permitted, in pursuit of knowledge. All Igor's own illicit gains had gone into supplementing his department's meager government funding. He was *so close* to a breakthrough, or so he hoped. There had to be *some* form of radiation or pressure that would show a seam in the poppers.

After the rifter came Mako, stepping carefully, with Morov leaning on him every once in a while but otherwise limping along tolerably well, if tortuously slowly. Then Barko, and Eschkov himself. Last of all, Brood trailed in their wake. The pale-eyed man moved almost as silently as the rifter. There were only tiny betraying noises—clinking pieces of his gear that weren't taped down, or the occasional grinding of his boot on some small bit of refuse. Mako had his rifle out, and Brood probably had his free, too. Some "protection" they turned out to be.

Eschkov peered at the misshapen buildings. Had some incredible flash-heat gone through here during the Event? But that was ridiculous; wooden window frames would have turned to ash. Nothing about this looked quick. The buildings should have crumbled; there was no scientific way they could be just... drooping.

Just like the trees at the bottom of the hill should not have come alive and eaten Tremaine. The kid, Aleks... well, caustic puddles of industrial waste were a danger out in the real world, too. *That* wasn't something that made Igor's head hurt with the sheer impossibility.

Still... why the hell had Igor himself agreed to this assignment? Kopelund could have just sent Barko and Tremaine. Or someone else. Maybe Aleks could have gone officially instead of trying to sneak in...

Igor's shoulders hurt. He eased the backpack straps, and a clattering jangle from the equipment hanging at the bottom echoed against the walls on either side.

The rifter stopped, so sudden and short Mako almost ran into her. Her head went up, an inquisitive animal movement; her nape was strangely pale and clean, a slice of white above her jacket collar. Her backpack wasn't as big as Barko's, even. She traveled light.

"What is it?" Mako whispered, very loud in the sudden stillness.

She half turned, ran a critical eye down their ragged little line. "Salvage," she said, finally. "Poppers, lampers, and probably other things. If you want them."

"Can we camp here?" Brood wanted to know. The sun was heading downward, and Morov's breathing had taken on a wheezing note. He was sweating, but then, so was Igor. Even in the shade it was greasy-humid, and the sudden damp made him shiver. His shoulder ached, and his left arm was cramping from holding the digicap. His fingers had gone numb. He hadn't even bothered to take a single snapshot of the buildings. It seemed... pointless.

But... science. He tried to lift the digicap, but his arm was too heavy. He tipped his head back, staring at the violet clouds. They looked like strands of hair combed over a bald patch. At least he had been spared *that* indignity.

"Two buildings up, there's a safe patch." The rifter made another one of those inquisitive little movements, listening to a sound none of them could catch. She glanced back once more, this time looking at Morov, who leaned on a rude crutch whittled from a sodden piece of scrap lumber. She'd even found a wad of cotton material that made an acceptable cushion, once the heat was run over it and some twine was scavenged to tie it on. "Can hop out from there to pick up shiny."

"Fine." Brood sounded like it was a done deal.

Mako, on the other hand, looked at Morov. "What do you say, Captain?"

Morov muttered something. Hard to hear. He was in bad shape.

Eschkov's head dropped forward. His arm hurt abominably. So did his shoulders, and his neck. This was not the place for a man whose brain did all the work. All he wanted was his own bed and a decent meal, perhaps reading a little Lipton and Ecke on quantum parsing at the canteen table at dinner, just to show his fellows he was up on the latest.

The rifter tossed another one of her little tails. It flew

normally, tracing an arc that regular equations could describe. When she set off, it took Eschkov a great deal of effort to totter after Morov's limping, crutch-ridden gait. There was a certain amount of physical misery that came with work in the field, he told himself. Then he told himself nothing, because placing one foot in front of the other became an endurance contest. A strange whooshing sound began in the distance, building as he stumble-staggered after Barko's bobbing bald head.

Did they hear it? How could they not? Nobody mentioned it. Was it the heartbeat?

He kept walking. Greasy sweat turned his yellowing undershirt into a chafing, sodden rag. His right hand clenched and released; his left clamped down, squeezing the digicap mercilessly.

The rifter reached the white strip of cloth. Picked it up with a smooth motion, halted halfway in rising from her crouch, and peered back along the line. Her mouth moved, but the rushing sound drowned her out. They *had* to hear it. It was bearing down on them, filling mouth and eyes and ears, a thick pumping accompanied by a high ringing whine. If Igor had eaten breakfast, he would have brought it all up in a painful gushing of acid and half-digested rations.

But he had not.

The horizon tilted. The rifter slid sideways, but she didn't fall. Igor's eyelids fluttered, a strobe of light and dark. His chest had turned to a black hole, and his left hand flew up to strike at the weight behind his ribs, the digicap's glass lens splintering on impact.

He was dead before he hit the ground.

# 42
# NO PART OF THIS PLACE

⊰⫞⊱

"Heart attack." Barko dropped Eschkov's pack in the corner with a clatter. "God *damn* it." This had been some sort of office, before the Event. This building wasn't as bulging-weird as the other ones, and that made him feel a little better.

Not enough. Just a sliver.

"God has no part of this place," Mako murmured, easing Morov down with a long-suffering sigh. It was a wonder the commander was still moving; his eyes were glassy with fever and his breathing was a series of shallow gasps until Mako got him settled. "Old man shouldn't have come."

"None of us should have." Barko rubbed at his face, his hands rasping against the luxurious beginnings of a beard. They should have found some way to bury Eschkov. It wasn't right to leave the man in the street. It just wasn't.

"Well, we're here now." Brood managed to fill up the tiny room, except for the space near the glass door. The rifter stood there, sunlight gilding the top of her head, showing a stubborn curl to the dark fuzz. Her large eyes moved over the terrain outside, her hands hanging limp-loose, each nail holding a crescent of grime underneath. A couple days outside had done wonders for her complexion. She would never tan, but at least the fish-belly pallor was gone. She didn't look quite as gaunt, either, even though Barko never saw her eat. "Hey," he continued. "Rifter. Start a fire."

She didn't turn, gazing out through dirty glass that wasn't bulging quite as much as every other window or pane on this street, for all the world as if she hadn't heard him. She scanned, her chin jutting a little, lips stretched over her large teeth as she sucked on them. The very picture of an unpretty woman deep in thought, deaf to the world.

No, not quite deaf. Barko began casting around for anything to use as fuel. There was faded lettering scratched on the front window—how long had it been since he'd seen pre-Event glass?

"Hey." Brood snapped his fingers. "Rifter! Get your scrawny ass making a fire, it's fucking freezing in here."

"Man, leave her alone." Mako crouched, digging in his pack. In the dimness, his broad, circular face creased with tiny black lines. Sweat and floating dirt, maybe, except there was no pollution in here.

No *human* pollution. Except this little group.

"I've got firestarters," Barko heard himself say. He sounded weary, even to his own ears. "Just find me something to burn."

"I'll go scavenge." The rifter pushed at the door, its hinges squealing with torqued distaste. She was a shadow in the afternoon light, distorted by dust and the blur of glass bent in ways it shouldn't.

If she was looking to piss off a sardie, she was going about it the right way. Brood's expression had hardened, and Barko hastily looked down, digging for the firestarters. Mako cracked open the medikit they'd been working off and glanced through the contents, squinting in the uncertain light. There were light switches in here, but no juice behind them. Each building might as well be a cave.

Barko found the foil-covered roll of firestarters. He began to carefully peel it open, his blunt fingers too clumsy. "We shouldn't have left him there," he muttered. "We should find a way to bury him."

"He has the whole Rift for a headstone." Mako peeled a skinstrip from its foil packet. Morov's half-closed eyes glinted, a glass doll's gaze.

"Fucking bitch." Brood stamped to the door. "How's he doing, Mako?" Without the rifter inside, his voice boomed off all the surfaces. Big man making noise.

Morov stirred. "Tired." A whisper-croak, barely audible. "Leg hurts like a sonofabitch."

"Fracture, probably." Mako smoothed the strip on Morov's damp forehead, then fumbled in the meds-case. "Another pop of painkillers, some rest tonight, and you should be good."

"We should leave him here with a medikit or two, go in, and pick him up on the way back." Brood crossed his arms, surveying the three of them with a proprietary air. His rifle, slung across his back, pointed its blunt snout at the top of the largest window.

"Fuck *that*." Mako came up with a one-use of antibiotic. The strip plastered to Morov's forehead was turning dark. "I say we sleep, then we head back for the outside. We've got almost fifty percent casualties here, and Morov needs some goddamn medical help that isn't field fuckery."

Morov croaked something else, and Mako nodded, his black hair standing aggressively up from his forehead, pushing Morov's sleeve up as far as he could.

"What was that?" Barko had an idea he knew.

Mako's round face had settled into a tight expression of distaste. "Who knows if the fucking rifter ain't deliberately leading us in circles? Better to just get out while we can."

"If you think she's leading us in circles, how do you propose we get out of here? Everything changes behind us, for God's sake." Barko kept peeling the firestarters, his eyes very carefully focused on the tear in the foil. It didn't need such concerted attention, but he didn't want to look at Brood. "I should never have agreed to this."

"What, Kopelund ordered you in?" Brood wanted to know, slinging his rifle around in front of him. He'd spread his legs, too, and ended up with one hand draped over the rifle at rest-but-ready, the familiar pose of every bored guard at a checkpoint since time immemorial.

"He didn't give me much fucking choice." A sigh—a deep one—caught Barko off guard.

Brood wasn't having any of it. His blond tips were more yellow now, and ragged. "Oh, go cry somewhere else. As if you egghead types wasn't dying for a chance to get in here. Poking and prodding everything. If your buddy hadn't gone down the hill and woke that tree-thing up, Morov wouldn't be dead."

"He's not dead yet," Mako objected, popping a patch of pain reliever onto the commander's upper arm. The inside of Morov's elbow was pale, strangely tender. It almost glowed.

"He's looking pretty goddamn dead to me. I give it a day, at most."

Morov coughed again. "Nice to know." For a second his voice was clear and hard as ever, if a little raspy. "Still the ranking officer, Brood."

The pale-eyed man shrugged. "Yessir." Two grudging little syllables staggering under a weight of sarcasm. With his hair lying flat and the blond tips dingy, he looked like a Hackala warboy ready to move up the ranks.

That put the conversation to bed. Barko broke off a bit of the firestarter brick and a packet of the catalyst, wrapped the rest of the brick with prissy care. The rest of the catalyst packs went into their pouch, and he felt Brood's gaze on him while he packed it all away. Eschkov had been carrying a lot of crap, but maybe there was something useful in there.

*There should have been a way to bury him, goddammit.* Barko's stomach was a clenched fist. The skinstrip was bright red, and there was no use in hiding it any longer. Morov probably was a dead man.

Barko had an idea Mako, with his questioning of Brood's authority—such as it was—would be next.

# 43
# HE'D FIND ME

꘎꘎꘎

Cabra rubbed her wet hands over her face, stripping away dust and sweat. Dribbled a little more water from her canteen and did it again. "Did you see him go down?" Dust coated her beaded braids.

"Didn't see a damn thing." Vetch leaned heavily against the brick wall of a pre-Event school. Half the bricks crawled with a reddish, branching growth, juicy blue-green knuckle-knotted vines burrowing into vitrified clay. A cramp seized his left side and he winced, leaning away from it, fighting the urge to hunch. You had to force the muscles on the opposite side to fire, to make the bastards relax. "Him *or* Il Muto."

*"Fuck."* She capped the canteen with a vicious twist.

"They know what to do." They'd either rift on their own and hook up further in, or head out and rendezvous at the Tumbledown. Probably the latter, since Sabby's nerves were gone. Vetch grimaced as the cramp gave one final, vicious twist before receding. He checked the sky and tried to taste the air, his breath coming in harsh gulps. They had a small bubble of safety here, not nearly enough, and it quivered around them, invisible seaweed. "We got to move."

Cabra didn't reply. She shoved her canteen back in its sheath-carrier at her belt, and her nostrils flared slightly. That was all.

"You comin'?" Vetch persisted, shifting from foot to foot without moving either, testing his balance. The stimtape on his boots glittered dully under the dust and blood and filth; his dungarees were spattered to the knees. His belt buckle held dots and slashes of bright crimson, too. Their small safezone wavered slightly, fraying at the edges.

Cabra examined him for a long moment. Finally, she shook her head. "I'm gonna find Sabby."

"He ent—"

"He'd find me." She bared her bright, thermabonded teeth. "You headin' for the Alley. I find him, we catch up."

"Fine." His eyes glittered, his proud nose lifting a little. "I ent splitting." If she was going to bug out now, there was no cut waiting for her, if he managed to get his hands on what Zlofter wanted. Except that wasn't really why he'd taken the job, and maybe she guessed as much by now.

That earned him a single contemptuous snort. "Didn't ask you to." She tapped the brick wall twice, lightly, and the sound was too hollow for such a solid structure. Which brought her up out of her crouch; she skipped away, each foot placed with a finicky drumbeat. Vetch jumped too, sensing the safe bubble closing like an iris shutter in a high-end corporate skyscraper. There was no good place to put his feet, and he went down on instinct, his shoulder hitting with a deep crunch.

A shimmer birthed itself into being above and between

them and Cabra yelled, a short, desperate sound. The thrill of weightlessness along each nerve turned painful, and Vetch continued rolling, on his side now instead of tumbling head over heels. Cabra thrashed, her right foot catching the brick wall, its fabric now turning friable as the shimmer warped at gravity. It spat her free with a sound like tearing cloth, but Vetch didn't wait to see if she hit the ground running or not. He was too busy gaining his feet with a muscle-splitting lunge, everything in his pack rattling now that he'd rolled over it, and searching for a safe direction to throw himself. The Rift pressed against him, sharp edges around a tender morsel, and he popped his hips left to avoid a sudden, half-seen danger. Running, then, with no mipsik herd to shield or carry him, the empty aching inside that made him a rifter dilating as he dragged his reluctant tired body along.

There. His feet found a thin, fraying thread, his boots slipping in greasy dirt that melted into rough pavement as he galloped along the expanding edge of a ripple. Not quite a pressure wall, merely a potential path, the breathless moment before lightning arcs between sky and earth.

Finally, the thread underfoot broadened into a ribbon, then swelled again into a pathway. Vetch slowed, his head swiveling, his left side gripping again with another monstrous cramp that threatened to empty his stomach and curl him into a witless worm on the ground. He denied it, sensing more than seeing the buildings rising around him and silver tape festooning a weird shape in the middle of their huddled group. The Rift had rolled him 'round like the small silver ball on the outside of a roulette wheel, and deposited him here.

He ducked aside, through an opening he barely saw, and

271

found himself in a small dark room. A hole in the wall was a shattered window, and a circle of potzegs glowed translucent-egg on the floor, the surface beneath it charred.

Vetch curled over, went to hands and knees. His sides heaved. He retched, then toppled and shook for a short while, listening to the wind play with the silvery flutters outside. Come night-fall, there would probably be boogaloos browsing on it. This place felt safe enough, and it also felt *used*. Someone had been here not too long ago, burrowing into the safe space and moving on before it was exhausted.

"Shine," he muttered, when he could breathe again. Another retch brought up hard sour liquid against the back of his throat. "Fuckbuckle *shine*."

He'd found her trail.

# 44

# COURTESY CALL

꘎꘎꘎

Kope's tetherphone buzzed; the little bell inside it smacked
mercilessly until he scooped the handset up. Nothing but
problems, goddammit. Already today his coffee tasted like
boiled piss and his pen ran out of ink halfway through a Form
38a. The goddamn thing had to be all finished in blue or black,
not a mixture of both. Not that anyone would care about anything it said, just if it arrived obviously piebald.

"What?" he snarled into the receiver.

It was Paks at the gate. "Kope, we got a shiny blackbird* with
an alpha pass headed up to you."

*Shit.* "How many heads?"

"Three. Driver, some egghead with a carrying case, and a
guy in a hair coat." Paks sounded nervous, and well he might.
There was no official visit scheduled for today, goddammit.
Kope had paid off the last inspection team to come through

---

* A commissioned officer who is clearly administrative instead of combative.

handsomely, and that was just last month. If the bastard had reneged, Kopelund was going to have to get creative.

"Thanks." A single brusque word, as if the general had been expecting this. He dropped the handset back into its cradle and cast a critical eye over the office as he surged up from his squeaking chair. The room was a fucking mess, paper all over the desktop, but that was to be expected. The window was half open, and the end-of-winter bite drifting through it was saturated with the smell of mud and the sounds of the drillyard. The second set of books was safely at home, behind a painting that looked glued to the goddamn wall since the Event. He ran a hand back through his hair and straightened his jacket, aware of hating himself for doing it but unable to stop.

The thought that it was someone from District was unpleasant, to say the least. He settled himself behind the desk again, opening a ledger from the stack to his left and bending over it, the very picture of a good little bureaucrat. Was it about Bechter? Nothing should be wrong with that little bastard's paperwork, and even in his haze of painkillers the snot had seemed to understand that his pension was dependent on Kope's goodwill.

Nothing but problems today, ever since he woke up and found out his wife had gone to visit her goddamn parents. Stupid bitch hadn't even *asked* him, or turned the coffee on. He should never have married the high-and-mighty praying mantis, even if her father had been a colonel.

When his visitors reached the door, giving only a courtesy knock, he found his palms were sweating. Hopefully it was a routine inspection, but his contact in the dispatch office should have given him a heads-up.

Two men. One, with a high pointed widow's peak of gray-ing fuzz and iron-rimmed spectacles, had the round doughy face of a pen-pusher and the watery blue eyes of a sadist who enjoyed watching his victims squirm over closed-circuit. Two, a broad-shouldered, rock-faced thug with a shoulder holster. Both of them had very fine coats, the pen-pusher's leather and the thug's woolen, and both uniforms sported the blue stripe next to the red that proclaimed Second Branch.

*Oh, fuck.* They could be from Central instead of District. If they suspected he'd sent resources into QR-715 ...

It was the one in spectacles who was running the show, because he was the one who spoke first. "General Kopelund?"

Kope let his gaze roam over both of them. A few seconds of silence, just to show he wasn't intimidated. "Appointments can be made with my secretary."

"He stepped away," the meat-slab said, his large mouth turn-ing into something just short of a smirk. He wore a wide leather standard-issue belt, but tucked discreetly back on his left hip was a small sheath that, unless Kope missed his guess, carried a set of brass knuckles.

"General Timor Kopelund?" Spectacles persisted. A bit of a pedant, then. He tilted his head back slightly, and the overhead lights glared off his spectacle lenses, turning his eyes into silver coins.

"I said, appointments can be made with my secretary. I am very busy. Good day." He bent back over the ledger, the stub of a pencil scratching in his sweat-greased fingers. A single word, repeated over and over again, just to give him the appearance of working.

Spectacles reached into his jacket pocket.

Kope braced himself. His right hand kept scratching at the paper. That word, over and over. He could salvage this, he just needed some time to think. His nose twitched, once.

Spectacles beamed gently, his cheeks bunching under those silver-coin eyes. "Agent-Major Ochki, Second Branch." The badge was legitimate, any idiot could see as much.

Which meant he was fucked, but he could perhaps bluff for some time. Kopelund shut the ledger with a snap and a sigh, and rose, heavily. Time to appear slow and stupid. He paced around the desk and approached his visitors, his hand itching for the service revolver slung at his side. One step, two. Three, and he was halfway across the office, drawing himself up to his full height, the steely glint in his eye and the cloak of authority resting secure as usual upon his shoulders.

"A courtesy call could have been made—" Kope began, and he barely saw the big man move.

A fist the size of a ham socked into his gut. Kope bent over, his tasteless breakfast threatening to leave him in a boiled-piss-coffee rush. All the air in the room had fled, and the only thing left was a heavy, colorless gas. It was too hot, despite the open window, and the lowest part of his belly felt suspiciously loose. Like his sphincters might give way after another hit like that. Kope hadn't been on the drillyard in years, and it had made him soft.

"There is no need for courtesy when dealing with corruption," Ochki was saying, but none of it reached Kopelund's staggering brain. "You've made yourself a nice little nest here, haven't you? Well, the feathers all had to come from somewhere." The dapper little man tucked his badge away, and his smile was almost benevolent. "Come now, sir. Do not be… undignified."

"—warrant," Kopelund wheezed, straightening as well as he could, just to show it hadn't hurt *that* much. *"Bastard."*

"Certainly." Ochki smiled. "I have it in triplicate, along with statements that will be produced at the court-martial. Some of them may even be *sworn* statements, if the investigation goes well. Which I think it will."

Now solicitous, the large man brushed at Kope's shoulders, tugging his uniform jacket to straighten it. "Sorry about this," he said, sunnily, with the absurd good humor of the subnormal follower of horrific orders. His tongue—strangely pale, as if starved of blood—flicked out, wet his thick lips, retreated. "Can't ever tell when a fellow will get a bit excited."

Ochki passed close by Kopelund, and the gasping man caught a hint of expensive aftershave, an expensive cologne the whores in town would call *Figsnap*, for a sickly sweet liqueur. *Run right through you and leave your bowels loose*, they would joke. These same women called Kope a word in their slurry-slang language loosely translated as *Pigfart*, for the unfortunate sounds he made during coupling.

Later, in the prison, he would be named something similar for the sounds he made during beatings.

>|||<

In the ledger, scrawled several times in pencil, with large looping consonants and small, cramped vowels, was a single word.

*Cormorant. Cormorant. Cormorant. Cor...*

And there, the marks died away.

# 45
# THE FISH YOU WANT

⋊┼┼⋉

Two bundles of scavenged wood carried on her back—they now had enough to last the night, if they kept the fire small—hit the floor with a thump. The tiny blaze, set behind what had once been a large reception desk to keep the heat from escaping too far, crackled merrily. This building was safe, but the dusk outside held hints of a funny heatless scent Svin didn't like. There would be no slipping away to explore the shifting margins of safety and feel out possible paths for tomorrow. No eating outside, where the walls didn't conspire to choke her and there were no avid little eyes focused on her mouth, either. A canteen was bad enough.

She could probably go *up* and find a quiet corner, but that would put them between her and the safe exit. And really, just because the building was relatively safe on the ground floor didn't mean some of the other floors didn't have things best left undisturbed.

The captain looked bad. He was shivering between fits of dozing, sweating through his clothes, and Svin didn't need a pic-dictionary to figure out the sly little glances Brood kept giving him. Or the worried ones Mako and Barko kept exchanging. At least they weren't stupid, but Svin had no illusions they would be able to stop the pale-eyed man or even slow him down. He was beginning to crack under the Rift's pressure, just like the goggles had. Only this sardie would take all of them with him, if he could, because that was the way he was wired.

The Rift didn't show you anything you didn't already know. It just peeled back the layers, and exposed the bedrock.

So they were locked in a room with a hungry wolf, like the old fable. Maybe it was time to tell them what they were really after.

"Good job." Mako, his eyes twin gleams, tossed her a silvery ration pouch. "It's warming up. Enjoy."

"Thanks." Svin didn't bother to tell him she had pouches of her own. It was probably his not-so-subtle way of trying to keep her at the campsite. "It feels bad outside."

"How bad?" Barko immediately wanted to know. As if she could put a number on the instinct.

"Just bad." She grabbed the strap around one load of wood, hefted it onto three other similarly strapped bundles. The other one—heavy because some of the pieces were larger, she'd had a hell of a time breaking them up—settled in its place, a neat pile instead of a mess. The ration pouch was indeed warm, welcome against her chilled fingers.

Brood, his rifle across his lap, was slurping from his own packet. His stubble was dark except for the scar dropping down from one side of his mouth and running along his jawline, a line of silver.

Svin hopped up onto what had been a kidney-shaped counter. This looked more like a waiting room than a shop. If she were rifting by herself, she would poke around a little, see if there was any salvage on this floor. It felt like a place poppers would collect, those little blue spheres with their secretive glow. Or lampers, the long metal cylinders with various effects—a few of them, when you twisted the central portion, would begin to hum and rise away from gravity's clutching fingers. Most of them emitted a glow from one end or the other, freed by that same twisting motion, varying in intensity from a halogen glare to a weak golden beam. They were impervious to human tools, and scientists—let alone mechanics—could not break them open to discover their secrets. There might be coils of that soft gray extrusion that could be used as a rope that wouldn't fray, or as electrical wiring that conformed easily to any contacts and could be passed even through a hair-thin hole. You could never tell what might turn out to be valuable; you had to rift enough the instincts would start to wake up and tingle.

Crouching easily, she folded the top of the ration packet and tore the spout with just the right amount of force. A slight whiff of steam rose, meaty, salty, with an undertone of floury noodles. Good enough, and there would be the sweeter portion at the bottom, once the rest of the paste had been swallowed. Once they'd figured out how to make it contain the required fiber, every military—even the pissant warboys—had laid in stocks of the pouches wherever and whenever they could.

Mako had even kneaded this one, so there were no little pockets of scorching almost-fluid. It was an unexpected gesture, but maybe he was just inherently thorough. Or the pouch had been squeezed and bumped around enough in his pack to make it smooth and conductive.

Morov didn't want to eat, but Barko pestered him with the

gentleness of a bluff blunt man unused to children or invalids. The bald scientist made sure the commander was swallowing the paste, then cracked open a small red box from the bottom of the medikit.

That got Brood's attention. "Wait a second. That's expensive stuff."

"Well, we're in a bad situation." Barko's reply was the essence of mildness. He slid the syringe free and examined it critically for breakage or bending. "Now's a fine time to wish I majored in biology."

"What did you major in?" Mako slurped at his own packet. Svin's had cooled enough to taste. Chicken something. Maybe even some cheese.

"Physics." Barko's expression turned set with distaste. The dirt veiling his head could almost be mistaken for stubble. "As if the shit in here doesn't violate every goddamn law I ever learned."

None of them looked at her except Brood. She controlled the urge to turn away, hunch her shoulders. It was never good to show any weakness to a brittle-skinned man. "You want the longer-gauge needle. Right into the muscle mass on the quads, if that's what I think it is." Svin suckled at her own pouch. The rations were meant to keep large men carrying heavy weights supplied with enough calories for combat. It was good to feel the hunger retreat, to feel her strong thermabonded teeth warm up with the paste sliding past them.

"Now she's a nurse," Brood muttered. "You shouldn't give that to him. He's a goner."

"He's not dead yet." Mako glared at Brood. "Regs say we don't leave our wounded."

"Fuck the regs. You think they matter in here?" Brood just

shook his head, the long-healed scar along his jawline flashing paler, and Svin sensed something ugly rising in the situation.

It wasn't time for that. Yet. So she finished a long slurp and wiped her mouth with the back of one narrow hand. "I'll tell you about the Cormorant."

That froze all three of them—Mako with a mouthful of paste, Brood with his index finger tapping the butt of his side-arm again, Barko's pupils dilated and his head turned to look at her. Morov's eyes glittered under half-shut lids, a fever-sparkle like the lights you saw over low-lying areas in a really active part of a Rift at night. Watching those foxfire pinpricks mass and flow was another good way to get hypnotized and end up dead.

"This is the Run," she continued. "The biggest Rift and the most active. Right in the middle is the Cormorant. You know why they call it that?"

Mako cleared his throat. His stubble was wispy instead of thick, and was curling at the tips. "The only thing I ever heard is it's a fountain and the water makes you young again."

"I heard that too." Barko dropped his gaze to Morov's thigh. "Gonna have to cut your trousers, old man. I also heard it was a statue. Solid gold. Some kind of bird."

"I don't think it's just gold." Brood's index finger wasn't tapping anymore. "Nobody knows *what* it is, just that it's worth more than all the other fucking trash in here combined."

Svin didn't correct him. She just moved a little, rocking in her crouch. "Do you know what it does?"

"Kills people?" Mako belched, his cheeks ballooning out briefly. "Like everything else in here?"

"No, you fuckbucklers. The Cormorant grants wishes."

The extraordinary statement dropped like a rock into a quiet pool. Brood let out a half-choked laugh; Mako rolled his eyes.

"Sure it does," Brood sneered. "A bird that grants wishes."

"They use cormorants to fish." Barko made a slit in Morov's pant leg, sawing at the tough material, exposing a patch of strangely innocent skin starred with black hair like pine trees on an icy hillside. Streaks of angry red reached up from the laceration just below, and a ripe, rotting-meat smell rose. "Tie a band around their throats so they can't swallow, send 'em after the fish like hawks after rabbits."

"That's fucking ridiculous." Mako's nose wrinkled. "Christ, Morov, you stink."

"Can't help it." The commander blinked, slowly. "That what I think it is?"

"Best money can buy, sir." Barko's mouth was a thin line. "This is gonna hurt."

"Do . . . it."

Svin exhaled sharply as the scientist popped the needle in and pushed the plunger down. Morov stiffened, his mouth falling open, a damp hole stretched into agony.

"Yeah." She tossed the words, one by one, down at the fire, while Morov gasped. "It'll bring you a fish all right. But maybe not the fish you want."

"Grants wishes," Mako snorted. "What the fuck next? Fairies and dragons?"

Brood's ghost-colored eyes had narrowed. That was all. Maybe greed would keep him from cracking, for a little while.

Svin busied herself with sucking at the sweetness in the bottom of her ration pouch. If she did it a little messily, none of them would see her small, satisfied smile.

# 46
# GOT QUIET, OR DIED

⊰⧦⊱

The sun had turned red, hanging above the western horizon; the river glittered fiercely, full of amber and molten gold. The smear of the stampede's passage cut across open lots and an industrial section, and, when viewed from halfway up a defunct metal skeleton that had once held powerlines, looked too short for the time spent running it. The wall had cut through houses, warehouses, and other structures, its drift clearly shown in the direction every building had been stretched. Like very resilient taffy, warmed and shaped before plunged into a cold bath. Little bits of siding, brick, wooden paneling, all sorts of outer surfaces were crumbling, the pitter-patter of falling debris intensifying as the setting sun breathed across the water.

Steel resonated under Cabra's hands and boots, plucked at by the low moaning that carried the reek of cloves, fear, and battlefield shit-stench up to her. She took her time, gazing along the smear, trying to see anything familiar. Asking the silence inside herself the same question, over and over again, and getting the same answer in return.

She couldn't spend all night up here, so she climbed carefully down, alert to any sudden change in the structure. It held her just fine, and when her boots hit dry earth again she shook her hands out, wishing she'd brought gloves. Scratches crisscrossed her palms and fingers, and it was going to hurt come tomorrow.

First, she had to get away, and find somewhere safe for the night.

Gaining the high ground was tricky, shimmers and squeezers crowding in a thick, milky stream down the first two clear hillsides she came across. There were safe paths up both of them, but those would require running, and her legs were already shaky. She reeked of sweat and mipsik, the heavy fug of cloves and fur wafting up from her clothes and turning her stomach whenever her back was to the breeze. Groping along, following what might turn out to be a false trail, turning back, keeping to a steady walk because if she slowed down she'd have to think about Sabby...

Too late.

Maybe she'd walk into the Tumbledown and see him there, nursing a shot of something while he waited for her, his golden hair tousled and his eyes probably already puffy-bloodshot. He'd ask if she got the payoff, she would have to shake her head, and his *told you so* would be louder because it remained unsaid, sitting on his face alongside the hangdog expression of a man who knew it was only a matter of time before something bad happened.

Cabra turned hard right, following the internal tugging. Most of rifting was learning to listen to that urging instead of drowning it in useless chatter. You got quiet, or you died.

There it was again.

The problem with that kind of listening was that you couldn't control what it told you. You ended up *knowing*, even when you wanted to believe otherwise. What it was telling her now was stupid, unbelievable, and true.

*He'd find me.* It wasn't a lie. If there was anything of Sabby left to find, she could have edged along whatever precarious path led to it.

Her route led circuitously up a gentle slope networked with residential streets, pre-Event houses set in weed-choked yards. Spiny bushes had invaded this neighborhood, and she kept an eye out for thornbacks or grazers. The sky had turned blue again, swept clean, and the sun beat almost sideways, edging each fringed leaf and serrated grassblade. The weeds, their nodding heads puke-yellow or fluffy white, fought with the thin green vines of merrywell with its prickle-periwinkle flowers. In the distance, the heart of the Rift glittered sharply, downtown's skyscrapers still throwing back their lying reflections. Easy work, opportunity, losing yourself in a faceless mass.

Really, the Rift was no different. The lie was just a little closer to the surface, its sharp edges poking like knifepoints stretching plastifreez. You ran the Rift until it caught up with you.

As she walked, her nimble fingers worked at her hair. Beads, hard and slick, rolled free, and she tossed them like strips-and-bobs, in front of her or off to the side, gauging how they fell. Step step step toss, step toss, step step step step, toss again. Rolling through each footfall, testing the pavement when she crossed a deathly quiet street, a bead glittering sharply as it plummeted through a pocket of gravity not behaving the way it should, slamming down with a sound like popcorn.

The trouble with rifting alone was having too much god-damn time to think. Her throat was full, her eyes dry-burning. Cabra rolled a gold bead in her scraped, bloody fingers, a blood blister under her thumb, the skin all over her roughening with the atavistic consciousness of being watched.

She tipped her head back, sliding the gold bead into her pocket. The pinchoks had returned, floating lazily through a darkening sky. Two of them were maybe clocking her, one of those overlapping-circle diagrams they had in school. She refused to glance at where Sabby should be, refused to think about how it had happened, *how* it had happened.

The safe path edged her along a dusty overgrown trail along-side a part-brick house, its rooms probably bigger than the shack she'd been born in. Certainly bigger than the room she shared with the Pooka over a bodega near Deegan. His clothes were there, and the clutter they'd made when packing for this run. His busted-ass guitar—he was always saying he was gonna get new strings. Gonna play her a song or two, just as soon as he could. Three years he'd been promising that, in and out of the Rift.

There it was again. She flicked a blue bead off her fingers; it flashed across an overgrown backyard with a faded plastic play-ground set quietly bleaching itself out under the Rift's seasons. The blue bead hit an invisible wall and dropped with a sound like wood snapping.

A stampede would get rid of the weak and the sick. Maybe that was part of the ecosystem of the Rift itself. Survival of the fittest, just like outside. Had she decided to go for Vetch's payoff because she knew Sabby would drop somehow, sooner or later?

No. Not that. Never that. Still, she wondered, as she wriggled through a hole in gray-weathered wooden fencing, not liking the way the lengthening shadows on the other side of the yard felt. That was the other thing about the goddamn Rift. Everyone was complicit, especially yourself.

Even when you...loved...someone.

Cabra glanced again at where Sabby should be, drifting in her wake, clinging to her safety. Swimming for so long with someone else on your back, you didn't feel lighter when they were gone. You just realized, in the silence, how tired you were, how tired you had always been.

She kept walking, unraveling her braids as she went. Her dirty scalp tingled at the sudden change. There was a safe hole very near, she could *sense* it, a snatch of melody overheard from a window the brain lightly teased at, trying to fit into a song.

Once she hit the blur on the way out, it would be time to look for another Rift. Otherwise she'd come back into this one, looking for what couldn't be found. Taking worse and worse chances until it caught her, too.

Or, she supposed, she could stop. Just stop hitting driftburn, take a cog-in-a-wheel job in a factory somewhere or just starve to death. Yeah. Sure. She could do that.

Surviving made you complicit, too. "Oh, Pooka," she whispered, tossing another blue bead in front of her.

It fell in a gentle arc, as if she were out past the slugwall already. Cabra's face contorted once, smoothed itself.

Carefully, cautiously, her eyes dry and her heart a knot of writhing thornback, the rifter moved on into the gathering dusk.

# 47
# STILL BREATHING

⋊╫⋉

The hallucinations were actually quite gentle. They reminded him of raindrops on a window, only the drops were huge, slow wheels of moving color. It was triphase plasma, his leg a red-hot bar of pain where the substance was freshly thermabonding a hairline fracture of his tibia as well as spreading up to fight the infection from the deep gash in his thigh above. Triphase was expensive because it fixed just about everything—if you applied enough of it. It was a minor miracle Barko had found a medikit containing a syringe that hadn't been stripped out and pawned by an enterprising sardie or janitor. Nowadays they put less spendy—and much less effective—stuff in the kits.

Morov watched the globs of color flow and meld. They were a little like the soap-bubble swirls of the Riftwall, but these colors obeyed laws. Red, orange, yellow, green, blue—they shifted through blessedly easy-to-name shades in a slow, logical rainbow, melting like ice cream but not merging. Each border was crisp and distinct.

His eyelids drifted up once, when a hazy shadow intruded

on his thoughts. Blinked, the movement stretched out into an eternity, a blackness lowering and rising. The pale smear above him was a face.

Someone crouched next to him. There was a dark crop of hair on the skull, so it wasn't Barko. Too chalky to be Mako. Too goddamn big to be the rifter.

It was Brood, his strange light irises disappearing and reappearing once as he blinked, too. His blond tips were darker than usual, wet and slicked-down. His breathing was even and slow, and when Morov moved slightly, the other man didn't flinch.

A cold fingertip traced down Morov's sweating spine. His hands were limp and useless, and even though the agony in his leg was retreating, it was still throbbing badly enough to make him want another painpatch. Or maybe a jolt of something, anything, even pine, just to take the edge off.

There was a sliding sound, cloth against a surface. A sharp, deep cough. Something moved, high up on a shelf—no, it was the rifter on the countertop, pushing herself up on one elbow and hacking like she was about to throw a lung. Sleeping up there, she was probably drier than the rest of them—it was damp in here, even though the heat-ray had sent little critters scurrying out of the carpeting and shattered furniture. The bugs were still here, even though everything else was gone. When humanity choked to death on its own blood, the cockroaches would take over. Maybe they'd make a better job of it.

The idea of cockroaches evolving to take on office jobs was amusing enough to distract him. It would be so easy to drift away.

He brought himself back to consciousness with a jolt, his vision sharpening. Brood's face, half shadowed, was calm and thoughtful. Why was he just *sitting* there?

The rifter finished coughing. There was another scraping sound, and the unscrewing of a canteen. She hawked and spat, a dry gobbet thoughtfully ejected toward the doorway instead of into the cubbyhole they were all sleeping in. A splashing—she took a mouthful of water, and the tiny glitters that were her eyes reflecting the punky glow of the fire were fixed on Morov.

Was she going to watch?

"Sir." The pale-eyed soldier's teeth showed, a facsimile of a smile. "Making sure you're still breathing." He slowly unfolded, towering over his commander, and Morov's sweat had turned cold and oily. How long had the bastard been sitting there, a vulture just waiting? Didn't they prefer rotten meat to fresh?

Well, Morov would rot soon enough with a knife buried in his femoral artery. Or his throat, maybe. Or Brood could do it the quiet way, the crunch of a neck breaking—the noise like a glass shattered under a towel. Or steady pressure against the carotid.

He could, really, do it anytime he liked. Was that why Kope sent him?

*No, Kope sent him to do for the rifter.* Still, he'd never liked Brood. The feeling was pretty mutual, kept in check by the routine of military discipline. One of those things on a back burner. Except here, everything was in front, and it was boiling harder the longer they stayed. The closer they got to the center and that goddamn Cormorant.

Brood stood there for a few more seconds, his weight shifting back and forth. Maybe his legs were cramping, or maybe he was considering doing both Morov and the rifter. That would be a fool's move, though, and while the blond-tipped motherfucker might be killcrazy, he wasn't an idiot.

He understood the rules, just like every other sardie who edged close to murder for the fun of it.

"Still breathing," Morov managed. His throat was dry as sanded glass. His gaze shifted past Brood, to the rifter. She was utterly still, only those betraying little sparkles of her eyeballs turning the shadow of her head into something recognizably human. "For now."

Brood's smile disappeared, or maybe he just turned his head. He sank down on his bedroll, and Morov realized he could hear Mako snoring and Barko's long, loud inhales. Was Brood on watch?

There was another gleam, very low, in the rifter's shadowed shape. A slight noise of metal releasing the tension of fleshly pressure. It was there and gone so quickly Morov thought it might be another hallucination, and the pain in his leg began to retreat on scorching little padded feet.

Every time Morov drifted out of thready, uneasy sleep, he saw the rifter's shape sitting upright on the counter. She was there all through the deepest part of the night, when the noises began outside. Creaking, groaning, the tossing of iron branches in a cold unforgiving wind. A rippling singsong screech in the distance turned into an agonized, throat-cut cry and ended with a gurgle. Soft sneaking footsteps pattered past the office door, but the rifter didn't turn, just watched Morov.

And Brood, from his bedroll, watched her.

She didn't lie down again until Mako woke up three hours before dawn for his watch. Brood passed a few murmured words with the other man, and soon he and the rifter were both asleep as Mako edged around the countertop and pissed in a corner instead of risking going outside.

# 48
# NO IMAGINATION

⋊╫⋉

The commander's office was a shambles of cardboard boxes, the full ones with official labels attached and a string of heat-tape sealing their tops. The half-empty ones were labeled in Ochki's spidery script, case number and evidence code written neatly but the number fields left blank.

Ochki, his suit jacket draped on the back of Kopelund's expensive chair with its ironed creases intact, glanced at the corporate drone with his shiny pompadour and little silver bead stuffed in his ear. The Second Branch agent neatened a pile of paperwork, tapping it against the desktop and setting it carefully in the current box. "I am not quite sure I understand," he said, finally. His round, steel-rimmed spectacles sent a tiny jet of light into the dark corner where the safe stood wide-open, its contents disarranged. Its mysteries would be thoroughly plumbed soon enough. The other safe, behind the painting on the wall in Kopelund's quarters, had been discerned but was not opened yet. Instead, the painting had been surgically removed and a blank metal face watched an empty room, the dial in its center just waiting for a thermaspray to turn it to mush but leave the safe's contents undamaged.

"Just a courtesy call, really." Zlofter's smile was smooth and plastic as the rest of him. "We had a close working relationship with General Kopelund."

Ochki nodded. Though he had taken off his jacket, he still wore his hat, and one could be forgiven for thinking it was to cover a bald spot. His suspenders, dove-gray and probably regulation issue, were well cared for and not new. His soft, shaved cheeks puffed slightly. "How close was that, Mr. Zlofter?"

Zlofter studied him for a moment, holding his very black, very expensive bowler. "Professionally close, Agent Ochki. We are shocked by the allegations."

"No doubt, no doubt." Ochki's round, pale face didn't change. "Shocking things here at QR-715. Unsanctioned experimentation. Graft. Quite a profitable side trade in government materiel. Yes, very shocking indeed." The window was not open, and it was much warmer in here than it ever had been during Kopelund's tenure.

Did Zlofter pale a shade or two? At the door, Ochki's slab of a bodyguard loomed. He was not blocking the entrance.

Not yet.

"We were only interested in legitimate—"

"Yes, the tracks were covered quite nicely. DynaKrom did request a prisoner transfer, all aboveboard and legal. Prisoner was remanded to the local authority, which would have been Kopelund."

"The prisoner?" Zlofter did not like the path this interview was treading. His welcome gift—a large fruit basket, with an envelope of hard credits tucked under burnished, glowing pears—stood forgotten on a side table. The agent hadn't even glanced at it. "The case was appealed, and since Kopelund had requested—"

"Indeed." Ochki picked up another sheaf of papers, glancing through them. There was a mote of dust on one of his lenses, and it was irritating. But he did not care for the idea of taking his glasses off just at the moment. "You were simply being courteous to the local military authority. Which is very much appreciated. We live in troubled times. Tell me, Mr. Zlofter, do you think he might have pulled it off?"

"I beg your pardon?" Yes, the corporate man was cheese-pale now. In a little while, that pompadour might begin to wilt. Even though he was merely a middling functionary, his mother corporation might make a certain amount of noise if one of its own disappeared in the scandal. DynaKrom was the local power, and a large source of tax revenue.

Such things mattered more than they should nowadays. But ILAC was tightening its hold, slowly and surely. The road was long, but it would end with more order. More safety. More sanity. Ochki looked forward to as much, though he would quite miss a certain amount of excitement, if it happened sooner. The very thought brought a half-pained smile to his moist, pink lips. "Kopelund. Do you think he might have brought something large enough out of that Rift to justify a quite surprising amount of resources wasted, despite the injunctions against such a thing?"

"I'm sure I can't guess." The corporate man had regained some of his aplomb, and sounded almost prim. His wristlet blinked, a sleepy green eye. It would be difficult to make someone who wore that type of tech disappear.

But it could be done. Oh yes, it could be. "If he did, I can't help but think he would have a buyer for the item in question already on the sidelines. In fact, I am *almost* sure of it." Ochki's watery blue eyes swiveled up, swimming behind the lenses, and the soft, almost paternal expression the black-uniformed dumpling of a man wore was by no means comforting.

Zlofter's throat moved, his Adam's apple bobbing as he swallowed. "You are?"

Ochki nodded, slowly. He sighed, a heavy, nasal sound when his mouth closed halfway through. It was a peculiar noise, and also not comforting. "But I am an old man, at the end of his career. Of course I see bad things everywhere; it has been my job for so long."

"It gets to you," Zlofter agreed. "Especially so close to *that*."

Ochki didn't ask what he meant. It was, in any case, obvious. The slugwall did strange things to people.

He tapped the next crop of papers into a submissive, neat little shape with his soft, clever little hands, well-cared-for nails brushed and buffed. "So I'm told. It was very polite of you to visit, Mr. Zlofter. DynaKrom can rest assured its investments in this particular installation will be in more…honest… hands, now."

The corporate man murmured a courteous, "Of course, of course. I shall leave you to it, then." He lifted his hat politely, but did not place it upon his pompadour, and took care not to hurry as he moved for the door. The big man had not moved, but it would only take a single glance from Ochki to change that.

The agent let him get within a step of the door. One more step, and he would be over the threshold and safe. The reedy little voice rose behind him. "Mr. Zlofter?"

"Yes?" The corporate man's hands clutched the brim of the new, custom-made, very expensive bowler. His palms were a little more damp than he cared for.

"QR-715 is a quarantine zone. We have new units arriving today with strict orders. Anyone attempting to enter the anomaly will be shot. And, of course, anything that comes *out* will be destroyed with whatever means are to hand. We simply cannot be too careful, now, can we?"

Zlofter's smile was a painted doll's grimace. "No. One can never be too careful."

"Good day, sir."

"Good day." There might have been something caught in the corporate man's throat. He stepped hurriedly into the hallway, and within minutes the soft rousing of an expensive engine echoed outside. Agent-Major Ochki, putting off retirement at the request of the Second Branch, shook his graying head. There was much more to be made here than a few crumbs from corporate scum, after all. Kopelund had no imagination.

Ochki indicated the fruit basket with a single contemptuous motion and told his faithful bodyguard to throw the offensive thing in the incinerator, bribe and all.

# 49
# SOMEONE MUST

ᛞᛟᛖ

Another clear, beautiful day. The clouds were now innocently white, the air fresh and clean, and something had happened during the night. The bulging buildings they had walked between yesterday glowed under sunshine, the surfaces on the left now covered with a sticky amber film, hardening as the light hit it. The sheet of material stretched across corners, rippling as it settled; it looked exactly like giants had plastifreez shrink-wrapped one side of the street. The right-hand side, bulging and sagging, groaned a little, dust puffing from seams and windows making that high thin singing noise as the glass was warped and bent, but would not break.

"Fuck," Morov breathed, a long drawn-out sigh of something too tired to be wonder. He could stand up without help, and even hobble without the crutch. All he needed was a stout short stick to act as a cane. The skinstrip on his forehead this morning had shown up nice and pale yellow.

It wasn't much of a victory, but Barko was grateful nonetheless. He rubbed at his head, wincing a little as gritty dirt scratched between palm and naked scalp. "I don't think it's a good idea," he said, again.

"Don't care what you think, baldy." Brood checked his rifle again, a completely unnecessary movement since he'd already done so twice. Maybe it was his version of a nervous tic. "Mako and I go with the rifter. We bring back this shitbird fairy-tale thing, then we all go home." His bloodshot gaze passed over the street in a brief arc, not quite apathetic. "Rifter says that shit down the road won't come here."

"I said I don't *think* it will." She stood a little closer to Mako than she had to anyone else, and he didn't step away.

"Still don't think we should split up." Mako's broad face was worried, a vertical line between his eyebrows and his wisp-curling stubble blacker than usual because of the dirt rubbed into his cheeks. Maybe it was camouflage, because he'd smeared it down his neck too, and on the backs of his hands.

"Didn't ask you." Brood's smile was wide, and white, and unsettling.

Mako looked at Morov instead. The captain nodded, wearily. "Go ahead, Mako. Get the fucking thing and come back."

"Yessir." Mako's nod was a salute, and pointedly did not include Brood.

The rifter examined Morov for a long moment, then nodded. "Back soon." She turned, smartly, tossed one of her little flying rags, and set off as soon as it hit the pavement with a sweet chiming. Mako trailed in her wake, and Barko thought it was quite possible the man's back was crawling at the thought of Brood behind him with a gun, even if there was little rifle ammo left.

At least, Brood said there wasn't much ammo left. He didn't say just how much he *did* have.

Morov watched as Brood ambled after the rifter and Mako, with a lazy hip-loose stride saying he had all the time in the world. His big shoulders were rigid, though, and before they turned at the end of the street he sped up, obviously not wanting to be left behind.

Barko squinted against the sunshine. Anywhere but here, he'd have called it a beautiful day. He opened his mouth, shut it, then decided what the hell, he could at least ask. "You think any of them are coming back?"

Morov's shrug looked painful, and he grimaced. "Maybe the rifter."

"Yeah. Can't tell if that's a shame." Barko's head hurt. For a few minutes, inside, he'd thought Brood was going to clear leather, go for Morov, and follow it up by shooting *him* for good measure. Morov's diplomacy had saved the situation— dealing with Kopelund all the damn time probably qualified the commander for sainthood *and* a spot in the arbitration hall of fame. The rifter had piped up, too, telling Morov that the next stage of the trip needed some agility, and he was in no shape to attempt it.

Maybe she'd even been telling the truth.

In any case, it was out of their hands now. Morov's drawn, suffering face was unreadable.

"Goddamn shame," he agreed. "At least they left some food."

Barko almost wanted to ask what the hell they would do if nobody returned, or how long they were going to wait. In the end, though, it didn't goddamn matter. It was out of his hands, always had been, and if he made it out of here the first thing he was going to do was quit his job and move somewhere much colder, or somewhere tropical. Somewhere the Rifts didn't stretch their soap-bubble fingers. "Yeah," he said. "This gives us time for coffee, too."

"Fucking optimist." One corner of Morov's mouth curled up. "You believe that shit, about the Cormorant granting wishes?"

What could he say? "Someone must." Enough to send them in here, to almost certain death.

"You think Kope does?" As if Morov hadn't had way more interaction with Kope on a daily basis. What was he asking Barko for?

"Looks awful likely." Barko headed back into the damp, nasty-smelling office cave. Smoke had blackened the ceiling already, and he didn't like the idea of staying here another night. He didn't say the rest; he didn't have to.

*Believed it enough to send us in here to die for it, sure.*

# 50
# OPTIONS

⋈

She wasn't even trying to hide her trail. Not that she could have, with a bunch of lundies tromping behind her. He could almost *taste* her, harsh soap and sweat on a woman's skin, the slightly spicy tang of a brunette woman's clean hair after healthy effort, the slight edge of ripe acridity that was a fully grown female used to hard effort and few showers. Overlaid with the oiliness of other males and their guns, metal and shiny ration pouches, a whiff of roughened fingers and the yeasty smell of men who drank. The last bit stayed even when they hadn't had anything alcoholic for a while. The body remembered, and it changed.

Vetch crouched, easily, right next to the corner of what had been a department store. Its window bulged outward a bit, dusty glass pregnant with a faint swirling glow. Faintly hypnotic, the streaks rotated counterclockwise, and the pavement under the window held soft dimpled depressions. The dangerous zone wasn't that big, but he was willing to bet whatever was under the paving ate well. Tossing a strip-and-bob into it might show him the thing's feeding habits, but it wasn't worth it. Best to stay in the little secure area, right in the window's blind spot, and think about things while his hands worked at his mapper, organizing by touch.

She was taking them up the Alley. It was just like her, really. Pick the most dangerous route to peel away a bunch of lundie motherfuckers.

Across the street, crumpled in the shade under a bank of similarly bulging windows over mounds of rubble—office buildings brushed by the edge of the pressure wall and consequently weakened—two pinchoks mantled on a skinny body. The lundie lay on his back with his arms crossed, a thin blue blanket from his pack crumpled a few feet aside. Looked like they'd weighted it down with bits of broken concrete, but the wall had stripped it away and mummified the corpse, turning its black-rimmed spectacles into high nodding curlicues of burnt plastic and spun glass. The pinchoks, their sharp shovel-beaks clacking, jostled each other. They had already stripped the muscle mass on the thighs and opened up the belly. Tatters of a white lab coat fluttered under their big, grasping-nailed feet.

Vetch's hands finished reorganizing his mapper. Next, his right hand dropped, and he eased the pistol free. Checked its clip, checked its sight, reholstered it without looking.

From here, he'd have to be even more careful. The last thing he wanted was any of his ripples touching the edge of her space. You could tell when someone was tracking you, if you didn't have a shit-ton of interference all around.

At least one casualty in her group. If she was taking them up the Alley, there were bound to be more. Was she just letting the Rift do its work, or was she after the Cormorant? Did she believe any of the stories? Had Ashe left a whisper, a word?

He wouldn't put it past the bitch.

Hearing the Rat had deezed hadn't really pleased him, but it hadn't *displeased* him either. He hadn't meant to come across her trail, but shit happened. The Cancún Rift—Xoch' Run—was the closest he could get to Guan, but it was a smaller bubble and had started to get crowded. Plus, a felon in solitary didn't get mail, not that she would have opened anything he sent, anyway. So he'd hopped a few freightsleds and palmed it the rest of the way, ending up in this stretch of the woods, figuring the biggest bubble would be the one they got around to attempting to officially map last. The Rat, sniffing around the corners of anything profitable, had beaten him to it.

Like always.

Vetch uncoiled, slowly, careful not to brush the concrete wall with his sleeve or dungaree leg. A layer of thick paint had turned bleached-beige, and bubbled up from an application of unimaginable heat. She'd stayed well away from this side of the road; the lundies probably had no idea how carefully she was threading from one safe path to another, hopping sideways when she had to, going in gentle arcs to minimize eddies in the current.

Good rifting. She hadn't lost anything, rotting in a prison cell.

What would he say?

No use in practicing a line. Vetch turned to his left, feeling for the path forward. It was there, and coming closer. Sooner or later the current would bring it right to this little safe patch, and he'd step off. Zagging across the street would bring him across her wake, and his palms were damp.

*We can do an appeal*, the gray-fringed lawyer in his seedy office had said while tropical sun beat down outside, *but it'll cost you.*

What the fuck else did he have to spend his marks on? Vetch waited, his heart beating high and hard. Cabra might have been wandering around looking for Sabby, but she had to know he was gone. Sabby and Il Muto, lost in the wave. Whether the wall had gotten them or a slip in the mipsik herd was immaterial. If she was smart, she'd head for the wall and driftburn out while she could.

Nobody to share the payout with, except *her*. He'd judge his time carefully. A man could hope for something. If he didn't get it, well, there were other options. The Rift was full of goddamn options.

*You worked for it. For once.*

Maybe it was the memory of that dismissive little headshake, the way she didn't even look at him full-on, that made him jump the gun. He shifted his weight a fraction of a second too soon, his toe touching down just before the safe path swung near him, and the pavement rippled. A high, popping, crunching noise echoed off the buildings, and Vetch yelled, more in surprise than pain.

It was when he landed that the agony started.

# 51
# CAUGHT THEIR FILL

>+|+<

The next slice of the Alley might have taken care of the problem, but Svin didn't like the way it felt. So she plunged off the main road and kept up a good clip, moving as if she had another rifter or two with her. Throw, watch, let her instincts tell her where to put her feet, don't overthink but don't get complacent, either. Feeling each step, testing it as the weight shifts, head up, everything around her hypercolored, her skin alive with sensitive prickles. The danger of the man's gun behind her was minimal for the moment; the far greater danger was letting it distract her from negotiating the single safe ribbon underfoot.

Mako kept up, his labored breathing echoing against the frowning walls on either side. He didn't step only where she did, and he clip-clopped like a blind horse.

No, not a horse. They probably had the good sense every other animal did. Svin had never seen one, but she thought they were probably much, much wiser than humans. Not to mention less murderous.

This road led down in gentle curves to the old riverport, taking advantage of the slopes to hide the bulk of the giant tumbled tangle of chemical plants and factories from those who lived above. Pipes sprouted from the plants like spines, buildings dozing in heavy midafternoon sun, having caught their fill of whatever the hard silver glitter of the river now carried. Smaller creeks were safest, you didn't want to go too near a lake or a river in a Rift. Too much could hide under the surface, and the water bounced interference around.

It was the river she aimed for, eyeing each of the sleepy buildings and deciding *no, no, no.* One felt too carnivorous, one not enough, one almost safe—she took note of *that* rickety wooden building, set at the end of a train spur. The rails had fuzzed with black honeycomb, and she hopped over them, not quite hearing the angry buzzing as the small metallic un-insects with their whorled bodies and large sleep-veined wings took notice of a shadow passing by. Mako, behind her, lumbered into an ungainly leap over them, and it was probably the sunny day-warmth that made them slow. They did not rise until Brood, lagging too far to see Svin's nimble hop and Mako's blundering, almost tripped on the rails and gave a short cry.

The brittlebees rose in a humming cloud, and Svin moved her skinny legs. Her feet beat on the crumbling pavement; she cut across the corner of another railyard, Mako right behind her. The building on the right was too dark, the one looming now on her left too ramshackle and innocent-looking, so it would have to be the one in the middle.

It wasn't perfect; it would have to do. The pale-eyed sardie wouldn't believe leading him over the tracks was innocent.

Which it wasn't, and now she'd tipped her hand. His rage would explode, his greed unable to keep it in check.

She snapped a glance back just as a military sidearm barked; chips exploded from the wooden face of the warehouse before her, exposing paler material beneath. Mako, sweat cutting clean tracks in the grime coating his face, barked as well, a single obscenity that told her he wasn't hit and she shouldn't slow down. She swerved, aware the ribbon of safety was fraying, and skated *just* on its outer edge, leaning to the left with her feet heel-to-toe like a child playing on a beam.

A massive door had not been fully closed the day of the Event. Now, molding and buckled, it sagged further; there was just enough space for her to nip into a caustic-smelling darkness. She dug her heels in as soon as she wriggled through the triangular aperture, her jacket tearing a little and her hipbag catching on a splinter. She lunged free, spinning to grab Mako's hand and *haul* him through.

Why? Well, he was a good shield, and he didn't want to kill her.

Yet.

"Come on!" she yelled, and his eyes were wide and rolling, their whites glaring. She found his wrist and heaved, his shoulders turning, and the gun behind them spoke again, along with the rising, nasty hum of angry metal shavings resisting a magnet.

*"Run!"* Mako yelled, shaking his hand free, gesturing her on. *"Run!"*

So he thought he was going to save her. Svin bent her knees, stuck her ass out, braced her grip on his wrist, and yanked backward as hard as she could, a long *hggggn* of effort escaping her burning throat. Wood splintered, and he fell through, his own jacket flapping and his rifle tearing more rotting wood from the door.

Inside, hummocks of yellow chemical dust rose and fell, an unbroken sea clinging to a thin strip of concrete shore along the walls. Svin took this in with a glance, and had to choose—yank the sardie up onto his feet and stand right there when Brood fired through the door, or leave the round-faced, *makhorka*-snorting man to whatever mercy the ghost-eyed asshole would dispense.

*Oh, fuck.*

Bullets plowed through the thin, dry-rotted wood in a deadly arc, tiny sharpened shafts of golden sunlight touching the dry yellow dunes inside. Puffs of nasty greenish steam rose wherever the light touched, and Svin, flat on the little strip of concrete floor next to the door, stared into Mako's dark, terrified eyes. His pupils had swollen, his mouth was loose, and she tried to tell herself she'd hit the ground because she'd somehow sensed Brood would aim high. It would have been stupid to risk herself for Mako, too stupid to be believed.

And yet. One skinny-ass rifter with a bad wire in her head, deciding to do something stupid instead of saving her own skin. Someday that was going to bite her.

Maybe today. Mako shuddered. Brood hadn't aimed too high, after all. Blood welled from the sardie's back, his filthy moon-shaped face very close to hers. Nose to nose, the sourness of his *makhorka*-tainted breath brushing her cheeks, she watched the light fade from those narrow eyes as he bled out.

Her hands, quick, clever little paws that they were, were

already worming their way under him, searching for clips. Grabbing what they found while she stared at him, watching a tiny spark carried to the end of the long black corridor of his pupils, vanishing under a gust of cold wind.

Brood yelled outside, a long wavering inhuman cry. No, his greed wouldn't stop him now. Men like him were built for one thing only, and in here where everything else was stripped from you but essentials, he could give full rein to the urge to beat, shoot, kill, destroy. Svin scrambled to her feet, her palms burning from the rough concrete. The yellow dust had found Mako's ankle and caressed it with a thin lapping tonguelet. His boot was already dissolving, tough leather sending up harsh angular steam.

She scrambled back, keeping to that too-thin ribbon of safety. Anything resting on the floor had been eaten away, iron stairs in the far back corner hanging instead of supported from below. Svin rounded the corner, her shoulder burning against the wall, and Brood kicked at the large warehouse door. A shower of splinters rewarded his efforts, and he kicked again.

Svinga jumped, gracelessly. Metal screamed as she pawed up the stairs, the entire world narrowing to a shuddering, swaying ladder under her palms and boots, blood torn free of her shredded fingers. There was a landing and a turn, and after that it was more solid.

*Bitch, look up!* It was Ashe's voice, the sharp clear tone of warning she used in the Rift. Svin's chin snapped up, a glaring shifting field of shadows and strange shapes—she ducked under the soft silvery streamers hanging from the ceiling, their tips stretching, fluttering to catch at her short, short hair. On hands and knees she scrabbled forward, along a narrow gangplank that had stopped quivering and shrieking under her.

*Now stop.*

Svin froze, not even daring to reach for the gun in her mapper. To her right and below, the dust moved, piled dunes slithering forward to caress Mako's prone form. He shuddered once, kicking, but that was only because Brood had shoved his shoulders through the hole they'd made and sprayed him with a short burst of rifle fire—maybe a waste of ammo, maybe not. The sound made the silvery streamers above move uneasily, overlapping echoes bouncing inside the cavernous building, falling dead against the sandy yellow dust. She gapped her mouth as wide as possible, breathing softly though her lungs cried out and her eyes were full of hot water. Her hands throbbed, but she hardly felt them, peering at the bright bar of golden light from outside.

Brood pushed through. Wood splintered and he almost tripped on Mako's outstretched hand. The dust made a dry rubbing noise, piling on itself.

"Motherfucker." Brood spat; the light from behind made him a monster shadow.

*The Rift don't do anything,* Paco Three-leg had said once, sitting across a small fire from Ashe with his otter-sleek head tilted and his hands wringing at each other. *It just lets all-us in-us loose.*

Ashe had just told him to speak for himself, and furthermore, to shut up because she wanted to sleep. She never did like philosophy. The Rift was there, they were walking in it, that was all the Rat ever needed to know.

"Oh, you little cunt," Brood half crooned, his rifle-muzzle sweeping across the dust-dunes. Svin didn't blink, barely breathed, watching his hulking dark shape in the flood of sunshine. One or two disturbed brittlebees buzzed in his wake, and as Svin's eyes focused she could see their stings on his cheeks, swelling and darkening rapidly. Maybe they were so heat-drowsy they hadn't been able to swarm him. "Come here. We got summin' to talk about."

He swayed, the rifle moving, its blunt snout seeking, seeking. The dust made a soft, subtle noise.

"Come out!" he yelled, making a stabbing motion with the gun. "All you gotta do is show me where it is, rifter!" His eyes narrowed. Svin's pupils, swollen just like Mako's now, began to pick out details. Thin grains of yellow spilling forward, cringing as they touched the sunshine. More green steam-smoke rose. It smelled like a freshly cut apple, but under that was the heavy nasty scent of digestive juices stirring raw macerated flesh.

He moved not to the right, as she had, but to the left, into deeper shadow. It was probably a good tactical choice, if he hadn't been in the Rift. Mako's body twitched again, and Brood's shoulder slammed the edge of the hole in the door as he leapt back, probably catching the motion in his peripheral vision.

"Come on," he muttered. The warehouse amplified the words, turned them back on each other. "Come on, sweetheart. Kope sent me to take care of you, make sure you were all nice and protected. I been good to you. Coulda done you a hundred times by now."

Svinga's lungs burned. Her eyes did, too, drying out. She refused to blink. Refused to breathe. Crouched silent and small as a rabbit, not even trembling. Quiet as a rat who knows the cat is outside its hole.

Brood stepped sideways again, his back to the wall. Maybe he didn't see the tangle of silver ribbons hanging from the ceiling, taking advantage of the deeper shadow next to the door's thin shield. The wall was thicker there, a shed attached to the main building insulating it even further from killing daylight. Maybe he didn't feel the slither of air against sweat-damp skin. Maybe he wasn't sweating at all, so certain he would flush out the rifter and—

Something flickered. He sent a burst into the yellow dust. The bullets pocked the dune surfaces, threw up tiny puffs of heavy, oily yellow grains. The sand began to whisper, an angry note creeping into its rasp. The gun clicked, a dry nasty sound.

He'd used up all the ammo in the clip. Did he have more?

"Fuck," he mouthed. Svin saw a single white gleam off his front teeth before the dingy bleached tips of his hair, standing up now that he'd run his hands through, passed within a millimeter of the lowest silver ribbon hanging from the roof.

*Fwump.* It dropped on him, the entire tangle slithering intestine-like over the interloper. A sucking sound carried it back up, and Brood screamed as he thrashed in its snarled embrace. The thick, shiny ribbons flushed, rubbing each other, and a pattering of crimson hit the dry floor and the yellow dust at once.

Svin let her breath out, softly, slowly. The knotwork mass of ruddy metallic tentacles convulsed once, and Brood screamed again. It kept massaging, a little at a time, and every once in a while that slurping, satisfied noise echoed against the walls. Sharp ribbon-edges rubbed against each other over Svin's head, but they did not drop on her. They thickened, pouring toward the uvula near the door that had caught a tasty intruder.

It took a long time for Brood's cries to fade into choke-muffled despair, and Svin watched every moment of it. After a while, she found out she was inhaling each time the mass tightened, and she waited for it to fall into its post-gorge doze before she began the slow, careful work of backing up, soundless, on hands and knees, praying the hungry ribbons in the roof wouldn't sense her own cargo of meat and copper blood.

# 52
# RED, RED RAG

>||‹

Dusk came with a thunderous red glow, russet clouds boiling over the shattered city at the heart of the Rift. Morov leaned on the cut-down crutch, mopping his forehead. Barko, right next to him on the sidewalk before the door to their malodorous hideaway, shook his head. "It doesn't feel any different."

"What, you're the rifter now?" There was no heat to it. Morov shifted his leg. The latest painpatch was wearing off; he grimaced. "Fucking Brood, man."

Barko nodded. His fingers twisted at each other when he wasn't rubbing the grime deeper into his scalp. His long, mournful face, dark circles under his eyes and his once-broken nose glaring-visible in the ruddy light, puckered itself. "I, uh, almost hesitate to ask. But do you think he...you know, Senkin?"

"Rifter didn't think so." And she'd watched Brood, for those long aching hours trembling on the knife-edge. Maybe she'd just wanted to see what would happen, but then, why would she have made any noise or sat up? Or was it just that with

Morov gone, whatever tenuous restraint on Brood he repre-
sented would also be gone?

"She just might not have said." Barko, true to form, found
the worst goddamn thing to worry about.

"True." Morov shifted again. He had only one cigar left, and
it was a whole one. "It's possible." A whole lot of shit was possible in here. You didn't even have to look at what was *likely*.
"Senkin would watch Mako's back."

"So he had to go?"

"Maybe. I don't know, baldy." He didn't even mind the chit-
chat. It kept him occupied, too.

"How's the leg?"

"Hurts a bit."

"Should have set it right before I did the plasma." Barko's
sigh was familiar. He did a lot of that. Some people were just
born to heave one after another. It was a pity, really. The scientist was a decent sort. Must've been why Kope sent him, to get
any morality out of the way.

Decent sorts didn't do well anywhere, inside a Rift or out.

"It's fine." Morov glanced up the street, scanning as if he
were on watch. The amber sheeting on the buildings on one
side ran with headache light, thick and golden as honey. It
had stretched over the buildings across the street from theirs,
too, and even the parts that were caught in shadow ran with
that same migraine glow. Red clouds overhead were strangely
shaped, blobs of heavier stuff than water vapor. Everything in
here was wrong, in one way or another.

"Hey." Barko straightened, shading his eyes with one broad,
filthy hand. "Look at that."

Morov turned, settling his leg a little more firmly. It ached like a sonofabitch. There was no more plasma left in the medikits; it was a wonder Barko had even found the one hypodermic.

A shadow at the far end of the block moved, hugging the ungolden side of the street. A ruby flutter, a lady's handkerchief waved from a window. It paled as it hit the ground, and in the rubescent glare, a thin shape swelled and shrank. Morov's hand dropped to his side, but found only an empty holster.

Losing your sidearm was a court-martial offense. The brig would seem like a goddamn holiday after all this. Asking himself who might have subtracted the piece was stupid. He sure as shit wasn't going to ask for it back and possibly piss her off.

Unless Barko had taken it, but somehow that didn't seem likely.

The thin, wavering shape drew closer, each time fluttering a red, red rag. Barko rubbed at his eyes, as if he didn't believe what he saw. Morov braced himself.

It was the rifter. The fuzz on her head was full of dust, standing straight up. Her face, in that awful glare, had turned into a sere, set icon, the expression that of a deposed queen disdaining the executioner. Tracks on her cheeks had been washed clean, but it was impossible to think of her crying. Those protruding eyes had become large and liquid, full of terrible blank knowledge, and her full, carved lips, barely covering her teeth, had swollen. A trickle of blackness slid from one long narrow nostril, and she bent to scoop up the handkerchief with a stiff, aching motion. Strapped to her back was another load of firewood—sticks, broken pieces of furniture, hedgehog spines that would carry the fire through the night.

There was nobody behind her.

# PART FIVE

✣

# CORMORANT

# 53
# ACTIVE SERVICE

⊰⊹⊱

...since the governing body has seen fit
to interfere, further investment in QR-715
is only mildly profitable at best. Attached
please find a dossier for A-MAJOR HAN K.
OCHKI, the replacement for GENERAL TIMOR
KOPELUND. You will note the gaps in OCH-
KI's CV, which seem to indicate some classified assignments. Our operative on the
ground feels said replacement is dangerous to engage, at least until secondary
sources can be plumbed. Said operative,
having disbursed funding for a secondary
and failed attempt at making objective C-3
(title: CORMORANT) viable, recommends a
"watch-and-wait" attitude. Given that said
operative has already made contact with new
staff at QR-715 and has recruited at least
three, as well as keeping contacts with the

rifter population, it is recommended that
Operative KARL E. ZLOFTER be given a com-
mendation and kept in active service...

    —Memo from the desk of Sidney Polkruv, Chairman
    of Section Committee QR712-QR716, DynaKrom
    Corporation

# 54
# WHAT YOU REALLY DO

⋊╫⋉

Barko handed her the ration packet. "He shot Mako?"

"In the back." The rifter swiped at her face with her red snot-rag instead of the blue one, but it didn't do anything other than smear the dirt around. "I ran."

"Sure." Morov didn't sound like he believed her. "And tomorrow you'll take us to the fairy-tale bird."

"If you want." She laid the rag on her knee. The thin cloth was too dirt-stiff to bend, but she didn't seem to care. "Might be best to go for the wall, though."

"Oh, yeah. Everyone fucking dead and nothing to show for it, that'll go over real well." The captain stretched his wounded leg out straight, wincing slightly. His cigar—unlit, a whole one—dropped from the corner of his mouth; he caught it, irritably. "Fuck that. We've come this far, I wanna see this Cormorant."

"You sure?" She massaged the silvery pouch with quick, rolling motions. The clean tracks on her cheeks were now smudged over. It didn't seem possible for this woman to cry. Maybe she'd run across some throat- and eye-scouring fume, again.

"Maybe heading out of this goddamn place would be best." Barko selected another ration pouch, handed it to Morov. The fire crackled, a cheery sound. "We don't have any more plasma, can't tell if the infection will come back. Or—" *Or an embolism,* he wanted to say. *Or any other goddamn thing.*

"Fuckbuckle your strap, baldy." Morov clenched the pouch in one dirty fist. "It's all the same. Either we go after this thing and die just like everyone else, or we step outside and have to deal with Kopelund. Might as well get something for all this shit. That is, if this bird-thing exists."

"It does." The rifter, solemn-eyed, kept working at her pouch. "Knew a rifter who went in."

Silence. She stared at the fire, flames reflected in her shining pupils.

"The fuck you did." But Morov only sounded weary. He gently removed the cigar, placed it carefully on his straightened knee, and began massaging his ration pouch.

"Ashe knew him too. Piotr Stepanovitch Vanich. Snaketooth, we called him. Always slithering out of trouble." Her mouth turned down at the corners, her swollen eyelids dropping a little, too. "It's a room. The very center of the Rift. You go inside, and it gives you what you want."

"A room?" Barko settled back on his heels. "Oh, for *God's* sake."

"A room." Morov stared at her, forgetting his pouch. It dangled from his dirty fingers. "You're *shitting* me."

The rifter shook her head. "Vanich. Family man. Went in.

Came out, rifted all the way to the slugwall. Found out his house been burned. Whoosh, and just like the house, fam all gone."

"Wait a minute. Vanich." Barko's hands had gone numb. "Almost a decade ago. It was big news. Big house, big family. Everyone dead, even the grandmother."

"Oh, yeah. Wife, kids, mother and father, mother-in-law, cousins. Good rifter, brought out lots of salvage. Fast and mean." She hunched her thin shoulders. "He told people he was gonna wish to be free. Tired of listening to everyone yelling at home all the time. Well, they weren't yelling no more." She folded the top of the pouch, carefully, and tore along the line to make the spout. "Rifters got other stories. It don't give you what you think you want. Just what you *really* do."

Barko shivered, zipping his backpack closed. "Didn't he end up hanging himself?"

"Yeah." She slurped at the pouch, lowered it, and covered her mouth with her hand when she caught him watching. A guilty little movement. So she didn't like anyone watching her eat. It was almost a relief to find out he'd guessed one thing correctly. Chowing down in the canteen must have been an act of strength, or just a plain fuck-you to everyone in the room.

"Son of a *bitch*." Morov stared, his mouth hanging open, his stubble tipped with ruddy firelight and his hair standing up stiffly in every direction. "A *room*? You didn't tell Kopelund this, now did you?"

She shrugged. Her shoulders had filled out a little. "Didn't ask."

"Oh, man." The commander shook his curly head. "You bitch. You lying, sideways *bitch*." He sounded, of all things, grudgingly admiring.

This earned him the briefest of nods. "Don't wanna go back to Guan."

"Who would?" Barko settled with his own ration pouch.

Morov raked back his sweat-stiff hair. "Son of a *bitch*," he repeated. Barko didn't blame him. "A fucking *room*."

The rifter made no reply. Barko began massaging his ration pouch. The heating-bead inside it gave under his fingers with a crunching snap, a smaller sound than Tremaine vanishing into the undergrowth or Eschkov hitting the ground.

"Kope wouldn't have come in himself after it." Barko's hands squeezed, released. He watched the fire leap to caress a few fresh sticks tossed on its heap of coals. "Would he?"

"Not without a whole goddamn legion." Morov sagged against his makeshift bed-pile. They'd have to treat it with the heat-ray again before they settled; the wind had risen at dusk and brought a damp chill on its back.

"He couldn't have covered that up. Not for long, anyway."

"Yeah, well." Morov shut his eyes, finally tearing open his rations with the ease of long practice. "He couldn't cover this up, either. Probably suspected what was coming."

"What do you mean, what was coming?"

A slight gleam from under one eyelid. "Well...shit, I might as well tell you. Remember when he sent in the Rat?"

How could Barko forget? He nodded, and the rifter tensed slightly, taking another long slurp from her pouch and covering her mouth again as she chewed. Or tried to chew, the slurry would slip right down your throat if you let it.

"Well, after that, I sent in a blacksheet." The commander took a mouthful of ration paste. "To Second Branch. Sent another one after Bechter, too. He was going to fuck with the man's pension, for fucksake."

For a few minutes, the fire did all the speaking. It crackled again, a few sparks rising idly on the updraft and winking out. The soot mark on the ceiling was spreading, condensation glistening at its edges, and if it got much damper in here they would probably wake up to find spots all over their bedrolls and clothing.

"You shady bastard," Barko said, finally. An anonymous report even hinting at Kopelund sending people into the Rift again would get a relatively swift response. ILAC bureaucracy ground slow, but it ground exceedingly fine. "So when we get out, they'll fucking arrest us, too."

"Not likely. Just following orders." Morov's tired grin stretched. Amusement made him briefly younger in the uncertain light.

The rifter made a small noise, a stifled chuckle. Barko's wasn't stifled at all. That set Morov off, too, and outside their tiny cave, the sound of human laughter brushed against a dense white fog rising from pavement and weeds alike.

# 55
# STILL IN THE TUBE

⟩╫⟨

*S*tupid. Clumsy. Almost lost a foot.

Vetch fed a few more dry sticks to his small fire, hunching his shoulders. He couldn't stand anymore, he was swaying and weaving too badly. His belt buckle gleamed dully, and his pack, laid right next to him, would be his pillow tonight. Sheer luck had saved him, thrown him back instead of out into the street, landing a hairsbreadth from the wall. His neck ached, and the back of his head was scabbed over. Dizzy from bouncing his skull off concrete, bruised all the way from heels to neck, he'd lain there stunned and thought, *What the fuck am I doing here?*

Didn't matter. A man did what he had to, and if he didn't want to examine why he was crouched in this precarious lean-to, smelling the flat mineral tang of the river and the heatless thick clinging of danger, nobody could force him. It wouldn't do any good, anyway.

Surviving through sheer luck was good enough. He hadn't lost anything, his mapper was secure and his gun was safe. His vision was doubling, but he'd still managed to cut across her wake and come out here, on the very edge of downtown, near what had been a street of high-end boutiques with gold leaf on their windows and well-mended sidewalks. This lean-to was post-Event, maybe another rifter's temporary refuge, and it was clean. Potzegs stacked in a ring in the middle glowed a little, milky opals.

He wasn't hungry, but he eased down to sit cross-legged and chewed at the protein bar anyway, washing it down with half the remaining water in his canteen. With that done, he dug in his mapper, dreamily, staring out the lean-to's triangular door. There was even a pad of overlapping bits of cardboard and scavenged fabric on the north side, far enough from the fire-circle to keep from going up but close enough to feel radiant warmth.

His left pupil was far bigger than his right. The world was a smear of fuzzy light and dark, and his fingers found what they wanted in the mapper. He drew out the capped syringe, tore the cap off, and had to try three times before he could tap it and clear any air bubbles.

Maybe he shouldn't have stopped to eat. He had to aim the needle at his own throat. Everything was whirling, and he had to jab twice before he found the right spot. Then he had to push the plunger down while the triphase plasma scoured up one side of his neck and down the other. Hoping it would get past the blood-brain barrier and the brain trauma wasn't too—

The sitting rifter toppled sideways, landing hard on the packed dirt. He didn't manage to roll onto the cardboard bed, and the syringe jutted up from his neck, half its cargo of glow-yellow plasma still in the tube.

Sometimes, when a rifter's luck ran out, it didn't kill him right away.

The fire, a chemical reaction, would continue as long as it had fuel. Outside the lean-to, tiny tongues of thick white vapor rose from the sidewalks and roads, thickening as the day's heat escaped the earth and made its way past layers of air and magnetism, out into the vacuum of space.

# 56
# WHAT WE CAME FOR

⋺╫⋲

Svin jerked into full alertness, her ears burning and her blanket almost sopping wet. She rolled off the counter without thinking about it, landing next to Barko with a thud. His deep, whistling breathing halted as he lunged into wakefulness, and she got her feet under her with a brief, thumping scramble, kicking his arm.

"Ow!" He was about to object further, but she clapped her hand over his mouth.

"Shhhh," she breathed. "Listen."

He shook his bald head, blinking furiously. He probably didn't hear it, so she peeled her palm away and hissed in frustration, grabbing his arms and shaking him with far more strength than her wiry little frame seemed capable of.

"Get up," she whispered fiercely. "Get your pack. *Now*."

"Whafuck?" Morov shifted on his bed-pile. Little scurrying sounds proved the heat-ray had been ineffective as he sat bolt-upright, groping for his rifle.

"Put that away," she told him. "We have to go. Now."

Thankfully, he didn't argue, just began struggling upward. Svin grabbed his arm and hauled, then grabbed the light pack she'd insisted he put together before they went to sleep. It was on his shoulders in a trice, but Barko was still rubbing his eyes and yawning.

"Hurry *up*," she whisper-yelled.

Poking and prodding, she got them to the door and peered out through the vapor-fogged glass. The sound drew closer, scraping against her nerves. A crackling, like ice forming on a river's skin. It was getting closer, too.

She *could* have just slid off the counter the other way, hit the door, and been gone before they woke up. It wouldn't have been hard.

The fog closed around them, but even its choking curtain couldn't deaden the noise. They heard it now, too, and Barko kept glancing back as she led them away, not on the left or right sidewalk but squarely in the middle of the road. Hexmoss grew on what had been painted stripes and the moisture had made it balloon, sending up tiny bright-red sacs on short thick stalks. When they burst, fluorescent green particles would scatter, whisked by stray breezes, and the moss might find another food source.

Svin very carefully didn't step on them, and neither did the men. They followed her closely, their breathing labored and loud in the semi-stillness. Barko looked over his shoulder again.

"Don't," she told him. She wanted to get out a strip-and-bob, but it wouldn't be any use in the fog. Instinct and other senses had to keep her alive.

"It's moving," he whispered back, two awestruck little words. *Of course it's moving*, she wanted to tell him. *Why do you think I got you out of there?* She knew what he was seeing—the amber resin, now tar-black and gleaming, running with moisture, creeping up the sides of the building they had slept in, making that slight icy-rubbing sound as it stretched bit by bit, flexing over iron, glass, wood, concrete, brick. When the sun rose, it would turn translucent, but she didn't intend to be around to see that.

Morov cursed, hobbling on his cane. Even at this speed they would outpace the black goo. The alleys slowed it down, tendrils throwing themselves from one wall and failing, splatting against the ground—or succeeding, splashing against the far wall and spreading, digging fingers in and thickening. It moved at a leisurely pace, but Svin was less worried about that than about the sense of dread in the fog. It was too thick to see very far ahead, though they could look back and peer through the hole in the vapor made by their passage.

"Stop looking back." She grabbed Barko's shoulder, dug her fingers in as hard as she could. "Don't make it notice us, for fucksake."

Then she let go and plunged forward again, into the mist.

>∦<

Sunrise found them an hour and a half later, working parallel to the river along a street that had once been high-end boutiques. Their antique signs creaked unsteadily in the freshening breeze, and the trees along either side of the boulevard had outgrown their spindly pollution-crippled phase. They stretched tall, wide, and gnarl-barked, naked limbs showing a fuzz of golden-green, circles of fallen leaves around each of the deciduous ones making wheeling patterns on pavement no step had disturbed for a long, long time. Some were bearded with gray moss that tinkled softly as the breeze shook by, and the tubs in front of some of the storefronts—a haberdasher's, a pharmacy, a milliner's and a fashionable atelier, a coffeehouse with its outside seating area full of rusting tables and age-spotted chairs—held remnants of ornamental flowers gone to seed as well as the rattling brown pods of winter-blasted weeds. Glancing downhill every time there was a break in the structures, Svin could see the river's false placidity. The fog was retreating in streamers for its watery refuge, and it had cleared enough that she could throw a strip when she felt uncertain. Uneasiness ran below her skin, a feeling like someone was breathing on her naked nape.

She kept them away from the buildings, because every window and glass-paneled door held thin threads of almost-breakage, a pattern of stress-stars as if something had hit from the inside, wanting to get out.

"If I'd known, I'd've brought a fucking bomb," Barko said. "Blow that shit up."

Morov's ersatz cane made a clicking sound on the cracked, bare street. "Why not just sell tickets?"

"Christ." The scientist dabbed at his forehead with a cream-colored snot-rag Svin had found in Eschkov's pack. "I know enough about human beings to guess it's a bad fucking idea."

"Money-back guarantee. But nobody would ever ask for it, or they'd have to admit they wanted disaster in the first place." Morov snorted a bitter little laugh. "We'd make millions." *Click-tap* went his cane as they paused for a moment, and his forehead was speckled with little beads of sweat. His eyes glittered, too, and the bandage on his upper thigh wasn't as pristine white as it had been. A thin spot of crimson had worn through at its center.

"I don't think I'd want to." The scientist glanced, a little guiltily, at Svin, who swung a bob lazily, deciding which direction to throw it. "What about you, rifter? You gonna go in?"

She shrugged. "Dunno."

"How can you not know?" Morov coughed, spat. The wad of phlegm splattered against a hexmoss-loaded stripe; tiny threads of violet steam rose. The red pods had shriveled—the moss would not be spreading along this street today.

"Not there yet." She checked wind direction, swung the bob some more. They were getting close. Each way forward felt hazardous. The problem was guessing which one was only mildly dangerous and which one was actively carnivorous. Cutting through an alley wasn't a good option for a few blocks; the shadows inside the ones on the left were too thick, and the right got them closer to the river. It would have to be the streets.

"But what do you think?" Now it was Barko persisting. Some color had stolen into his cheeks under his gray, thickening beard, but his head was as innocent of hair as ever. A few thin scabs at his temple, mere scratches. His stride had grown longer. He didn't look cheerful, but he was certainly a little more spry.

Some people took to the Rift despite themselves.

The sun had just broken the eastern horizon. In the distance, birds were serenading the return of the daystar. Around them, though, a bubble of silence swelled. Here and there, in the circles of fallen leaves around the frowning trees, flashes of discolored bone showed. Tiny skeletons, some subtly altered— no squirrel had teeth that sharp.

Yes, staying away from the buildings, and the trees, was a good idea here.

"We're close," she said, finally. "I can still take you back to the wall. You could cross later today." She didn't look at either of them, focusing instead four or five blocks down where the fog slithered across the street, a gliding, glinting greasepaint rope. "Probably safest."

Morov coughed again. This time he didn't spit. "Might as well get what we came for," he said, finally. "Barko?"

The scientist took his time. Maybe he was thinking it over. Or maybe he was just struggling against the inevitable. Svin didn't care to look at him and figure out which. If they decided to go back to the slugwall, she'd take them. The odds were in favor of them surviving passage through, and Morov could get his leg treated. They might even be called heroes, surviving QR-715. Kopelund, with his piggy little eyes looking for the next angle, might even listen when they told him the Cormorant wasn't what he thought.

For a moment she thought about *him* coming into the Rift. Now *that* would have been interesting.

"Are you sure?" Barko finally said. "You don't look so good, Morov."

"Fuck you," was the commander's equable reply. "Let's go."

Svin tossed the bob at an angle, watching its rise and rapid descent. She didn't wait to hear more, just began walking again.

# 57
# THE MEMO THAT SHRANK

⊰╫⊱

His tibia had thermabonded wrong. Each step was a corkscrewing reminder, and his hip had begun to hurt with a dull deep ache as well. Morov followed the rifter's skinny shoulders, watching the bag bouncing on her hip, envying how she tested each step before she committed her weight. Behind him, Barko lumbered, and he envied the scientist's plodding, normal steps as well.

His thigh hurt, too. If they'd had another hypo of plasma, he might have been okay. As it was, the throbbing from the deep gash was returning, and so was the fever.

He was going to die while they slept tonight. Or he was going to stagger into whatever piece-of-shit hole the rifter said granted wishes, and die there.

The boulevard widened. They were in the belt orbiting downtown now, and the sun beat down once more. The fog had vanished, and the buildings on either side were covered with long yellow vines exhaling a weird, sweetish rot-smell. Their leaves were long and knife-edged, clacking when the wind rose in irregular cycles. Moving air whistled between the rising structures. Soon they'd be in the skyscrapers, and he couldn't shake the idea that if any of the buildings had decayed or been shattered by the Event, they might collapse on the tiny animals at their feet. The rifter's nuts-and-hankies wouldn't keep *that* disaster at bay.

There was also the uncomfortable feeling that the Rift was, well, *breathing*. The whooshing between buildings down toward the river halted every once in a while, paired with a funny head-lightening sensation until the next bellows-squeeze. Each time the breeze rose, sweat cooled on his forehead, cheeks, nape, hands. The light pack weighed him down, straps cutting cruelly. Was this what Eschkov had felt right before he keeled over?

Nope, Morov's heart was fine. He kept walking, aware the rifter was slowing to match his cane-clicking pace. Frustration boiled in the bottom of his belly. He deserved better than this. Kope shouldn't have sent him in here. Shouldn't have sent Tolstoy or Senkin or Mako either. Who knew what that motherfucker Brood had planned for, with that cold-blooded cocksucker in charge?

The rifter's dim shape as she watched Brood loom over him... the bitch had saved his life, but that didn't mean much. He'd been dead the instant grenade shrapnel pierced his thigh. Should have turned around and headed for the wall then. Proper medical attention and sending another blacksheet in. They were anonymous, of course, and this was a juicy bit of dirt to have on your commanding officer. Kopelund probably would have sent someone else to take care of him in a hospital bed, though, especially if he suspected what Morov had done.

The rifter wasn't anything great—for Chrissake, she'd eaten

a man's *eye*—but at least she'd been there when it counted. Brood might have just clamped Morov's nose and mouth shut; he'd been too weak to struggle. A little bit of choking, a little bit of twitching, and it could have been all over.

Morov stared at the pavement. Pre-Event concrete was a lot better and more durable than the current stuff. The shock to the world economy meant that even though they knew how to make higher-quality shit, they didn't have the resources. It had taken twenty goddamn years to get back to seventy-five percent of pre-Event GDP in most places.

They stopped so Morov could drink from Barko's canteen. The rifter found water, God alone knew where, but she wouldn't say how she did it.

Barko said something, and her reply was too quiet. Morov's head jerked up. "What?"

"I asked if she thought it was aliens." Barko sloshed his own canteen a little. "The Event. We're getting close to the center, or at least, I *think* it's the center."

"It is." The rifter crouched in the middle of the street, an arm's length away from that vile, nasty moss with shriveled red beads all over it. "Right smack zero."

"So, do you?" Barko persisted.

"Dunno." For a moment, it looked as if that was all they were going to get out of her. Then her chin rose and she gazed thoughtfully at the skyscrapers looming close. "Ashe said maybe. Knew a guy who thought it was us."

"Us?" A mouthful of tepid water smoothed Morov's throat. The goddamn cane made his shoulder hurt, too. His deepest fucking desire right now was for his leg to be fixed and a good bed to sleep for a week in, as well as some chow that wasn't heated in pouches. An apple. Maybe a hard, sour peach, puckering up his mouth and filling his nose with hot saline. God *damn*, but that sounded good. "The shit you say."

"Maybe not us now. But in the future. Salvage is tech, right? Some scientist gets his pet project going and it rips something up. Either *then* or now. This the biggest Rift, and lots of government all over before the Event."

Barko let out a short sharp sound that tried to be amusement and failed miserably. "Wouldn't that just be the shittiest joke ever. *We* made the Rifts."

"Or it could be things from outside," she continued, by far the most Morov had ever heard her speak. "Time's funny in here, gravity too. Things from outside our space. Eggheads like him been fiddling around ever since the world wars. Breaking atoms, breaking every fuckbuckle thing they can. What if something saw them doing it? Came to have a look around, found out we're fucking meatsacks, and left? All this just fucking trash left after a picnic."

Barko's mouth hung slightly open as he regarded her. He probably never thought someone who didn't talk had enough brains to grind up a question that fine. "Never thought of it that way before," he said, screwing the cap back on his canteen.

She made a small spitting sound, and craned her neck to examine Morov. He stood, because getting down into a crouch was impossible and once he sat down he wasn't sure he was going to get back up again without help. When she unfolded, he realized again just how small she was. Malnutrition and solitary in Guan would turn anyone into a rag of their former self. Maybe her eyes and teeth weren't too big, they just hadn't gotten the memo that shrank the rest of her.

Her tongue flicked out, wet those lips. With some more weight on her, they would be lush instead of oversized. She might even grow some hips and tits.

"You sure? We could make the shimmer near here by dusk." She pointed, a brief movement with a thin, dirty finger extended, its nail bitten all the way down. "That way. It's near, and it wants us gone."

So *had* she been leading them in circles while the group was whittled down?

Did it matter? Morov decided it didn't at the moment. There was only one thing that did. "Which way's the Cormorant?"

She pointed in another direction, a forty-five-degree angle. There was a street heading that way, a concrete canyon already losing what little sunlight had managed to reach its floor. It looked cold, and the Rift exhaled again, soft wet paintbrushes flicking over Morov's cheeks.

"I told you," he said. "I want to see what we came for. Let's get on with it."

Barko didn't argue, but he did dig in his pack and bring out one of his little handheld devices. A strap with sensors went over the scientist's chest, and Morov thought of ancient warriors needing help with their armor before a decisive battle. So he hobbled closer, and buckled what he could with his thick, clumsy, swelling fingers.

# 58
# WHITE WINGS

⊱╬⊰

The sun, halfway between noon and horizon, was a glaring golden eye glimpsed between high concrete spires, their tops afire with its gaze. There was a clatter as Morov dropped his cane, and Barko grabbed the younger man's arm before he could topple. "Shit," the scientist muttered. "Should have put the plasma in a little higher on the leg. Or more of it."

"Doesn't matter." Morov leaned on him, awkward but not overly heavy. "Damn thing slipped. Sorry."

The rifter wrapped a scrap of cloth around the head of the splintered bar-support, tying it with quick neat fingers. It would soak up the sweat—Morov was wet all over, and his breath had started to wheeze again. Barko walked beside him, sometimes stepping ahead to toe chunks of fallen concrete out of the way. Every once in a while the rifter would stop dead, and moments later tiny pieces of concrete or metal would peel from the edifices around them. Even a pebble could kill you if it dropped from high enough, and Barko's back prickled painfully each time he heard the clattering from other parts of downtown.

The buildings began to crumble more thoroughly the further they traveled. After a while, the sunlight was scouring half-tumbled monuments of twisted rebar and vaporized concrete, the road starred with wreckage. Even further, as the shadows lengthened and a soft breath of a warm spring afternoon reached its zenith, creeping between the ruins, the stresslines from some unimaginable almost-explosion became clearly visible, raking across the buildings. The rifter had chosen the one street that was relatively clear, but Morov had to be helped over wreckage too big to skirt, and eventually the rifter took the captain's pack and carried it as well as her own. The skyscrapers melted away, crumbled into dust, and strange yellowish-green grass with fleshy pods at the bottom of each blade and full, nodding seedheads began to spring up. Trashwood reared in the more sheltered corners, scrub brush daubed with bright fresh green. One or two spiny copse-clots appeared, but the rifter kept them well away. She threw her little rags more frequently now, and often paused even when one did what it should and fell without shredding, or hovering, or being smacked aside with a terrific *crack*, as if hit by a cricket bat. Birds—or birdlike things—rose and fell, diving into the grass or twittering among the bushes; there was a gray flash of something that could have been a rabbit once or twice.

Morov's cane sank into the damp earth more than once, but they didn't have to go far. The pasture was roughly circular, in the very heart of downtown, the sides of skyscrapers shearing away in irregular curves at its borders. The rhythmic breezes were softer here, and rustled the undulating grass in discrete, discreet lines.

"So this is the center," Barko whispered. The spectra, strapped securely to his fist, was showing off-the-charts readings in recognizable patterns. Each time the Rift took another breath, every damn emission it could read hit a plateau, then slowly fell off. Nice, even, regular—he could barely believe his eyes. Where was the randomness? Where was the—

Morov coughed, wheezing. "Shit," he said, very loud in the stillness. "Can't breathe."

"Almost there." The rifter pointed, her scabbed palms dark and her dirty fingernails brutally short.

After the wrecked buildings and the sudden grassland, it was almost absurdly anticlimactic. A weathered shack perched on a slow rolling rise, its west wall snug against a huge gray-barked tree in full leaf. The closer they got, the warmer it became, until the temperature settled on a balmy summer's day with just enough wind to keep the sweat cooled but not enough to raise a dust storm. The tree looked normal, except for that smooth, sheer bark. The leaves were somewhat oakish, with deep-fingered fringe, but its seeds had a maple's whirling wings.

The shack's silvered, weathered wood was the exact same shade as the tree bark. The scientist blinked, trying to decide whether the house had been built or had simply *grown* there, an abscess on the tall, graceful, leafy column.

The door faced them. Sagging leather hinges did not squeak, but the wood itself made a scraping, singing noise as the breeze pushed at it. The rifter's dark fuzz of hair moved a little under the wind; Barko's stubble tingled, trying to stand straight up like the hairs on his arms and chest and back and legs.

Morov kept coughing. He'd gone alarmingly cheesy-pale, and it occurred to Barko that moving around after the application of plasma might have worked a blood clot free inside the commander's body. Embolism. Those little bastards tended to lodge in the lungs. "Oh, shit—" he began, but Morov dropped the cane and staggered forward. The rifter, her head tilted slightly, watched them with her wide, dark eyes, and for a moment Barko saw it again—the unconscious, regal beauty a stray angle could give her in this summer afternoon light.

Anything could be lovely, if you turned it the right way.

Morov staggered, coughed rackingly, made it another few steps. The rifter didn't move to help him, and Barko hesitated. Throwing him into the house, the Cormorant—if that was what this was, and not just another random, deadly piece of the Rift—what would that do? Stopping him so he could choke out his last staring up into a sky that was too blue, with fluffy white clouds that looked like pendulous breasts and streaks of black-oil shimmer that hypnotized the unwary, was that the right thing to do?

Barko couldn't tell.

The captain tripped, his wounded leg bending with a crunch, and fell over the threshold. He screamed breathlessly, a despairing sound cut short with a lungwhistle, and the entire shack shuddered. The tree shook its leaves, and white flashed among its branches.

Butterflies, or something close to it. They poured out, fringed white wings holding black spots in their centers, and Barko half yelled, half moaned, stumbling back in disgust. They looked *wrong*, their long fleshy bodies too heavy for those papery wings to keep aloft. Some circled the rifter, who simply stared, her generous mouth slack instead of tight with pain; a few fluttered toward Barko, who dumbly raised the spectra as if it would ward them off. The majority cascaded onto Morov's legs and flashed into the gloom over the threshold.

They had short-stubby proboscises, and the sound of those tiny blunt needles sinking past fabric and into skin was a pick-pocking murmur that threatened to bring the last ration pouch Barko had ingested out in a painful acidic rush. They spread their wings and preened, and Barko's vision blurred. Hot water slid down his cheeks.

After a short while, he became aware of his own voice, raggedly repeating Morov's name, and one other thing.

"I'm not going in...I'm not, I can't. I'm not going in there. Morov...*Morov*, you asshole..."

Neither he nor the rifter had a chrono, so they had no idea it was precisely 4:37 p.m.

>╫╫<

They camped at the edge of the grassy circle, their backs against a chunk of concrete that had once been a statue of a dictator. It lay facedown and broken, but it sheltered them from both the wind and from any prying eyes. No fire, but at least the ration pouches were hot, and they had Morov's blankets as well as their own.

The rifter made herself a nest in the most acute angle, scooting back until she could rest her head against the torn inside of what had been a broad strapping statue-chest. She settled, slurping from her pouch and covering her mouth afterward with that same half-guilty movement. Barko did his best not to look at her during mouthfuls, staring instead out over the undulating grass. The sunset was beautiful—masses of fire dying under a slow assault of ink, the colors between night and the end of weary day bleeding rapidly through too many shades to count, too many shades for the human eye to distinguish all at once.

When they had both finished, Barko swallowed the last of the dessert syrup—something probably meant to taste like cherry—and chased it with the flat, tepid water from his canteen. "Ozymandias," he said, finally.

The rifter rested her chin on her thin knees. "What's that?"

"Poem." He indicated the shattered statue. "About a guy seeing a statue of a conquerer, lying in the dirt. *Look on my works, ye Mighty, and despair.*"

"Huh." She thought this over, or maybe she just dismissed it. Was there any poetry in her thin frame? She didn't seem like the sort.

"Did you go to school?" He could no longer see the smear halfway to the horizon that was the listing, horrifying little shack.

She nodded, but didn't add details.

Barko closed his eyes. Wished they could have a fire. "What happens out here at night?"

A short pause, and he could almost see her thoughtful expression. Another man might have mistaken it for stupidity, but nobody stupid could have survived the past few days. Then again, brains was no indicator of survival ability, either.

"Dunno," she said, finally. The wind rustled through the grass. "Feels safe enough."

"Okay." He thought about it, and decided—much to his own surprise—that she was right. "That's funny. It does."

"Make a rifter of you yet, bald man." A hint of a smile, and the bloody sunset light made her regal again for a bare moment.

He shuddered so hard his pack, sitting obediently next to him, made a small *whoof* noise. "No, thanks. I just want to get out of here." He tilted his head back, examined the sky. A few stars glimmered, and he wondered if they were the same ones he'd see outside the Rift. "Was that really the Cormorant?"

"Yes." Short, definite, crisp.

"Do you think he wished for—"

"He was dead before he crossed the drift, baldy."

Was she lying? How could she tell? Did he believe her?

Some things it was best to just not think about at all.

"Are you coming out with me?" He didn't mean it to sound so wistful.

"Maybe." Her face dropped into her knees and her breathing lengthened, and that single time, Barko knew beyond a doubt she was lying.

# 59
## COOLING ENTROPY

✦✝✦

Inside a slumping triangular lean-to on the edge of downtown, thin wisps of smoke rose from a bed of cooling ash. The fire, having hugged all the fuel it could find, settled into cooling entropy. The side-lying shape in deeper shadow, an amber spine protruding from its slack neck, lay in a single bar of sunshine from a rent in the roof. The golden light glinted off a large, twisting belt buckle, its grooves and whorls darkened with grime.

# 60
# OLD ENOUGH TO KNOW

⋈

With just the scientist, it didn't take as long as Svin thought it would to reach the slugwall from the core. Some ways were shorter than others, and while the Rift might resist you going in, it generally didn't mind so much when you were heading *out*.

She stopped more than she had to, though, thinking carefully about each part of the route. No reason to get lull-stupid.

The scientist plodded behind her, and after a while, he stopped talking. It was a relief. He didn't start again until lunchtime, when they halted at the edge of a residential district. The houses had transformed into spongy, resilient material exuding an acrid moisture. The day was clear, no caustic fumes, but dark oilslick clouds were gathering over the river. Looked like a sweep starting, and if it hit before she could reach a safe hole, she might end up just as dead as Morov.

"Funny." He broke off half a dry-ration cracker, handed it to her. "Ashe said I'd never go into a Rift."

Svin's chest threatened to cramp. She breathed out, softly,

and examined the pressed bar of dehydrated fiber packed with sweeteners and ersatz vitamins. The jagged edge where he'd broken it showed the striations—gigantic machines had extruded this, dried it, packaged it, sorted it into boxes. Then it had been shipped and unpacked, put in kits, shipped again to a storeroom, requisitioned for this trip, and now it was going into the machinery of her body, that marvelous thing that turned everything she put in her mouth to shit.

A lot of trouble for too small a return, really. Just like everything else.

"So she was wrong." Svin nibbled at the bar, holding her free hand cupped to hide her lips and to catch any crumbs.

"She wasn't wrong about much."

*Who gonna be my sweet thing?* A faint faraway voice. Memory was like the old pressed-wax cylinders, it wore out after a while. At least, some things did. Then there were things like the screams when a tangle of living metal sucked the fluids from a man, contracting to draw out more and more before it began to drip with red resin to strip out all the minerals and fat-soluble nutrients. And things like Ashe next to her in the dark, her mouth a sticky delight and lightning playing through Svinga's veins.

"You could Rift, if you wanted," Svinga said, finally. She took another nibble, gauging just how dry and old the bar was. After she swallowed the small wad of tasteless cardboard, she decided to tell him the whole truth. "But you'd die soonish. You don't listen enough."

He nodded. Once he got out, he'd take a shower, and that head of his would be polished bright as ever. He'd go back to the gray drudgery of daily routine, but he might even appreciate it now.

He didn't ask her *listen to what?*

Maybe he was already old enough to know.

>+|+<

This part of the slugwall looked deceptively like a straight line, and the swirls in it moved almost sluggishly. They jerked instead of flowed, at least at first. Svinga crouched, watching the blur, tasting it in that secret place far back on her tongue. Barko settled beside her, much more easily than he would have at the beginning of the expedition. Exercise did him good. He looked younger, too—the circles under his eyes had lessened despite the rough sleeping conditions, and his incipient paunch had faded. He looked wiry now, much fitter, and the hodgepodge of stuff attached to his pack made him look like a soaker.* There were rifters who swore people could live inside, subsistence farming and stripping enough salvage to get by.

The idea had its attractions.

The slugwall began to soften. Barko watched, his eyebrows drawn together, and he probably felt the change coming. "Hey." He shifted his weight a little. "You gonna go in *there?*"

No need to ask what he meant. "Ashe thought I should."

"Yeah, well." He didn't have to say any more.

He straightened his legs and began the process of getting up slightly before she did. She made sure his pack was well strapped, and his precious spectra was lodged in his palm. The energy wall might fry it, but he just shook his head when she pointed it out. "So I lose a hand," he said. "Big deal."

---

* A long-term rifter—someone who goes in meaning to stay for more than a few days.

"You could lose all the data."

"I got everything from the center backed up on buffered chips. Kope won't be happy, but he can at least sell *that*." A curious look went over his dirty face, but he shook his head when her eyebrows rose inquiringly. "Doesn't matter. It's coming, isn't it."

She nodded. "Few minutes at most."

"You waiting with me?"

"Of course." She didn't add, *you fuckbuckle idiot*. Or anything else, like *be careful* or the most useless words of all, *good-bye*. Instead, she repeated herself. "Go fast. Hit it at the angle I push you at. Soon's you're through—"

"—Drop and roll. And breathe out right before you hit."

She clapped him approvingly on the shoulder, and the moment came along too soon, tearing through the surface of *now*. She shoved him at the right angle, taking a few running steps to add her force to his, coiled her arms, and pushed off with legs and arms both as hard as she could.

Barko the scientist vanished through the blur. It rippled, the weak point in the fabric eddying as the blur closed around the dark smear, and there was nothing left of him on this side. He hadn't been cut in half midstream, his legs on this side and his trunk over there. She'd done the best she could.

She sank back into her waiting position, and *listened*.

Finally, it came, faint and faraway. *What you doing?* Ashe whispered.

"Thinking," Svin whispered back. "Shut up." Her chin relaxed, and the corners of her mouth tilted up. Her eyes swelled with hot water she blinked away, and finally, she rose and turned away from the wall, feeling for a bob.

# 61
# THE CLOSEST THING

✴╫╳

OR-715 Admin Center bustled with fresh activity. Sardies from the garrison sweated on the drillyard, new sergeants and captains barking orders. In the corridors, janitorial staff scurried. There was no more loafing like there had been under Kopelund, no more comfortable little niches, no more thriving illicit trade in government supplies. In a little while, the new power in the administration would begin the delicate process of extending his reach, but for right now, spring cleaning was in order. Scientists were called to the head office and given packets from Central with fresh directives, along with the warning that there would be tight deadlines for further papers submitted, and the loopholes in the funding system had been closed.

Kopelund's office was much less polished and much more active now, the window firmly shut even on hot days. Paperwork was ruthlessly organized and filed as soon as the new leader had perused it. Two full-time secretaries from Second Branch, both young broad-shouldered men with crewcuts and smart red-sashed uniforms, kept the appointment schedule running clockwork-neat. The fleet of leavs and transports was being refurbished—amazing, really, how much funding there was once the holes in the dam were plugged.

After a frugal lunch—a blushing-red apple from the market, a crumbling slice of bryndza,* and a quarter-round of coarse black bread, washed down with a flagon of very weak beer— Agent-Major Ochki suppressed a belch and settled in the hard slatted wooden chair he had requested instead of Kopelund's cushioned monstrosity. He had cleared the desk before leaving precisely at noon, but there were already three reports sitting in his in-box. It was the nature of the work, of course. In a few months, he would hand this installation over to someone a little less...weak-minded than the unfortunate Kopelund.

The first report was on the discovery of some very expensive medical supplies in a disused corner of the storerooms, includ- ing quite a few syringes of triplasma from the older medikits. The person responsible for squirreling them away had not been found yet, but the junior agent in charge of that sector of the building had a few suspects. Ochki initialed precisely in the box provided, to show he had read the report, then picked up a blue pencil and noted that said junior agent could use whatever methods necessary to discover the thief.

Ochki turned to the second report, which had a red stripe at the top. That denoted some kind of border incident, and he settled his spectacles more firmly, peering through them. In ten minutes his bodyguard would come in with a tray bearing the coffeepot and two mugs, and Ochki looked forward to that

---

* A type of sheep-milk cheese.

postprandial cordial. It was one of the few pleasures he allowed himself in these benighted times.

The timestamp was 4:37 p.m., yesterday. Apparently the fellows watching Sector H-13 had shot at something emerging from the Rift's energy wall. Ochki frowned slightly—they were requesting alcohol rations, a practice he did not see the utility of in many occasions, but it was traditional.

The "something" turned out to be a scientist from the physics sector, filthy and disheveled, carrying a pack crammed with rations, equipment, and attached to a mangy bedroll.

Ochki tut-tutted softly. He knew, of course, about Kopelund's little fantasy. Well, *that* was best swept under the rug, and quickly. A tinge of impatience married to annoyance was swiftly quashed—his superiors trusted him with delicate matters, and whispers of something in the middle of the largest Rift in the world needed careful handling. In fact, the last of many anonymous blacksheets sent in to detail Kopelund's less-savory activities had only reached higher levels because of that strange, silly word.

*Cormorant.*

It took him a few moments to find the requisite forms. Half the alcohol ration was approved, the corpse and everything it carried was to be processed in D Wing with the specialists he would have to request from Central. No doubt everything would be riddled with bullets. Ochki would have to question the tower guards personally, to ascertain if anything the physicist carried had "vanished." Perhaps more of Kopelund's hapless group would stumble out of the Rift in the upcoming weeks, though the odds were—to put it mildly—extremely low. Though there had been movement in the B sector not too long ago, and a patrol had found nothing but a collection of blue and yellow beads scattered haphazard across half-frozen grass near the slugwall itself.

By the time Artev the bodyguard arrived with the expected coffee, Ochki was stapling together the last of the forms. His Incident Report Form only needed a second reading and a signature, to make everything official. The bodyguard read Ochki's expression with a flicker of his dark, good-natured eyes, and called for a secretary.

It was good to be efficient, Ochki mused. Next week he would process death certificates for the rest of the group Kopelund had sent on that foolish little escapade.

The third report was a routine personnel transfer request, and Ochki gave it his full attention while he sipped at his coffee. The rats were fleeing the tightening ship, indeed.

He had already filed away the unlucky physicist's name, the closest thing to forgetting it.

# 62
# THE BEST JOKE

⤜╫⤛

Black clouds swelled, streaming up from the river. Scorch-white spears jabbed from earth to sky and back again. A heavy petrichor fume rose from the bending grasses, the just-leafing trees and the evergreens, the flowers and the weeds. Rain was coming, and with it what the rifters called a sweep—a pressure wall amped up to eleven, a tsunami of air or energy or both. You didn't want to stand in the way of that leveling wind, or test your luck with the jabbing crackling discharges that changed whatever they touched. Some told stories about Rift-lightning striking an unlucky structure or animal and converting it to glass, or giving birth to several spinning grav anomalies that didn't have to get near you to kill you—they just had to fight over your molecules, and you could be shredded in an eyeblink.

Over the small gray shack with its sheltering smooth-barked tree, a single patch of clear night sky lingered. Around it, the sweep whirled and collided with itself, clouds stacking and tearing at each other, chaos flickering between billows of ink starred with rending crashes of pallid energy.

The tree's glossy gray trunk creaked as the wind freshened, flirting near the sorry structure. Something white lay on its doorstep—the butterflies clung to their shelter, their legs and proboscises still buried deep. Their wings fluttered. The black spots on each had swollen, and the wings were now edged with black as well, resembling nothing so much as wavy dark hair. A single unlit cigar, thrown free, lay discarded in the flesh-bulbed grass near the doorway, its seedheads flattening in the breeze.

There is something else on the doorstep, too.

It is a white rag, tied to a heavy, ordinary nut. It has been arranged with care, and under its small weight is a threadbare piece of paper with careful childish writing. It flutters, like the wings. It has not managed to cross the threshold.

The sweep, when it achieves its full strength, might drive it into the Cormorant despite the layer of peace that surrounds the structure, a fish leaping into a mouth too constricted for its cargo of longing.

Is there movement, deeper in the gray shack's interior? It doesn't look like much—four flimsy walls, a roof more holes than solidity, no sign of interior partitions for bedroom, kitchen, a hole for shit to drop into. Yet overhead, there are stars in an oval slice of sky darker than the ink-swirl clouds, gem-bright fires no earthly observer would recognize.

Through the noise of the storm, of resin shattering in the Alley and windows creaking elsewhere, concrete falling and rising as the Rift turns uneasily in its half sleep, wood snapping and shrieks of the boogaloos cowering in huddled masses wherever they can find some shelter, howling from whatever predators would ride these wild waves, mipsiks singing their half-hooting, half-human songs, and the wrack of any storm, comes a single thread of sound.

*Listen.*

It is laughter, a nasal wheeze at one end, the kind of belly-holding merriment when a good friend has told the best joke and every meeting of their gaze with yours provokes a fresh cascade of helpless laughter. It's also a familiar sound; once you've heard that particular rasp-edged voice, you don't forget it.

*Listen harder. Listen again.*

Somewhere in the sweep, Ashe the Rat is laughing.

Laughing, in fact, fit to die.

# extras

orbit

# meet the author

LILITH SAINTCROW was born in New Mexico, bounced around the world as an Air Force brat, and fell in love with writing when she was ten years old. She currently lives in Vancouver, Washington.

# if you enjoyed
## CORMORANT RUN,

### look out for

# TRAILER PARK FAE
## Gallow and Ragged

### by

## Lilith Saintcrow

*Jeremiah Gallow is just another construction worker, and that's the way he likes it. He's left his past behind, but some things cannot be erased. Like the tattoos on his arms that transform into a weapon, or that he was once closer to the Queen of Summer than any half-human should be. But now Gallow is dragged back into the world of enchantment, danger, and fickle fae—by a woman who looks uncannily like his dead wife. Her name is Robin, and her secrets are more than enough to get them both killed.*

# extras

Jeremiah Gallow, once known as the Queensglass, stood twenty stories above the pavement, just like he did almost every day at lunchtime since they'd started building a brand-new headquarters for some megabank or another.

He was reasonably sure the drop wouldn't kill him. Cars creeping below were shiny beetles, the walking mortals dots of muted color, hurrying or ambling as the mood took them. From this height, they were ants. Scurrying, just like the ones he worked beside, sweating out their brief gray lives.

A chill breeze resonated through superstructure, iron girders harpstrings plucked by invisible fingers. He was wet with sweat, exhaust-laden breeze mouthing his ruthlessly cropped black hair. Poison in the air just like poison in the singing rods and rivets, but neither troubled a Half. He had nothing to fear from cold iron.

No mortal-Tainted did. A fullblood sidhe would be uncomfortable, nervous around the most inimical of mortal metals. *The more fae, the more to fear.*

Like every proverb, true in different interlocking ways.

Jeremiah leaned forward still further, looking past the scarred toes of his dun workboots. The jobsite was another scar on the seamed face of the city, a skeleton rising from a shell of orange and yellow caution tape and signage to keep mortals from bruising themselves. Couldn't have civilians wandering in and getting hit on the head, suing the management or anything like that.

A lone worker bee, though, could take three steps back, gather himself, and sail right past the flimsy lath barrier. The fall would be studded and scarred by clutching fingers of steel and cement, and the landing would be sharp.

If he was singularly unlucky he'd end up a Twisted, crippled monstrosity, or even just a half-Twisted unable to use glamour— or any other bit of sidhe chantment—without it warping him

376

further. Shuffling out an existence cringing from both mortal and sidhe, and you couldn't keep a mortal job if you had feathers instead of hair, or half your face made of wood, or no glamour to hide the oddities sidhe blood could bring to the surface.

Daisy would have been clutching at his arm, her fear lending a smoky tang to her salt-sweet mortal scent. She hated heights.

The thought of his dead wife sent a sharp, familiar bolt of pain through his chest. Her hair would have caught fire today; it was cold but bright, thin almost-spring sunshine making every shadow a knife edge. He leaned forward a little more, his arms spreading slightly, the wind a hungry lover's hand. A cold edge of caress. *Just a little closer. Just a little further.*

*It might hurt enough to make you forget.*

"Gallow, what the hell?" Clyde bellowed.

Jeremiah stepped back, half-turned on one rubber-padded heel. The boots were thick-soled, caked with the detritus of a hundred build sites. Probably dust on there from places both mortal and not-so-mortal, he'd worn them since before his marriage. Short black hair and pale green eyes, a face that could be any anonymous construction worker's. Not young, not old, not distinctive at all, what little skill he had with glamour pressed into service to make him look just like every other mortal guy with a physical job and a liking for beer every now and again.

His arms tingled; he knew the markings were moving on his skin, under the long sleeves. "Thought I saw something." *A way out.* But only if he was sure it would be an escape, not a fresh snare.

Being Half just made you too damn durable.

"Like what, a pigeon? Millions of those around." The bullet-headed foreman folded his beefy arms. He was already red and perspiring, though the temperature hadn't settled above forty degrees all week.

Last summer had been mild-chill, fall icy, winter hard, and spring was late this year. Maybe the Queen hadn't opened the Gates yet.

*Summer.* The shiver—half loathing, half something else—that went through Jeremiah must have shown. Clyde took a half-step sideways, reaching up to push his hard hat further back on his sweat-shaven pate. He had a magnificent broad white mustache, and the mouth under it turned into a thin line as he dropped his hands loosely to his sides.

*Easy, there.* Jeremiah might have laughed. Still, you could never tell who on a jobsite might have a temper. Best to be safe around heavy machinery, crowbars, nail guns, and the like.

"A seagull." Gallow deliberately hunched his shoulders, pulled the rage and pain back inside his skin. "Maybe a hawk. Or something. You want my apple pie?" If Clyde had a weakness, it was sugar-drenched, overprocessed pastry. Just like a brughnie, actually.

Another shiver roiled through him, but he kept it inside. *Don't think on the sidhe. You know it puts you in a mood.*

Clyde perked up a little. "If you don't want it. How come you bring 'em if you don't want 'em?"

*Insurance. Always bring something to barter with.* Jeremiah dug in his lunchbag. He'd almost forgotten he'd crumpled most of the brown paper in his fist. Daisy always sent him to work with a carefully packed lunch, but the collection of retro metal boxes she'd found at Goodwill and Salvation Army were all gone now. If he hadn't thrown them away he had stamped on them, crushing each piece with the same boots he was wearing now. "Habit. Put 'em in the bag each time."

She'd done sandwiches, too, varying to keep them interesting. Turkey. Chicken. Good old PB&J, two of them to keep him fueled. Hard-boiled eggs with a twist of salt in waxed paper, carefully quartered apples bathed in lemon juice to keep them from browning, home-baked goodies. Banana bread, muffins, she'd even gone through a sushi phase once until he'd let it slip that he didn't prefer raw fish.

*I just thought, you're so smart and all. Ain't sushi what smart people eat?* And her laugh at his baffled look. She often made little comments like that, as if...well, she never knew of the sidhe, but she considered him a creature from a different planet just the same.

"Oh." Clyde took the Hostess apple pie, his entire face brightening. "Just don't stand too near that edge, Gallow. You fall off and I'll have L&I all over me."

"Not gonna." It was hard taking the next few steps away from the edge. His heels landed solidly, and the wind stopped keening across rebar and concrete. Or at least, the sound retreated. "Haven't yet."

"Always a first time. Hey, me and Panko are going out for beers after. You wanna?" The waxed wrapper tore open, and Clyde took a huge mouthful of sugar that only faintly resembled the original apple.

"Sure." It was Friday, the start of a long weekend. If he went home he was only going to eat another TV dinner, or nothing at all, and sit staring at the fist-sized hole in the television screen, in his messy living room.

Ridiculous. Why did they call it that? Nobody did any *living* in there.

"Okay." Clyde gave him another odd look, and Jeremiah had a sudden vision of smashing his fist into the old man's face. The crunch of bone, the gush of blood, the satisfaction of a short sharp action. The foreman wasn't even a sidhe, to require an exchange of names beforehand.

*I'm mortal now. Best to remember it.* Besides, the foreman wasn't to blame for anything. Guiltless as only a mortal could be.

"Better get back to work," Jeremiah said instead, and tossed his crumpled lunchbag into the cut-down trash barrel hulking near the lift. "Gotta earn those beers."

Clyde had his mouth full, and Jeremiah was glad. If the man said another word, he wasn't sure he could restrain himself. There was no good reason for the rage, except the fact that he'd been brought back from the brink, and reminded he was only a simulacrum of a mortal man.

Again.

# if you enjoyed
## CORMORANT RUN,

### look out for

# SIX WAKES

### by

# Mur Lafferty

*A space adventure set on a lone ship where the clones of a murdered crew must find their murderer—before they kill again.*

*It was not common to awaken in a cloning vat streaked with drying blood.*

*At least, Maria Arena had never experienced it. She had no memory of how she died. That was also new; before, when she had awakened as a new clone, her first memory was of how she died.*

*Maria's vat was in the front of six vats, each one holding the clone of a crew member of the starship* Dormire, *each clone waiting for its previous incarnation to die so it could awaken. And Maria wasn't the only one to die recently...*

## THIS IS NOT A PIPE

*Day 1*
*July 25, 2493*

Sound struggled to make its way through the thick synth-amneo fluid. Once it reached Maria Arena's ears, it sounded like a chain saw: loud, insistent, and unending. She couldn't make out the words, but it didn't sound like a situation she wanted to be involved in.

Her reluctance at her own rebirth reminded her where she was, and who she was. She grasped for her last backup. The crew had just moved into their quarters on the *Dormire*, and the cloning bay had been the last room they'd visited on their tour. There they had done their first backup on the ship.

Maria must have been in an accident or something soon after, killing her and requiring her next clone to wake. Sloppy use of a life wouldn't make a good impression on the captain, who likely was the source of the angry chain-saw noise.

Maria finally opened her eyes. She tried to make sense of the dark round globules floating in front of her vat, but it was difficult with the freshly cloned brain being put to work for the first time. There were too many things wrong with such a mess.

With the smears on the outside of the vat and the purple color through the bluish fluid Maria floated in, she figured the orbs were blood drops. Blood shouldn't float. That was the first problem. If blood was floating, that meant the grav drive that spun the ship had failed. That was probably another reason someone was yelling. The blood and the grav drive.

Blood in a cloning bay, that was different too. Cloning bays were pristine, clean places, where humans were downloaded into newly cloned bodies when the previous ones had died. It was much cleaner and less painful than human birth, with all its screaming and blood.

Again with the blood.

The cloning bay had six vats in two neat rows, filled with blue-tinted synth-amneo fluid and the waiting clones of the rest of the crew. Blood belonged in the medbay, down the hall. The unlikely occurrence of a drop of blood originating in the medbay, floating down the hall, and entering the cloning bay to float in front of Maria's vat would be extraordinary. But that's not what happened; a body floated above the blood drops. A number of bodies, actually.

Finally, if the grav drive *had* failed, and if someone *had* been injured in the cloning bay, another member of the crew would have cleaned up the blood. Someone was always on call to ensure a new clone made the transition from death into their new body smoothly.

No. A perfect purple sphere of blood shouldn't be floating in front of her face.

Maria had now been awake for a good minute or so. No one worked the computer to drain the synth-amneo fluid to free her.

A small part of her brain began to scream at her that she should be more concerned about the bodies, but only a small part.

She'd never had occasion to use the emergency release valve inside the cloning vats. Scientists had implemented them after some techs had decided to play a prank on a clone, and woke her up only to leave her in the vat alone for hours. When she had gotten free, stories said, the result was messy and violent, resulting in the fresh cloning of some of the techs. After that, engineers added an interior release switch for clones to let themselves out of the tank if they were trapped for whatever reason.

Maria pushed the button and heard a *clunk* as the release triggered, but the synth-amneo fluid stayed where it was.

A drain relied on gravity to help the fluid along its way. Plumbing 101 there. The valve was opened but the fluid remained a stubborn womb around Maria.

She tried to find the source of the yelling. One of the crew floated near the computer bank, naked, with wet hair stuck out in a frightening, spiky corona. Another clone woke. Two of them had died?

Behind her, crewmates floated in four vats. All of their eyes were open, and each was searching for the emergency release. Three *clunks* sounded, but they remained in the same position Maria was in.

Maria used the other emergency switch to open the vat door. Ideally it would have been used after the fluid had drained away, but there was little ideal about this situation. She and a good quantity of the synth-amneo fluid floated out of her vat, only to collide gently with the orb of blood floating in front of her. The surface tension of both fluids held, and the drop bounced away.

Maria hadn't encountered the problem of how to get out of a liquid prison in zero-grav. She experimented by flailing about, but only made some fluid break off the main bubble and go floating away. In her many lives, she'd been in more than one undignified situation, but this was new.

*Action and reaction*, she thought, and inhaled as much of the oxygen-rich fluid as she could, then forced everything out of her lungs as if she were sneezing. She didn't go as fast as she would have if it had been air, because she was still inside viscous fluid, but it helped push her backward and out of the bubble. She inhaled air and then coughed and vomited the rest of the fluid in a spray in front of her, banging her head on the computer console as her body's involuntary movements propelled her farther.

Finally out of the fluid, and gasping for air, she looked up.

"Oh shit."

Three dead crewmates floated around the room amid the blood and other fluids. Two corpses sprouted a number of gory tentacles, bloody bubbles that refused to break away from the deadly wounds. A fourth was strapped to a chair at the terminal.

Gallons of synth-amneo fluid joined the gory detritus as the newly cloned crew fought to exit their vats. They looked with as much shock as she felt at their surroundings.

Captain Katrina de la Cruz moved to float beside her, still focused on the computer. "Maria, stop staring and make yourself useful. Check on the others."

Maria scrambled for a handhold on the wall to pull herself away from the captain's attempt to access the terminal.

Katrina pounded on a keyboard and poked at the console screen. "IAN, what the hell happened?"

"My speech functions are inaccessible," the computer's male, slightly robotic voice said.

*"Ceci n'est pas une pipe,"* muttered a voice above Maria. It broke her shock and reminded her of the captain's order to check on the crew.

The speaker was Akihiro Sato, pilot and navigator. She had met him a few hours ago at the cocktail party before the launch of the *Dormire*.

"Hiro, why are you speaking French?" Maria said, confused. "Are you all right?"

"Someone saying aloud that they can't talk is like that old picture of a pipe that says, 'This is not a pipe.' It's supposed to give art students deep thoughts. Never mind." He waved his hand around the cloning bay. "What happened, anyway?"

"I have no idea," she said. "But—God, what a mess. I have to go check on the others."

"Goddammit, you just spoke," the captain said to the computer, dragging some icons around the screen. "Something's working inside there. Talk to me, IAN."

"My speech functions are inaccessible," the AI said again, and de la Cruz slammed her hand down on the keyboard, grabbing it to keep herself from floating away from it.

Hiro followed Maria as she maneuvered around the room using the handholds on the wall. Maria found herself face-to-face with the gruesome body of Wolfgang, their second in command. She gently pushed him aside, trying not to dislodge the gory bloody tentacles sprouting from punctures on his body.

She and Hiro floated toward the living Wolfgang, who was doubled over coughing the synth-amneo out of his lungs. "What the hell is going on?" he asked in a ragged voice.

"You know as much as we do," Maria said. "Are you all right?"

He nodded and waved her off. He straightened his back, gaining at least another foot on his tall frame. Wolfgang was born on the moon colony, Luna, several generations of his family developing the long bones of living their whole lives in low gravity. He took a handhold and propelled himself toward the captain.

"What do you remember?" Maria asked Hiro as they approached another crewmember.

"My last backup was right after we boarded the ship. We haven't even left yet," Hiro said.

Maria nodded. "Same for me. We should still be docked, or only a few weeks from Earth."

"I think we have more immediate problems, like our current status," Hiro said.

"True. Our current status is four of us are dead," Maria said, pointing at the bodies. "And I'm guessing the other two are as well."

"What could kill us all?" Hiro asked, looking a bit green as he dodged a bit of bloody skin. "And what happened to me and the captain?"

He referred to the "other two" bodies that were not floating in the cloning bay. Wolfgang, their engineer, Paul Seurat, and Dr. Joanna Glass all were dead, floating around the room, gently bumping off vats or one another.

Another cough sounded from the last row of vats, then a soft voice. "Something rather violent, I'd say."

"Welcome back, Doctor, you all right?" Maria asked, pulling herself toward the woman.

The new clone of Joanna nodded, her tight curls glistening with the synth-amneo. Her upper body was thin and strong, like all new clones, but her legs were small and twisted. She glanced up at the bodies and pursed her lips. "What happened?" She didn't wait for them to answer, but grasped a handhold and pulled herself toward the ceiling where a body floated.

"Check on Paul," Maria said to Hiro, and followed Joanna.

The doctor turned her own corpse to where she could see it, and her eyes grew wide. She swore quietly. Maria came up behind her and swore much louder.

Her throat had a stab wound, with great waving gouts of blood reaching from her neck. If the doctor's advanced age was any indication, they were well past the beginning of the mission. Maria remembered her as a woman who looked to be in her thirties, with smooth dark skin and black hair. Now wrinkles lined the skin around her eyes and the corners of her mouth, and gray shot through her tightly braided hair. Maria looked at the other bodies; from her vantage point she could now see each also showed their age.

"I didn't even notice," she said, breathless. "I-I only noticed the blood and gore. We've been on this ship for *decades*. Do you remember anything?"

"No." Joanna's voice was flat and grim. "We need to tell the captain."